CLUB FANTASY

JOAN ELIZABETH LLOYD

KENSINGTON BOOKS

KENSINGTON BOOKS are published by

Kensington Publishing Corp.
850 Third Avenue
New York, NY 10022

All Kensington titles, imprints and distributed lines are available at special quantity discounts for bulk purchases for sales promotion, premiums, fund raising, educational or institutional use.

Special book excerpts or customized printings can also be created to fit specific needs. For details, write or phone the office of the Kensington Special Sales Manager: Kensington Publishing Corp., 850 Third Avenue, New York, NY, 10022. Attn. Special Sales Department. Phone: 1-800-221-2647.

Kensington and the K logo Reg. U.S. Pat & TM Off.

ISBN: 0-7394-4592-8

Printed in the United States of America

Chapter

1

"Glen asked me to marry him last evening," Jenna Bryant said as she put her Garfield mug on the table beside the cozy overstuffed sofa and propped her feet on the coffee table.

Marcy let the dead leaf she'd pulled from one of six cyclamen on the living room windowsill fall from her fingers, and dashed across the small room to drop onto the couch beside her sister. She wrapped her arms around her ninety-five-seconds-younger sibling and shrieked, "That's wonderful!" Marcy's grin almost split her face. "I'm so happy for you. I knew you and Glen were perfect for each other. He's a great guy."

Jenna eased her sister away, heaved a deep sigh and squared her shoulders. "I told him no." Jenna watched her sister's face turn from elation to disbelief to uncertainty and somehow it appeared to confuse her still more.

For several moments Marcy just stared, then she said, "It happened around ten last evening, didn't it? I was sitting watching TV and something spooked me, frightened me from the inside."

"Yeah, that was about the right time." Although the two women always made fun of the alleged connection between identical twins, they couldn't deny that occasionally strong emotions seemed to be transmitted from one to the other.

"Tell me," Marcy said softly as she settled at the other end of the nubby oatmeal couch, curled her feet beneath her, and reached out to take Jenna's hand. Jenna marveled at her sister's calm strength. She was a wreck.

Although the women were twins, their mother had always tried to bring out different characteristics in her two daughters. Thus the two women were very different. Where Jenna was spontaneous, Marcy was a planner. Jenna's desk was covered with little slips of paper. Marcy had a neat, organized day-runner.

Physically they were unlike as well. Although their features were identical, Jenna constantly dieted and worked out at a gym three or four times a week while Marcy allowed her tendency to be overweight to take over her eating habits and had ballooned until she weighed almost forty pounds more than her sister. At five foot seven, Jenna's 130 pounds looked wonderful, with large breasts and flat abs. At 170, Marcy was a size sixteen and, although she was what some might call zaftig, behind her back others bluntly said she was fat.

Both women were attractive but, where Jenna used cosmetics to enhance her large gray eyes, soft full lips, and high cheekbones, only occasionally did Marcy even spread on light lip gloss. Jenna's light brown hair was softly layered, falling to her shoulders; Marcy's was longer, usually caught behind her neck in a wide barrette.

It was only ten o'clock on a spring Sunday morning and while Jenna had pulled on a pair of forest green, stretch pants and a soft yellow, SUNY Albany sweatshirt, Marcy wore her uniform: black sweat pants and an unadorned black sweatshirt.

"It should have been so lovely," Jenna said, remembering. "We went to dinner at Miragio's, and Glen had arranged for champagne and special flowers on the table." She shrugged. "I knew he was going to ask me."

"And," Marcy said, gently, when her sister paused.

Jenna felt her stomach muscles tighten. "He's so nice and I'm so fond of him. He looked so wounded and I feel like such a shit, Sis. I've known how he felt for several weeks, and I realize now that I've been trying to sidestep that moment hoping I wouldn't have to hurt him. Finally, last evening, I couldn't avoid it any more."

When Marcy took a breath to speak, Jenna held up her free hand. "Let me say this my way." Explain. How could she explain it to her sister when she didn't fully understand it herself? She loved him, didn't she? Did she?

When Marcy nodded and squeezed her hand, Jenna continued. "Glen's a wonderful guy but the closer we got the more restless I became. As he drew me nearer, somewhere inside I wanted to break away. Don't get me wrong. He wasn't doing anything that didn't flow naturally out of our relationship. After almost a year it's natural that he'd think in terms of something—something more permanent." She huffed out a breath. "Listen to me. I sound like some guy who can't even say the word marriage without stuttering. But when I think about it, my stomach hurts."

She disentangled her hand from her sister's, picked up her mug and sipped, more as a prop than from a desire for the tepid coffee. "After a leisurely dinner, dessert and coffee, he took the predictable blue velvet ring box from his pocket, opened it and asked me. I froze."

Just the thought of it had her on her feet pacing the small living room, from the curtained windows that faced a quiet residential street to the fireplace, its mantle topped with framed, family photographs and a vase filled with recently cut lilacs. "It was everything a woman could want. He told me he loved me, wanted to spend the rest of his life with me. He said he wanted a house, kids, but we'd wait with either or both if I wanted. He laughed and said that, since we had no folks to ask, he had considered asking your permission to marry me, but in the end, he said, I was the only one who mattered." Jenna felt her eyes fill. "It was so romantic, so perfect."

When she didn't immediately continue, Marcy said, gently, "But you told him no."

"I saw myself ten years from now, still here in Seneca Falls." Her tone hardened as she continued, "Gateway to the Finger Lakes. Two-point-six kids, a house with a white picket fence around it, a dog, all the things that lots of women want. I felt like I was being crammed into a box. All I could hear was that song. Something about 'You'll cage me on your shelf' and 'I'll never get the chance to be just me first, for myself.' I felt my throat close and my hands sweat. I was totally panicked. I heard my heart pound in my ears. I couldn't catch my breath. While he sat there across the table looking at me with such expectation in his eyes and that damned ring box in his hand, something in my head was banging on the inside of my skull trying to get free. I couldn't do it. I just couldn't do it." As she told the story, she felt her fingernails dig into her palms and her chest tighten. "I haven't been leading him on. I thought it would work out, I really did, but when push came to shove I couldn't."

What she couldn't discuss, as close as the sisters were, was that she also wanted more out of her sex life than Glen offered. He was workmanlike in bed, and amazingly predictable. She'd often suggested more creative activities and Glen always obliged, but he quickly slipped back into his boring pattern. There must be more to sex than this, she found herself saying over and over. Like Glen, Marcy wouldn't understand, Jenna thought. They're both just too straight. *I need more*, she cried silently.

"It's okay, Jen," her sister said. "You don't have to do anything you don't want to do."

Jenna unclenched her fingers that ached with muscular tension. "I know. And I know that you'd give your eyeteeth for that kind of life. You wouldn't be the flighty one who slammed someone so nice." She swallowed the urge to cry, picturing Glen's handsome face fall as she refused his offer.

"I'm me and you're you, Jenna. We may have lots of genes in common but we are two different people. What I might want and what Glen wants have nothing to do with you. You've got to be true to yourself. Marriage is forever, or at least it should be."

Jenna sniffled and swiped at the tear that was trickling down her cheek. "You always know how to say the right thing, don't you, Sis?" She sat back down in an unintentional mirror image of her sister's pose, legs tucked beneath her. "So I told him that I couldn't marry him. He was totally shocked and I guess I was too. What was worse, I couldn't really tell him why. I tried to explain but he just shut the ring box and stuffed it back in his jacket pocket."

She picked up her mug and played with the handle. "Then I did a really bad thing. I tried to lessen the pain by saying that we might talk in six months or so. Maybe Thanksgiving or Christmas. He grabbed on to that. I should never have said it." She felt her eyes fill with tears of both pain and frustration. "I have no idea whether there is any hope, but I gave him some.

"I wanted to leave him right then but we had come in his Nissan. He dropped a few bills on the table and, like the polite guy he is, helped me into my coat, and then into his car. You should have seen his profile. It could have been carved out of the side of a mountain. His jaw was locked, eyes straight ahead. From the moment we left the restaurant to pulling into our driveway, he didn't say another word." More tears flowed down Jenna's face and Marcy sniffled in sympathy. "He put the car in park, draped his arm across the back of my seat and said, 'I love you, and I'll wait as long as it takes.' Then he looked at me with those gorgeous brown eyes. I got out of the car and didn't look back." Jenna sniffled. "He didn't leave until I was in the house and had turned off the porch light." It had been so final. Was she right to be so selfish? Yes. She had to do this. "I hate myself for not being more forceful. Don't wait, I wanted to say. Make a new life with someone who loves you more than I do."

"Do you love him?"

"I don't know. I thought I did, but could I do this to him if I loved him? I'm not sure I know what love is. Watching him last evening broke my heart, but it didn't change my mind."

Marcy unfastened the barrette that held her hair and clenched it between her front teeth. She reflexively combed the straight brown strands through her fingers and refastened the clip as she did dozens of times a day. "What now?" she asked.

"I was up most of the night trying to figure that out. I must look like death warmed over." She tucked her shoulder-length, chestnut hair behind her ears.

"You look just fine, nothing a good night's sleep won't cure. What's done, is done and it's time to move on. Glen will do okay. He's tough. You need to look out for number one, you."

"I know. I'm so confused that I don't know who I am or what I want any more." She shuddered. "This isn't easy for me to say, Sis, but I made a difficult decision at about five this morning." God, she was going to hurt someone else; first Glen, now her sister. "I've got to get away from here. I love you but I've got to take some time to be by myself." As she watched her sister's face close up just the way Glen's had, she wondered how she was going to get through the day. She had to make Marcy understand, better than Glen did. She just had to. "Do you realize that we're almost thirty-one and we've never lived alone?"

"You mean I'm part of this too?"

"It's not you. I love you." She stared at all the family pictures on the mantle, then turned to her sister. "It's being twins. As different as we are, we've always been part of a set, maybe not to anyone else, but to me. Jenna and Marcy. The girls. We had the measles together, got poison ivy together, started menstruating on the same day. Remember when we each broke an arm within a week of each other? Big joke, but it's not a joke at all. It's not you, it's us, with a capital *U*. I'm drowning in US."

Marcy slumped back onto the sofa cushions. "I never realized that you thought of it all that way."

"I don't think I ever focused on it until last night. It feels like a giant case of claustrophobia. Once it surfaced it was as if it had all been there forever."

"I'm sorry you resent me," Marcy said, her voice tiny.

Jenna saw her sister's face reflect all the hurt she must be feeling and almost changed her mind. *No, I can't or it's going to be this way for the rest of my life.* Hadn't Marcy ever felt any of the same things? "I don't mean to hurt you, Sis, even a little, but think very hard for a moment. Can you honestly say that you've never wanted to be an only child?"

"Of course not," Marcy said immediately.

"Think harder. Is that your final answer?"

Marcy sighed. "Maybe occasionally."

"If you think about it a little more you might discover that it was more than occasionally. I don't mean to play amateur shrink and you know I love you more than anyone, but I think we both need space." Was she just rationalizing doing something so traumatic to her sister? "Maybe we should have done this when we came back here after graduate school, but it was so easy just to move back into the folks' old house and with AAJ based near here, the rest just seemed to happen."

With an almost uncanny ear for languages, the two women had majored in comparative linguistics at the State University of New York at Albany and had both obtained masters' degrees. They spoke half-a-dozen languages fluently and had gotten jobs as translators for AAJ Technologies, a multinational computer manufacturing firm based between their hometown of Seneca Falls, New York, and Syracuse. Their parents had died in their final year in graduate school, and had left them their house. So, after graduation, they had moved back into their old rooms and had flowed along that way for almost eight years.

Jenna had met Glen, a lawyer who had represented AAJ in several high-profile cases, when he had needed a German translator for a patent dispute. They had dated for almost a year until the previous evening.

"So what are you going to do now?" Marcy asked, her voice small. "Are you really going to move away?"

Although this was almost as difficult as saying no to Glen had been, she was becoming more and more sure as she spoke. "Yes. I'm going away. I have to."

"You're just going to pick up and move? Where will you go? What about a job?"

"I have an idea, but I need to make a phone call first." She leaned forward and hugged her sister. "I didn't mean to hurt Glen but, much more important than that, I don't mean to hurt you."

Marcy's face brightened and the lost little girl look faded. "I know that, silly. I'm just taking a moment to brood and wonder how much truth there is to what you said about wanting to be separate."

"And . . . ?"

"I think you might just have had the courage to realize things I didn't know were there. That's really duckspeak, isn't it. I only thought I was happy."

"Some of this might be duckspeak and I'll admit I don't have a clue how much. I just know that I have to get away for a while."

"Where are you going?"

"I'm going to make a phone call. Then I might have some answers." Leaving Marcy still deep in thought, Jenna went upstairs to her room.

Fifteen minutes later, when Jenna returned to the neat living room, Marcy was still sitting in the same position on the corner of the sofa. "I've been thinking about it," Marcy said, "and, although I want to punch myself for admitting this, you might be right about some of the things you said. The thought of your moving away, if only for a short time, is like having part of myself amputated, but I think it's probably right for both of us." She smiled. "Not for forever, I hope, but for a while maybe." She hesitated. "The thought of being here by myself scares the shit out of me and that makes no sense. We're two independent women."

"Who are closer than most women ever get." Jenna picked up her mug and sipped her now cold coffee, flopped back onto the sofa, and propped one ankle on the other knee. She and her sister had made a concerted effort to develop different friendships during college, worried that they were becoming almost clones of each other. "Do you remember Chloe Whitman?"

She watched as Marcy flipped through her mental filing cabinet. "Sure. She was in our undergraduate class in Albany. I didn't really know her but you and she were pretty close for a while as I recall. Chloe Whitman. All I remember about her is that she was tiny, with huge brown eyes. I always thought she looked like one of those Keene paintings of the kids whose faces were all eyes."

"That's her. Pretty quiet, with a few girlfriends, myself included. God, the guys used to go crazy, wanting to protect her, spoil her, but she kept pretty much to herself. Anyway, Chloe and I have kept in touch over the years. We had dinner together several times when I was in New York City on business.

"She e-mailed me about six months ago that her aunt had died and left her a brownstone in Manhattan. She said that she was living there with lots of empty space and invited me to visit sometime. I just got off the phone with her. I asked about staying with her for a while, and she jumped at it. She even looked in the Sunday paper while we talked and found an ad for a temp agency specializing in translators." She took a deep breath. "She invited me to move in as soon as I can spring myself from AAJ."

"Oh, God, Jen," Marcy said, her eyes filling. "It's so fast. My brain says it's the right thing for both of us, but my soul is bleeding."

"I know, Sis," Jenna said, wrapping her arms around her sister. "I know."

Marcy was in pain. Her sister was leaving and she felt as if she needed to mourn. No, that was stupid. Phones work two ways and we'll visit often. Anyway, she'll be back. Won't she? Marcy pushed any negative thoughts down and concentrated on the upside. Jenna was doing something so brave, something Marcy could never have done. She gazed at her twin and marveled at her ability to do something so momentous. Her sister had always been spontaneous, easy and relaxed about changes in plans. "You're really going to do this, aren't you?" she asked

"I am. I have to."

"What about your job at AAJ?"

"I'm going to try to get a leave of absence but if they won't do that, then I'm going to quit."

Marcy's eyes widened. How could Jenna be like that? Marcy found herself envious. She would have been making out budgets, lists of pros and cons. It would have taken her weeks to make a decision. "What about all your friends, the bowling league, your library volunteering? What about all that? You'll be leaving everything you know. What if you don't like Chloe in close quarters?"

Jenna chuckled and patted her sister's hand. "Stop worrying, Sis. I've saved a bit of money over the years so I can be flexible. If I don't like it there I can move somewhere else, or I can come back home." She grinned her most charming grin, one Marcy had succumbed to her entire life. "Don't rent out my room so fast."

"Sorry. I guess I do get carried away." Marcy shook her head ruefully. "It's just that you boggle my mind. You're going to pick up and go. Just like that, when there's so much to plan."

"What's to plan?" Jenna asked. "Chloe's got a place for me to stay at least for a while. I've got enough money to tide me over until I find work. What more is there?"

Marcy's mind whirled. "You've got to pack, for example. What will you take? Will you take lots of suitcases or should we mail boxes? You'll need to change banks. No, maybe you won't. Is there a branch of your bank in New York? What about your car? Will you take it with you? If you don't, will you sell it or put it on blocks or just let it sit while you're gone?"

Marcy stopped talking as Jenna held her hand up to stem the flow of words. "Sis, relax. It will all work out."

Marcy stood and headed for the kitchen, her brain moving at a million miles an hour. "I'm going to make some fresh coffee and get a pad and pencil." She stopped in the kitchen doorway. "We can begin with a list of what's to be done."

When Jenna smiled her indulgent smile, Marcy said, "Okay, I'm organizing again, but it's necessary. It keeps my mind busy so I don't have to think about the hurt."

"I know, and I'll leave all that to you. Let me know what I have to do and I'll do it."

"Jenna, I can't make decisions like these for you."

Raising an eyebrow, Jenna said, "I've made the big one, you just get to make the little ones."

Marcy huffed an exasperated breath. It had been like this all their lives. She did all the planning and Jenna went along. Their parents had always teased them. Jenna would be in charge of deciding the important things, like foreign policy, campaign finance reform, or whether America should go to Venus. Marcy, they said, would make all the small ones for all of them, like what to have for dinner, what courses to take in school, and where to go on vacation. It had always been her responsibility, one she'd taken on willingly. Hadn't she?

As she carefully measured decaffeinated coffee into the white paper filter, Marcy thought about what life would be like for her after her sister was gone. One moment she thought about how empty the house would be, the next she realized that she could have dinner at nine o'clock or leave dirty clothes in the living room if she wanted to. It was going to be difficult but she had to admit that it would have its benefits. She could stop being a constant role model for her sister, trying to teach by example.

She started the coffee brewing and grabbed a handful of jelly beans from the glass jar on the counter. As she chewed, she got a pad and pencil from the kitchen counter and headed back to the living room, already making notes.

Glen Howell hadn't slept at all the previous night, and now sat in the small living room of his tiny condo several miles from the Bryant house. Stretched out in a lounge chair, he tried for the hundredth time to figure out what had gone wrong the previous evening. He'd sensed for several weeks that Jenna was putting him off, trying to avoid his proposal, but he'd figured that when the moment arrived she'd agree. After all, they were so right together.

He remembered the day they'd met. He'd been stunned, not by her good looks—although she was lovely—but by the force of her intelligence. Not only could she do a running, perfectly correct idiomatic translation of a complex legal conversation, but she did it with a calm style that impressed both him and his counterpart. He had realized at the time that she had sped the negotiations with a few well-thought-out suggestions and had wanted to see more of her, professionally and personally.

He'd asked her out to dinner and, to his surprise, she'd accepted. They'd begun seeing each other more and more frequently until they had slipped into a comfortable, almost married life. And the sex was good too.

He traveled back in his mind to the first night they'd made love. Neither of them had been virgins, of course, but they had come together new to each other. Since that evening they'd made love at least once a week. They had tried a few sexual experiments together, but he preferred standard missionary-position lovemaking. Now it was pretty much routine, but he was quite sure she climaxed most of the time.

If it wasn't the sex, why had she said no to his proposal? He'd planned the evening so carefully, from the violets on the table to the vintage of the champagne. He'd even arranged for the restaurant to play some of their favorite music, mixed with a little cool, soft jazz. He could still hear it. They'd had such a wonderful time. Finally, over brandies, he'd taken the ring from his pocket and watched her face tighten. He still couldn't understand what he had seen. If he hadn't known better he would have thought she'd looked like some cornered animal, like she'd been asked to do something illegal or immoral.

He remembered exactly what she'd said. "I need time. I need space. I can't do it. I just can't do it." He had no clue what that meant. What kind of space and how much time? Did she really mean six whole months? Thanksgiving? Christmas? He reached for the phone, then pulled his hand back. He loved her, so he'd give her what she needed. But what about what he needed? He picked up the receiver and dialed Jenna's number.

"Hello?"

"Hi, Marcy. Is she there?" Funny, although the two women teased him about it, he always knew from just a hello which was which. He heard some muffled conversation, then Marcy said, "She is, but I think you'd be better off leaving her alone for a while."

Glen sighed and let his shoulders droop. "I want to talk to her, make her understand that I'll give her whatever time she needs, although, frankly, those will be the longest months of my life. I want her to know, too, that I'll be there for her whenever she wants to come back." When, not if. He didn't want to think about his life without her in it.

"I think she knows that but I'm afraid that it'll be a while," Marcy said, then added, "If ever." It was said so softly that he wasn't sure he'd actually heard it.

He allowed his body to slump back into his chair. "I know, but we'll still see each other at work. That'll have to be enough for now."

He heard Marcy's heavy breath. "Glen, you know I think you're a great guy, but I have to be honest with you. She's planning to go away for a while. She's arranged to move to New York City and stay with an old friend, temporarily. I don't know what that means for you and her but I wouldn't hold out too much hope."

Shit, Glen thought. *She's leaving. Temporarily.* Marcy had said temporarily. "I need to talk to her before she leaves, tell her . . . Please." What could he tell her that she didn't already know?

After another moment of muffled conversation, Marcy returned to him. "She won't talk to you. Not now. Maybe not ever. Maybe you should just move on."

Move on? Glen felt his throat close and he swallowed hard. "Is she mad at me for asking her to marry me? I thought she'd be happy."

There was a pause. "She's in a panic right now. She feels that she's never been by herself so she can't consider becoming part of a new pair. I sort of know how she feels. We've always been part of a very intimate twosome, one maybe only twins can understand, and now she wants—maybe *needs* is a better word—needs to be on her own for a while."

Glen realized that Marcy was right about the sisters' closeness. They had gone to college and graduate school together and had lived in their parents' house ever since returning to

Seneca Falls. "Isn't there anything I can say or do? I could send flowers or something."

"Glen, give her some time. I'll let her know how you feel. I think she knows how much you care but, in my opinion, it would be best if you just let her go."

Glen sighed again. "What choice do I have? It's May now," he said, and, ticking the months on his fingers, he continued, "so by Thanksgiving, this will all be in the past."

"Let's say that you'll let her go until Christmas. And, Glen, during that time get out, do things. Don't sit home and dwell on this. There's a good chance she won't be coming back."

No. She'll be coming back. Christmas. She'll be home for Christmas.

In a four-story brownstone on Fifty-fifth Street, Chloe Whitman lay stretched out on her bed. She'd invited Jenna without question, but now she wondered. How would the straight-A student from the middle of nowhere react to her lifestyle? "Oh well," she whispered, running her tiny hands over her sweat-covered body. *Time will tell*, she thought. With a loud purr, she rolled over and stretched out over the naked man beside her, undulating so her nipples rubbed against his chest, her mound pressed against his rampant erection. "Purr for me, baby," she growled.

A long moan made his chest rumble, the vibrations flowing from her nipples through her belly to her soaked pussy. How long could she tease him? she wondered. Maybe just a little longer. She slid her body down the length of his, licking his hairless chest, delving into his belly button and finally arriving at his massive cock. God, he was so hot.

She flicked her tongue over the end of his enormous erection. She'd never had sex with him before and wondered whether something the size of his penis would fit into her body. Or her mouth. She'd find out part one first. She opened her mouth and sucked gently on the head of his cock, wrapping her lips around and slowly drawing it into her wet cavern. No, she realized, it wouldn't all fit into her mouth. She could only take the first inch or two inside. Would that mean that he wouldn't fit into her body either?

She straddled him, one knee against each side of his ribs and held her body still, drawing out the pleasure, then slowly lowered herself and rubbed her sopping folds with his cock. Would he fit? God, she couldn't wait to find out. Slowly, ever so slowly she lowered herself, taking first an inch, then two, of his massive erection into her body. Slowly she allowed her body to be stretched to its fullest by him. Then she had him, totally within her. As he moaned again, then bucked his hips, she levered herself up on her knees and dropped onto him again. She squeezed her vaginal muscles and they came together, spasms of heat echoing through her body as she felt his answering pulses.

Much later, she again thought about Jenna. *Oh well*, she thought. *Time will tell.*

Chapter
2

The advisor Jenna saw in human resources the following Monday morning was surprised at her sudden decision to leave. "I understand what you mean," a woman named Henshaw told her as she scanned Jenna's personnel folder that lay open on her desk. The way the older woman said it, it seemed to Jenna that she didn't understand at all. "Sometimes you just need to spread your wings and try something new, I suppose. I would love to find some way to convince you not to go. I've seldom seen such glowing evaluations." She closed the folder and gazed at Jenna.

"I'm really sorry," Jenna said, flattered by the woman's kind words, but frustrated at her lack of understanding. "I'm afraid this is something I just have to do."

"Is it a matter of money?" When Jenna shook her head, Ms. Henshaw continued. "Are you sure? I think we can come up with a nicer package for you."

When Jenna shook her head again, Ms. Henshaw continued, "All right, then. I'm certain we can make this a leave of absence if that's okay with you. How about we make it six months, renewable for another six if you want it? That way we just might be able to lure you back when you've seen the 'big city.' "

Jenna wanted to throw her "big city" crack in her face, but she realized that a leave of absence was just what she wanted. Freedom with a safety net. "I think that might work out just fine," she said, pasting a congenial smile on her face.

For the first time, the woman's face softened. "Good. You know about your non-compete, of course. You can't work for anyone in any of the businesses AAJ's involved in. No trade secrets."

"Of course not," Jenna said, disgusted to think that Ms. Henshaw thought for one minute that she'd violate any confidences.

"Well, that's fine, then," the woman said, her professional smile reappearing.

During the next two weeks Jenna and Marcy spent a considerable amount of time at the mall. Although Ms. Henshaw's "big city" crack had enraged Jenna, she realized that she needed clothes more fitting to life in New York City and her conversations with Chloe had reinforced that fact. Her friend had called the agency she'd found in the paper and relayed to Jenna that there were always temporary openings for experienced translators and the daily fee mentioned was substantial. Of course she'd be paying rent for the first time in her life, and living expenses were going to be more in New York too, but Jenna would cross those bridges when she came to them.

Since most of the time she'd gone to work at AAJ casually dressed in slacks or jeans, cotton shirts or bulky sweaters, she'd need more businesslike clothing for working in Manhattan. The sisters roamed the malls after work, picking up pantsuits with matching, sheer sweaters, slender skirts with matching vests, and, of course, high-heeled shoes and purses to match. In one boutique, Jenna found a beautiful, slender leather belt and, as she handed it to the check-out clerk, she watched Marcy jot down a note in a small notebook. "What are you writing?"

"Just keeping a list of everything and checking what you'll pack and what you'll have to mail."

Jenna quickly snatched the notebook from her sister's hand. "Stop making lists. It will all come together. I promise."

Marcy smiled ruefully. "I know. It just helps me to keep from crying. If I can make it all seem like a project, I don't think about the distance from here to New York City."

"We each have unlimited nationwide calling on our cell phones, so I know we'll talk often," Jenna said around the lump that had formed in her throat. She handed the notebook back. "Okay, Sis, keep your lists. And I love you for it." She took her sister's hand and squeezed.

At odd times Jenna found her mind wandering back to Glen. She saw his handsome face, hair falling over his forehead, his deep brown eyes, the sexy dimple in his chin. Was she being a complete ass? Maybe she should call him, try to get him to understand, to wait for her. Wait for what? For her to come back from her silly little excursion to the "big city"? It wasn't just a whim, she told herself over and over. She needed this and it was best for Glen to forget about her. In her heart she halfway hoped he was pining away for her and would wait, desolate, until she came home, if she came home. Whenever she had thoughts like that, however, she chastised herself for her uncharitable ideas and quickly wished that he'd find someone wonderful and create a new relationship.

The Friday before her flight, her friends at work threw a lunch at the best restaurant in town, oddly the same one where, two weeks before, she'd turned Glen down. Everyone brought gag gifts, and by the time all the packages had been opened Jenna had four cans of mace, several sets of sexy lingerie, and a package of locks for her apartment door. One woman had bought an *I Love New York* tote bag and filled it with a flashlight, candles, batteries in three sizes, bottles of water, and over a dozen different varieties of candy. "An emergency kit for blackouts," she explained. Jenna felt badly that Marcy wasn't at the celebration. "Those are your friends," she'd said. "Let them enjoy you, and you have fun with them."

It seemed only moments after the night Glen had proposed that Jenna was at the airport, heading for a commuter flight to LaGuardia. As they approached the security checkpoint, the two women hugged. "This is as far as you can go," Jenna said. "I'll call . . ."

"I know. When you can. I won't count on it and I promise I won't worry."

Jenna took her sister by the shoulders and turned her back the way they had come. "No long good-byes. So long, Sis," she said, lightly slapping her on the bottom.

"So long, Jen."

Jenna put her shoulder bag and purse on the conveyor and walked through the metal detector. As she picked up her things, she looked back. Marcy was waving and, with a damp-eyed grin, Jenna waved back.

Jenna had been in Manhattan several times before on business so she knew her way to baggage claim at LaGuardia Airport. The weather was perfect for a Memorial Day week-end, with temperatures in the high seventies and a clear blue sky with just a few white, puffy clouds. With the one suitcase she'd brought rolling behind her and her carry-on bag and purse over her shoulder, she made her way to the taxi stand and gave the driver Chloe's address. As the taxi drove toward the Midtown Tunnel, Jenna reflected on what she had begun. She'd left her job, packed several boxes and sent them to Chloe's brownstone, and talked to her friend several times, most recently just the previous evening.

"I can't believe you're really coming," Chloe had said, her tone almost giddy.

"At this time tomorrow I'll be in Manhattan. I'm not sure I can believe it, either. It's really all right, my staying with you until I can find a place?"

"For the 'leventy 'leventh time, yes, it's okay. You can stay as long as you like. I'd love the company, actually. This place is so big I think my voice actually echoes."

"You're sure you don't need anything? I can—"

"Stop right now," Chloe said, interrupting the flow of Jenna's words. "I don't need stuff, I don't need my own space, I don't need anything. I want you here and that's that."

Jenna knew that she'd said the same things over and over but she needed to be really, really sure it was okay.

"Let it go, Jen. It's a done deal. Just show up tomorrow."

"Okay, if you're sure."

"I'm hanging up now. See you tomorrow."

Jenna replayed the conversation as she watched the familiar skyline slide past the taxi window. This was the right thing to do. She pictured Marcy seated at the tidy desk in her room, poring over her day runner, organizing her tasks for the following week. She saw Glen's hopeful face as he proposed. She'd spotted him in the halls of AAJ twice since that awful evening, but she'd ducked into a side corridor before he'd seen her. He'd called several times during the past two weeks but she'd refused to talk to him. Maybe she was a coward, but it seemed kinder that way, both to him and to herself.

She'd called Marcy from the airport to tell her that she'd arrived safely and the two women promised to call several times during the following week. This would be their first extended separation and, although it was her choice, Jenna was still choked up. Now she was here, she thought, as the taxi arrived at the address she'd given the driver.

She opened the taxi door and stepped out. The brownstone was four stories tall, with two steps leading to a small stoop. She tipped the driver as he set her suitcase beside the front door, and watched him drive away. She was really here. She'd done it. This was day one of the rest of her life. That phrase might be a cliché but it was as true for her as it could be.

She inhaled deeply. She was here, where she belonged. She

was startled at the thought but somehow it was true. Manhattan felt like home. Seneca Falls was a small, touristy town, pleasantly nicknamed the Gateway to the Finger Lakes and she'd spent a good deal of time in Syracuse on business. Large as Syracuse was, it was nothing like this. Manhattan hummed with life and action. Sounds of cars, trucks, taxi horns, and garbage cans clanging, interspersed with sirens, pounded the air. The city smelled of pavement, the bagel cart on the corner, and the Pakistani restaurant in the middle of the block. She raised her face to the brilliant blue sky, only a narrow strip of it visible between the buildings, and she couldn't keep from grinning. She was really here. She took a deep gulp of city air and let it out slowly, then pressed the doorbell.

Almost immediately the door flew open and, with an almost childlike squeal, Chloe propelled herself out and threw her arms around her friend. "You made it," she said.

Jenna leaned down and embraced her. "I did. The flight was uneventful, just the way I like a flight to be."

Chloe backed up and gazed at her, taking in her bright red Minnie Mouse tee shirt and denim vest over her jeans and sneakers. "You look just terrific," she said. "It's hard to believe it's been more than nine years since Albany."

Jenna hugged her again. Chloe's lush figure was barely contained in a pair of navy blue short shorts, a white tank top covered with a sheer, kelly green overshirt, tied beneath her breasts. Her auburn hair was seemingly uncombed, a riot of curls all over her head. Her feet were bare and Jenna could see that her manicured toenails were the same shade of shocking coral as her fingernails. "Closer to eleven, but who's counting. Anyway, Chloe, we've seen each other lots of times since then. Every time I've been in New York, actually."

"Right, all three times. I'm just glad you're here."

"I'm glad you're glad," Jenna said, shaking her head in wonder. "You haven't changed, you know. You still look about sixteen years old." She knew that, like she and her sister, Chloe was in her early thirties.

Chloe shook her head sadly. "I still get proofed at most of the places I go. It's the bane of my existence."

"Most people would love that. I always envied you. All the guys in school wanted to cuddle and cosset you, but you kept it all under control. Me? All they wanted to do was get help with their assignments."

"They still want to cuddle and cosset me, and more," Chloe said, then grabbed Jenna's arm and pulled. "Come inside and let's really catch up."

Jenna walked through a small entryway with black and white checkerboard tile and a small chandelier. Chloe led her past a spacious living room, furnished with homey pieces that made you want to sit down and curl up. Two large, gray upholstered chairs, a leather lounger, and an overstuffed sofa upholstered in a rose and gray tweed and covered with a dozen pillows in various shades and patterns, all in black and white. A fifty-two-inch TV set stood in the corner, and when Jenna admired it, Chloe said that she had a friend who loved sports and had bought it for her so they could watch together. As Jenna took a breath to ask about the friend, Chloe said, "Come on back to the kitchen. I'll show you around in a little while, but let's take some time to catch up first."

As she walked through, Jenna fell in love with the house. Warmth and charm seemed to radiate from the very walls. The kitchen was small but contained all the necessary appliances, including a microwave with more controls than a small jet plane and something Chloe called a convection oven. "I don't cook much, but when I do leftovers and TV dinners, those are the best and fastest." The *pièce de résistance* was the small garden in the back of the building, accessed by a door covered by a wrought-iron trellis which, Jenna imagined, was both protective as well as decorative. "I love what I've seen so far, especially this backyard." Jenna pointed to the door that led out the back. "May I?"

"Sure. The key's on the hook." Jenna dropped her suitcase on a kitchen chair and grabbed the key. She quickly unlocked the backdoor and stepped outside. "This is amazing," she said as Chloe followed her into the miniature garden, surrounded by a seven-foot-tall fence of classically weathered wood. The late spring air was thick with the smell of roses from several climbing vines that snaked their way up the brick wall, almost covering the kitchen window. "I have to keep cutting them or I wouldn't be able to see out at all," Chloe said, following Jenna's gaze.

A small patch of earth was filled with red and white impatiens and petunias. There was a tall wrought-iron pole with a bird feeder hanging from each of its curved arms. "I can't get over it." Off to one side was a small fish pond with several large goldfish and a tiny rock-strewn waterfall. "I would never have expected this in the middle of Manhattan."

"I know. It's a lot of work but I just love it. I still remember when Aunt Elise and I sat out here as adults and equals for the first time." There was a melancholy smile on Chloe's face.

"I'm sorry about her death."

"Yeah, me too. She was quite a lady," she hesitated, "and quite a pisser too. Wait until I tell you about her."

Jenna said, "From the little you've told me I'm sorry I never met her."

"Me too. You'd have liked her."

"I want to put my things away but let's sit out here for a while first and catch up. I'm just blown away by this garden."

A few minutes later the two women were stretched out on a pair of white wrought-iron lounge chairs covered with thickly stuffed red and white striped cushions, tall glasses of sweetened iced tea in their hands. "Tell me all about you," Chloe said and, slowly at first, then more definitively, Jenna told

Chloe about Glen and her feelings about him and about herself.

"He sounds like a keeper. What could be wrong with a good-looking attorney? Wasn't he any good in bed?"

Jenna blushed slightly. In college, the last time they had spent any real time together, Chloe had been quiet and demure but, in the time since, her friend had become surprisingly outspoken.

"He was fine in bed," Jenna said, finding it strangely easy to talk about it. "Actually, fine is a good word. It was very okay and not much more."

"No spark? No earth moving or sky rockets?"

"Sadly, no. I think I could have dealt with the rest if I hadn't felt so," she hesitated, then blurted out, "bored in bed."

"The death knell of any relationship."

"I felt like such a shit telling him no as he sat there with a ring in his hand. But Chloe, there was more to my leaving than Glen. His proposal made me focus on where I was headed and how I was living. I've never been just me, alone. When he asked me to marry him, I suddenly felt, well, almost claustrophobic. It was like the walls were closing in. I couldn't breathe." She slumped.

"I know exactly what you mean and that's why I'm so glad you're here," Chloe said. "I've no intention of settling down right now, either. Frankly, I'm having too much fun. I'm less into finding Mr. Right as I am into Mr. Right Now."

Jenna smiled at Chloe's candor. Suddenly she felt she had to get it all off of her chest. "It's Marcy too. We've always been so close that the thought of going from such a close relationship with her to another intimate one was strangling me. I want some aloneness, if that word has any meaning. I need to be me!"

"I realized that you two were trying to make separate friends. Maybe that was why she and I never got close in school."

"We really did try to be separate but once we were back in Seneca Falls, it all fell back into the same old pattern, and I didn't really mind for a while. Actually, I think Marcy would have been content to have us go on living in the same neighborhood, doing things together with our respective husbands."

"She's married?"

"No, but when she does, it will probably be to Mr. Seneca Falls and they'll have two-point-three children." Jenna stopped herself. "Sorry. That's not fair of me at all. Marcy's wonderful and my best friend. It's just that we're too close. I had to get away."

"Of course you did," Chloe said, sipping her iced tea.

"You understand?" Jenna said, a bit nonplused. Her friends in Seneca Falls had looked at her blankly, and then told her she was crazy. A few sympathized, but most were small-town people at heart and viewed New York City as some kind of Sodom and Gomorrah, a center for terrorism, robberies, and rapes.

"Don't look so surprised. I can't really relate to what goes on between you and Marcy," Chloe said, "being an only child and all, but I can understand what you're saying about being yourself. I've become a different person since I moved in here, so maybe the space will help you to get everything back into proportion."

"You do seem more alive than when we were in school. You were always so, I don't know, closed sort of. Now you've blossomed."

"Thanks for that," Chloe said with a grin. "Actually, when I came back home after I graduated, I got a job on Wall Street and became a staid, boring stockbroker. Business-casual clothes, business-casual lunches, business-casual friends, and a business-casual life. It was okay, but just okay."

"You seem anything but 'just okay' now. What changed besides you not being a boring stockbroker any more?"

"Aunt Elise changed me," Chloe said. "Let me get some more tea, and then I'll tell you about her. Want some?"

Jenna sensed the pain in Chloe's voice when she talked about her aunt. The two had obviously been very close. Jenna looked at her glass and said, "Sure. Let me give you a hand."

"Not necessary. Right back." As Jenna started to rise, Chloe grabbed the glass and motioned, "Sit, sit. I'll just be a moment. This is the last time I wait on you, however. From now on, you live here and you're on your own."

Settling back into her chair, Jenna thought about Chloe. The two women had had rooms close together in the dorm during their freshman year and had become closer and closer as their college years passed. By the end of their senior year they had been the best of friends, and the wrench she'd felt when Chloe had gone back to the city had been difficult. The two women had kept in touch in the intervening years, keeping each other up to date on their business lives. Socially they hadn't shared much, until now.

Jenna was jerked from her reverie by the sound of the back-door slamming. Chloe handed Jenna the refilled glass and settled back on the lounge chair. She sipped, then said, "Okay. As I wrote you, Aunt Elise died about six months ago."

"I'm sorry about her death. You seemed so devastated. You didn't talk much about her back when we knew each other."

"We got much closer after my folks died. She was the only one left of either of my parents' families. It was a tough year. First, my dad went from cancer; then my mom just sort of wasted away. During all that time Aunt Elise was there for everyone, giving as much of herself as anyone needed. I hadn't known her very well before that, but for all those months she was our rock. At first I loved her for helping, then I just loved her. She was a wonderful, classy, alive woman and she pulled me out of the depression I fell in after my folks were gone." Chloe sipped her tea, pain radiating from her body. "I'm sorry.

It seems so silly for me to still be upset. After all, it's been more than six months since she died."

"Stop apologizing. We all grieve in our own way and get over it at our own speed."

"I know, and Aunt Elise wouldn't want this. Exactly the opposite. She was the one who made me realize that we only go around once in this life and we should do things that give us joy."

"She sounds like someone I'd have liked."

"Oh, you would have hit it off with her and she'd have loved you too." Chloe gazed off into space, then said, "She was almost seventy when she got sick. We looked alike, you know. She was tiny, like me, with soft, curly, brown hair and striking blue eyes." Chloe smiled. "Her auburn hair probably came out of a bottle.

"So after my folks were gone, Aunt Elise and I got really close. We spent a lot of time together. She called me her alter ego. She was the kind of free spirit that I had always wanted to be but never thought I could, especially where her love life was concerned. She still had several men friends when she got sick."

"I'm so sorry. Her death must have been difficult for you, especially after living through it with your parents."

"It was." Jenna watched Chloe take a deep breath. "Her last years weren't easy. She was diagnosed with cancer about three years ago and died last November."

"I'm so sorry," Jenna said. Two and a half years. Jenna's parents had died suddenly in an auto accident when the two girls were in their final year of graduate school. The shock had been devastating, but now that she thought about it, how difficult must it be for someone to have to deal with it for two and a half years.

"Me too," Chloe said. "Before that, she was the most active, interested and interesting woman I ever met. We took vacations together, went to the theater and movies, and just enjoyed life. We spent so much time together and I began to change, to be like her. It became more and more important for me to do things that gave me pleasure. It didn't take a rocket scientist to discover that I hated being a stockbroker, and we talked at great length about what I wanted to do. She convinced me to go back to school to study art, not the fine arts stuff but graphic design. She helped me with the cost of my courses and gave me a party when I finally got up the nerve to quit my Wall Street job. As you know, I'm still working at the same advertising agency I started with back then. It's not nearly as much money as Wall Street, but I really love what I do."

"She sounds like a very generous lady." Jenna and Marcy had had to work part-time throughout school to supplement their scholarships, Jenna waiting tables in the local watering hole and Marcy writing short stories for a magazine and articles for the local paper.

"Yes, she was. At the time it seemed okay to let her help and I agreed to pay her back when I could but, after a while, I realized that although she spent like she had lots of money, things were getting tight for her. Then she was diagnosed with cancer. It sucked, long and messy. She was in and out of the hospital and, during those final months despite insurance, the out-of-pocket for her medical care was astronomical. She went through everything. When I show you around, you'll see that the downstairs and my bedroom are pretty much the only parts of the house that are still furnished."

"Why didn't she sell the building? It seems that something like this," she gazed around the brownstone, "in the middle of Manhattan, must be worth quite a bit."

"I tried to get her to sell but she was incredibly stubborn. She loved this house as much as I do now and wanted me to have it after her death. I argued but she wouldn't change her mind, obstinate old darling. So I helped with whatever I could. I emptied my meager savings account, secretly paying part of the costs of almost everything so she could have the illusion that she could afford it all. At the end, she had hospice care and passed away right here in this house. She wanted that very much." Chloe sniffled and Jenna pulled a Kleenex from her purse and handed it to her. "I was holding her hand when she died."

"I'm so sorry. It must have been very difficult for you."

She sniffled, then brightened and said, "That's in the past now, but I love this building so I'm here, and I'm going to stay here for as long as I can manage. The tax payments are tough and that's where your rent money will help a lot."

"Of course. This should work out just great, and give me time to figure out my life."

"There's one more thing that we need to talk about. I lead a pretty active social life and I hope we won't get in each other's way."

"We won't. I don't think I'm going to be doing much dating, at least until I get my head together." She didn't want to get into a relationship and have to tell another guy no the way she had with Glen.

Chloe looked horrified. "Of course you'll date. That's what you're here for."

"No, it's really not. I need space and time to figure myself out."

"Nonsense. From what I hear, you need to experience everything and that means a social life and a sex life. Sky rockets, earthquakes and all. You need to find out whether Glen is the one or not and you can't do that without other men to compare him to. Take it from me, good sex is the best cure for whatever ails you. You said he was just average. It's time you found someone who makes your toes curl."

Was curling toes a cure for her confusion? "I'll think about it."

"If I have anything to do with it, you'll do more than just think about it."

Chapter
3

The two women talked for several hours until the lowering sun and the shadows of the nearby buildings darkened the little garden and voracious mosquitoes forced the women inside. They talked about nothing and everything and quickly all of Jenna's remaining unease about the living arrangements lifted. Chloe was still the same easy-to-be-with, caring person she had been in college. Although Jenna and Chloe had been friends in school, she hadn't felt as close as they did after that one long afternoon.

When they eventually went inside, Chloe took Jenna on a quick tour of the brownstone. The charming four-story building consisted of a living room, dining room, kitchen and one bedroom on the main floor with three bedrooms of varying sizes on each of the upper floors. "I sleep down here," Chloe explained, "and you can have the larger bedroom on the second floor."

"I'll take a smaller room," Jenna said quickly. "I don't need much space."

"Actually there are only two bedrooms with furniture, mine and the one I picked for you. I put your boxes there, so let's just leave it the way it is for now. I'm happy where I am."

"There's no furniture in the other rooms?"

"Oh, there's a bed in most of them, and a dresser in some, but not much else. Aunt Elise was into antiques so when she got sick we sold off most of the contents of the upstairs. We also replaced the good pieces downstairs with stuff from discount stores. She liked to think of it as redecorating."

"I didn't realize that money had gotten that tight."

"She had been a collector of sorts and spent freely, so the furnishings were worth quite a bit. Between that and my secret supplements she had private-duty nursing and the best food from good restaurants. Remember that scene in the movie *Arthur*, when he brings the butler the meal on the cart? I took that to heart. At the end, eating was her only real pleasure."

Chloe opened the door to her bedroom. "Aunt Elise took over this room when she got sick and I moved into it after she died." Like the living room, Chloe's bedroom gave the immediate impression of being comfortable. It was just big enough for a queen-sized bed with a bright crazy quilt topped with brightly colored pillows, a rocking chair with flame red seat and back cushions, a narrow dresser topped by a large mirror, and several white ginger jar lamps. A TV stood on the corner of the dresser, arranged so Chloe could watch in bed. The thick, moss green carpeting matched the drapes.

"This is a great room," Jenna said. "Inviting, welcoming somehow."

"Except for putting the regular bed back instead of the hospital one, it's not too different from when Aunt Elise lived in here. I hope you don't think it's ghoulish but I feel closer to her with her rocking chair and quilt still here."

"It's not ghoulish at all."

Chloe showed Jenna her large closet, stuffed with clothes, a wardrobe that must have cost a small fortune. "Wow," Jenna said.

"Yeah. I love nice clothes and you know how I love to shop."

Chloe backed out of her room and led Jenna up the stairs.

She opened the door to the room on the left. It was as cheery as Chloe's room, with soft rose carpet, a queen-sized bed with a mauve satin quilt as a bedspread, sprinkled with small roses and matching pillow shams. One wall held a triple-width dresser and a desk/makeup table combination with a small upholstered chair. "I got new linens and stuff when you told me you were coming." She stroked the quilt. "I had a ball in one of those giant bed-and-bath stores. I got you new towels and mats too."

"You didn't have to spend the money. I don't know how long I'll even be here." Jenna knew that Chloe hadn't fully recovered financially from her aunt's illness and so felt slightly guilty. She hadn't wanted Chloe to spend anything on her. "I offered to send anything we might need."

"I know it wasn't necessary but I just couldn't help myself. I want you to be comfortable."

"Thanks." Jenna was starting to understand why Chloe had trouble making the tax payments on the building. Maybe she could help her friend get her financial house in order. It was usually Marcy who made budgets but Chloe certainly needed help if she was going be able to stay in the brownstone.

Chloe opened the door to the double closet and Jenna saw her boxes, neatly stacked off to one side. "Those were heavy," Jenna said, shaking her head. "I hope you didn't try to carry them upstairs by yourself. I fully intended to help you."

Chloe winked. "Don't worry, I didn't carry them myself." She batted her eyelashes. "When you're five feet tall, no one lets you do anything. One look at me and the UPS guy called me honey, carried everything upstairs, and put it all in the closet."

Jenna couldn't suppress a chuckle. "Doesn't playing helpless get you down from time to time? From what I remember you're as helpless as a barracuda."

"I know that, and you know that, but when it suits me"—she batted her eyelashes again—"no one else does."

Jenna burst out laughing. "Okay. I give."

Early on Tuesday morning, Jenna took the copy of the advertisement in the *New York Times* and made her way to the temp agency Chloe had found. She explained to the manager that she didn't want a permanent position since she didn't know how long she'd be in town. With her letters of reference from AAJ and her scores on the computerized exams she took, she was immediately welcomed into the cadre of translators at a generous hourly rate. "It says you've specialized in simultaneous translation. I've got something for you for tomorrow if you're ready to begin working. I've got some textile importers from Hamburg coming to negotiate with the president of a small firm in the garment district. I had intended to send someone else but, if I can arrange it, I'd like him to stay on the long-term assignment he's on. I had just about given up hope of finding anyone."

"Sure. Sounds great." A job already. *This is going to work out fine.*

Just before nine the following morning she arrived at Paramount Textiles, in the heart of the garment district. She'd dressed carefully for this, her first job. With Chloe's help, she'd selected a beige linen pantsuit with a black, knit, short-sleeved top and black flat-heeled shoes. She'd kept her jewelry simple, wearing only a slender gold necklace and matching earrings.

She fought her way across west Forty-seventh Street, weaving between rolling racks of dresses and slacks in every color of the rainbow and triple-parked trucks, finally arriving at the ancient but spacious building just on time. As she got off the elevator on the fourth floor, she was almost tackled by a tall, angular man of about thirty-five, with lots of deep brown hair, touches of grey already gracing the temples, and large, flashing brown eyes that glared at her from behind rimless glasses. He was scowling and pacing the front office. "If you're Jenny Bryant, the translator the agency sent," the man said without preamble, his face flushed, "let's get started."

"Are you Mr. McBride?" When he snapped a quick nod, she continued, "I'm sorry if you've been waiting for me but I was told to be here at nine."

The man glanced at his watch, then huffed and looked chagrined. "Call me, Toby, and I'm the one who's sorry." When his eyes softened, she realized that he was really quite nice looking. "I'm very anxious about these negotiations and I guess I let it get to me. You're actually right on time, Jenny. Can we begin?"

"Of course," she said, realizing that she probably had more experience at such meetings than Toby had. "And it's Jenna."

"Jenna?"

"My name is Jenna."

"Jenna. Unusual name. Would you like some coffee?"

"No, thank you. I'm fine. Why don't we just get started?"

He led her into a room with a wall of windows, and she placed her purse on the long wooden table covered with papers, bolts of fabric, and a large assortment of swatches. He introduced her to two men, Herr Schuller and Herr Morgen. They nodded to her, and they exchanged a few words with Jenna in their native language.

"What did you say to them?"

"I just asked which part of Germany they were from and how they liked New York. Sorry, I was just trying to put them at ease. I sense that they are as nervous about these talks as you are."

"Really? That's very good to know."

There was another interchange, then Jenna said, "They complimented you on your written proposal."

Toby raised a quizzical eyebrow. "There was more than that. You blushed."

She found herself embarrassed as she said, "They also complimented me on my pronunciation."

His sudden smile lit his face but there was an edge of irritation to his voice as well. "That's great. You're getting along with them better than I am already."

He's off the wall, Jenna thought. Calmly, as if to a frightened child, she said, "Since I'm an extension of you it's good for both of us."

Toby nodded and began to speak. For the next three hours, the three people bargained, haggling over delivery dates, quantities, and shipping costs, with Jenna easily keeping the conversations straight. At just after twelve, Jenna said to Toby, "I don't know what your plans are, but I'd suggest a nice lunch about now. I think they're close to agreeing to most of your terms but they need some time to let it all gel." This was a common tactic at AAJ and Jenna had been part of dozens of such lunches.

She watched Toby consider it, then nod. "Good idea. Why don't you mention it to them?"

After a few minutes of discussion, a restaurant was agreed on. "If you don't mind another suggestion," Jenna said, "when we get to the restaurant, I'll go to the ladies room and stay a while. Maybe you can arrange to get a phone call so they can have a few minutes to talk things over in private."

"Okay. Great idea. You're really good at this," Toby said, his eyes glowing with obvious admiration. "I'll set that up when we get there."

By midafternoon, all terms had been set and the contracts were being drawn up in English. "Can you come back tomorrow and translate the terms and conditions for them?"

"You'll have to arrange that through the agency. You know that they'll have to have their own people go over the documents in detail back home."

"I know, but I'm hoping to make them more comfortable with everything before they leave. If there are any last-minute hitches, maybe we can take care of them then."

"Sure, no problem."

"Thanks for being so patient with me. This deal is my first venture into the international market. I was a bit nervous about it."

Dryly, Jenna said, "I never would have guessed." Toby had the good grace to look chagrined, and then they both burst out laughing.

By the time she left at five-thirty, her agency had given her the go ahead for the second day, and had given her a two-day assignment for the following week.

At dinner that evening she told Chloe about her day. "That's great," Chloe said. "You seem to have been a hit."

"Yeah. Toby called the agency late this afternoon and gave me a glowing recommendation."

"Is he cute?"

Jenna blushed. She thought he was very attractive but that wasn't a businesslike thing to admit. "I didn't really notice," she said, uncomfortable with herself for sounding a bit stuffy.

"Right. And I don't notice when I look at that guy from *CSI Miami*. The cute one with the great biceps."

"Really, I didn't pay any attention to his looks. This was business."

"Of course it was. So, do you think he'll ask you to dinner tomorrow night?"

Chuckling, Jenna said, "You're incorrigible. Okay, yes, he's very good looking." She hesitated. "He looks sort of like Glen."

Chloe frowned. "Stop obsessing about your ex. He's in the past, or at least that's where you should put him if you don't want to get serious with him. It's kinder to both of you." Chloe bit down on a burger she'd brought in from a restaurant down the street. "So, if he asks, will you have dinner with him?"

Would she? Maybe she needed to get back on the dating horse. She mentally shook herself. This was all silly. He wasn't going to ask her to dinner.

"How about having dinner with me?" Toby said, the following afternoon after the two Germans had left. "I'd like to get to know you better."

"Let me be perfectly honest with you, Toby," Jenna said. "I'm just out of a long-term relationship and I don't know whether I'm ready for anything else right now."

Toby stared at her. "I asked you to have dinner with me as a friend. Relax. I haven't devoured a dinner partner in weeks. I just wanted to thank you properly for all your help these last two days. You sped things up and made some very helpful suggestions." All at once he looked like a little boy. "And you kept me sane."

Jenna felt perfectly silly. Here he was thanking her for her skill and she was acting like a ninny. "Sorry. I guess I'm a little gun-shy. Sure, I'd love to have dinner with you."

He asked whether she'd ever had real authentic Indian food and she admitted that she hadn't, but that she'd love to try. An hour later they were sitting across from each other at a quiet restaurant near his office, sipping red wine.

"Tell me a little about yourself," Toby suggested, moving the small lamp to the side of the table where it was out of the way.

By the time the appetizers arrived, she'd given him a capsule version of her days at SUNY Albany and her experiences with AAJ. She'd even told him a very brief version of her relationship with Glen. "Tell me what everything is," she said, pointing to the plate of assorted finger food, "and warn me what's hot."

"Are you afraid of hot things?" he asked smoothly, and Jenna wondered whether he had meant the double-entendre.

Deciding to ignore it as her imagination, she answered, "Not at all. I just like to be warned." *Phew,* she thought. That answer could have the same kind of double meaning. She was about to correct any misinterpretation when she reconsidered. *Why not flirt a little? After all, Chloe's right. I do have to move on, so why not try my wings.*

His smile was warm and open. "Okay. I promise I'll warn you." He held her gaze for just a moment longer than necessary, then pointed out the tandoori chicken, mango chutney, vegetable fritters, and a sausage-looking thing called kefta or something like that. "Oh, and this," he said, indicating a crisp, flat bread covered with black specks, "might be spicy. Sometimes it is and sometimes it just tickles the tip of your tongue."

There was nothing in what he said that was in the slightest bit suggestive, but his tone was warm and invitational. To change the subject, she said, "You've heard the condensed version of my life story, how about yours?"

"Fair enough." Between bites, Toby told Jenna that he had graduated from NYU with a degree in business and had taken over his father's company when his dad had retired several years before. He had been married for four years, a marriage that had ended two years previously. They discovered that they shared a love of classical music, but while Jenna worked out three times a week, Toby was a couch potato and enjoyed watching vintage sitcoms. During a meal of chicken saag and a moderately spicy lamb curry with rice, two kinds of bread, and a delicious concoction of cucumber, yogurt, and mint, they discovered that they generally agreed politically but disagreed on the administration's handling of the trouble in the Middle East.

Toby ordered an orange-sherbert dessert that arrived in hollowed-out oranges, and as she ate, Jenna found herself telling him about Chloe and her recent arrival in New York City. When she mentioned Marcy and her need to get away from her twin sister, he asked, "Are you two identical?"

"Our genes say we are, but except for things that we can't change, like our height and eye color, we're really very different. She's a planner and I'm a by-the-seat-of-the-pants kind of girl. She's also more of a couch-potato type, like you." She heard what she'd just said. "I didn't mean that as an insult, you understand, it's just different from the way I am. I like to stay in shape. I mean—" She swallowed. "I'm sorry. None of that came out right."

"I understood exactly what you meant. There's no need to apologize. I gather that your sister is still back home in—?"

"Upstate. Seneca Falls to be exact and, yes, she's still there. She does document translation for the company I used to work for."

"You're both translators. Maybe you're not as different as you might think."

Jenna thought for a moment. "Yeah, maybe."

As the waiter stopped at the table for the third time in five minutes, asking whether there would be anything else, Toby looked around, then at his watch. "I think they are giving us a hint."

Jenna glanced around and saw that they were the only ones left in the restaurant. "I think we're overstaying our welcome."

"It's after ten and I guess they're ready to close up." He took out his credit card and handed it to the hovering waiter.

Jenna felt incredibly awkward. She and Glen had always gone Dutch, but she didn't know whether it would be an insult to mention it. Toby seemed to read her mind. "This is a business dinner to thank you for all your help with those Germans."

"I was only doing my job," she said.

"You did quite a bit more. You're bright and quick and you have a great people sense. You seemed to know exactly how to handle them, when to push a bit and when to back off. You were a real asset."

Glowing with the unexpected praise, Jenna said, "Thanks."

"I told the folks at the agency too." He took her hand across the pink tablecloth and gazed into her eyes. "Now that we're done with the business end of this, let me say that I really enjoyed our dinner and I'd love to see you again. I really mean that."

Jenna's hand warmed at his touch and she felt her pulse

speed. "I'd like that," she said, realizing that she meant it. "Let me give you my cell-phone number. I don't know whether I'll bother getting my own phone, so I'll use my cell for personal calls for now." She gave him the number and he wrote it down on a piece of paper that he carefully put in his wallet. She wrote down his home number as well.

He signed the credit-card slip, and then the two of them walked out into the warm, late-spring night. "I live in a converted loft not far from here," Toby said, "but I'd like to see you home."

"Don't be silly," she said. "I'll get a taxi."

He stood with her while they flagged down a passing taxi. As she climbed in, Toby said, "Take care and I'll call you. Maybe we can get together one evening next week."

"That would be wonderful," she said, then gave the address of the brownstone to the taxi driver.

Since she had no assignment for the following day, Jenna wandered around New York City doing tourist things while Chloe was at work. She took the elevator to the top of the Empire State Building and stared in awe in all directions. She took a subway to Ground Zero and found her eyes filling at the sight of the massive empty space and the memories of that awful day, then pulled herself together and walked to Chinatown for lunch. In the afternoon she visited the United Nations Building, wondering whether she'd ever work there. They probably have all the translators they need, she thought, but it would be exciting to be part of international peace negotiations or something equally dramatic.

She arrived home, marveling at the fact that she already thought of it as home, at about five. She poured herself a glass of iced tea, stretched out in the back garden and called Marcy, knowing her sister would have just arrived home from work. "How did your second day at Paramount go?" Marcy asked.

"Just great. I felt really good about my part in the negotiations. I think I really greased a few of the wheels."

"You always do, Jen," Marcy said. "Tell me about the boss. You were less than candid when I spoke to you on Wednesday."

Jenna could hear the unbridled curiosity in Marcy's voice. "I didn't mean to be evasive. He's nice." She lowered her voice. "He took me to dinner."

"What?"

Louder, she said, "He took me to dinner. We had real Indian food. You'd have loved it. We had—"

"I'm not interested in the dinner menu. Tell me about the man. Come on, give."

"He's very nice. Midthirties, divorced, like that." Somehow, for the first time, she found she didn't want to go into all the details of her evening. Although it was nothing more than a dinner between business acquaintances, it felt personal.

"Okay," Marcy said, no trace of ire in her voice. "I understand if you want to keep this to yourself. One of the things we vowed was to build separate lives while you were gone." She paused, then continued, "By the way, I saw Glen today. He said to tell you that he'd give you all the time you want but he's still hoping you'll come back. He's still acting as if you'll be back by Christmas."

"He's so focused on that six-month thing. I wish he'd just let go."

"I know, but he's really in love with you. I think you really threw him a curve when you turned him down. He seems a bit lost now."

Jenna uncrossed and recrossed her legs. "You've always been fond of him. Take him to dinner and try to get him to understand. Take him to dinner just because."

"I'm not horning in on your boyfriend, Jen."

"He's not my boyfriend any more, and if you're interested, nothing could make me happier."

"If you're trying to push a relationship, let me make this clear. Glen's a nice guy and I like him as a friend but I'm not interested in him. I'm not interested in anyone. I'm very happy just the way I am."

They had had this discussion several times recently. Jenna worried about the way Marcy seemed content to sit around with little or no social life. Maybe her dates with Glen had been a bit predictable but at least she'd had dates. "I know that. I just wish—" she stopped herself. It did no good to restate something that Marcy already knew. "I love you, Sis, very much."

"I love you, too, Jen. Call me when you want and I'll do likewise." The connection ended.

Chloe arrived home a few minutes later. "How about going somewhere for dinner?" Chloe believed the old joke. What she made for dinner was reservations.

"Sure. Where to?"

They settled on a noodle house a few blocks down on First Avenue. "I've got a date tomorrow night," Chloe said, neatly eating her soup with spoon and chopsticks. "He's got a friend in from out of town. Any interest?"

"I don't think so," Jenna said, juggling a spoon in one hand and awkwardly using chopsticks with the other, trying not to spill down her shirt. "Thanks anyway."

"I wish you'd give it a bit of thought. I know the other guy and he's really nice. He's not Glen, of course, but he's intelligent, interesting and has a great sense of humor. It would be a great favor to me."

"Why are you so anxious to set me up?" Jenna asked, deciding to tuck a napkin into the neck of her sky blue tee shirt.

"I worry that you'll spend a few months here, then scurry back to the safety of Seneca Falls, having experienced nothing of what there is to experience here."

"And that's sex, right?"

"It's variety. It's men, good food, good conversation, flirtation, and that wonderful heat when two people begin to dance around the attraction they feel. And, yes, it's sex."

Jenna squirmed under Chloe's scrutiny. "I've been sexual. Glen and I had some pretty wild times."

"Yeah, you told me," Chloe said, raising a quizzical eyebrow.

Slightly annoyed, Jenna said, "Stop putting me and Seneca Falls and Glen down like some collection of small-town people with nothing exciting ever happening. It's not like that."

"I'm only quoting you, Jenna. You said you were here to experience things and this is how. Wouldn't you feel like a horse's ass if you went back and discovered, sometime down the line, what you'd been missing? There's more to life than Glen. You're chomping at the bit to do something but you're too chicken to reach for it."

Jenna sat back and put her spoon and chopsticks down. She wanted to rail at Chloe, tell her that she should mind her own business, but she also was enough of a realist to accept that some of what her friend was saying was true. She had come to New York to grow, to reach out for things. "This would be just a date," Jenna said finally. "No prior commitment or understanding. No tacit agreement for sex afterwards."

Chloe made a face. "I wouldn't do that to you," she said, putting her utensils down. "Not a chance. Harry is a thoroughly nice guy who I've been seeing for several months on and off. His friend's name is Brand and he's in town from Dallas. As a favor to Harry I arranged a friend for Brand when he was last in New York. The four of us had dinner, went to a movie, and that was that. No strings. No nothing. Stop being so suspicious. Yes, I want you to get out and experience life but whether or not you get laid is completely up to you."

Jenna had to smile at Chloe's blunt language. "I'm sorry I got so carried away." She realized that people at nearby tables were leaning closer to hear the rest of the conversation so she lowered her voice. "That's the second time this week. I guess I've got ulterior motives on the brain."

"No problem," Chloe said with a dismissive wave of her hand. "So, will you come with us? We're thinking of seeing that new Jack Nicholson film."

Jenna let out a long breath. "Sure. Okay. That sounds fine."

"Great. I'll call Harry when we get home."

Chapter
4

After a delightful evening with Chloe, Harry, and Brand, Jenna lay in bed thinking about the way her life had progressed since arriving in New York City just a week before. She'd had dates with two different men and had had fun with each. Where Toby was serious and sexy, Brand had been just plain fun. She and Toby had discussed a myriad of subjects, while with the foursome earlier that evening she had laughed more than she could remember. Harry and Brand tossed one-liners back and forth, keeping the women laughing with genuine good humor.

Toby was very attractive and sexy looking and made her heart skip a beat or two, and, while Brand was ordinary looking, with thinning toast-brown hair, a thick nose, and a body like a fire hydrant, she quickly forgot to notice his looks at all. Two different men with two different personalities, both of whom she had enjoyed.

As she thought about dating, her mind inevitably drifted to sex, and, while Brand was fun, it was Toby who filled her mind. Thinking about Toby she imagined how his mouth would feel against hers, how his hands would feel on her breasts. Would his touch excite her differently than Glen's had? She remembered her last sexual, rather ordinary, experience with her ex and sighed. Her ex. Interesting way to think of him, but she guessed that that was exactly what he was. *Ex-what*, she didn't know, but he was history, at least for now. Would she consider going back to Seneca Falls and her old life with him? Certainly not right now.

Where was this all going? What was she here for? Was Chloe right when she said that getting back on the sexual horse was the perfect way to begin to sort things out? Maybe, but that didn't mean tackling some man on a first date. But what about on the second or third? She quickly realized how awkward it would be to bring some man back to the brownstone with Chloe's bedroom right off the living room, possibly entertaining there or in the main room. As Jenna fell asleep, she realized she'd have to talk to Chloe about it.

The following morning the two women were sprawled in the living room, surrounded by pieces of the Sunday *New York Times*. After a long period of silence, Jenna said, "Chloe, there's something we need to figure out."

Chloe pulled off her reading glasses, ones she wore only at home to give her eyes a rest from her contact lenses. "Sure, Jen. What's up?"

"This is a bit embarrassing. I was thinking about last evening. I had a great time, by the way, and thanks for kicking me in the behind and getting me to accept the invitation. Anyway, the guys dropped us off and avoided an awkward moment by simply saying good night and getting back into the taxi. But what do we do about inviting a man back here for, well let's just call them, extracurricular activities?"

"Extra . . . Oh, yeah." Her face took on a hopeful expression. "Are you starting to think about real dates? Like with sex afterward?"

"Don't go jumping to conclusions, Chloe, I just want to think things through in advance." And, yes, I'm thinking about sex.

"I understand what you're getting at. Living here, together, is like having a college roommate, except that you can't just hang a ribbon on the door and ask the other guy to come back in three hours. I've actually been thinking about it."

"Any ideas?"

She crossed her legs. "How about this? What if we set up a second living room upstairs? We have all those just-about-empty rooms. Let's get a small sofa, a chair or two, and stuff. That way you can have the upstairs and I can have the downstairs. If I'm in the living room and you and a friend want to go upstairs, just move quietly and we'll all pretend not to notice."

"That's a great idea, but won't furniture cost a lot? I'm really not sure how long I'll be here, after all. It sounds like a giant undertaking for what might only be a month or two." She knew that, at best, Chloe's finances were precarious. Although a second living room was a great idea, she wasn't about to spend much on it, or allow Chloe to.

"Shopping will be such fun. Hold on a minute." Dashing from the room, Chloe returned with the Yellow Pages. Flipping through the much-used volume, she said, "Let's see where we can start."

"Chloe," Jenna said, stemming the rush of shopping enthusiasm bursting from her friend, "I don't have money to spend on furniture and you don't either."

"I know, but shopping's such fun."

"It might be fun but we can't afford it. Isn't there another way? Do you know anyone we can borrow some stuff from?"

Chloe deflated, then brightened. "Wait a minute. I remember seeing something in here." She began rapidly turning pages, wetting her middle finger occasionally.

"Do you read that thing in your spare time?" Jenna said sarcastically. "It's worn and dogeared like an old bible or something."

"The Yellow Pages is a gas to browse through. You'd never believe what goes on in this town, and you can find such interesting places to shop and stuff. Lots of people are switching to using the Internet, but to my mind computers are a great mystery, except for graphics, of course. For me the good old Yellow Pages does the trick." She flipped a few more pages, then said, "Here it is. Furniture rentals."

"You can rent furniture?"

"Sure. Several guys I know come to town for several months at a time on business. Their company finds a sublet and sometimes they need to add a few pieces. So they rent." She scanned the page. "Look. There are several places right around here. We can pick up a few big pieces on a month-to-month basis and fill in with small stuff. Looks like they all deliver, pick up, and everything." She tapped one finger on a large display ad. "This one's even open on Sunday."

"Only in New York," Jenna muttered.

That afternoon, after deciding which room would work out best for a second living room, Chloe and Jenna visited a nearby rental company and picked out a nondescript sofa, side chair, end and coffee tables, and a couple of lamps. The salesman did a few calculations and came up with a surprisingly reasonable monthly charge. Since Jenna had only two days of work booked for the following week, they arranged to have the pieces delivered midweek. After that, Jenna would see how the room shaped up and decide what little touches she wanted to add.

Every day she'd fallen more in love with the house, and it seemed more and more important to help her friend with the taxes. She found that, to compensate for Chloe's extravagance, she was suddenly reluctant to spend money. Jenna vowed that they would eat home every night and that when she worked she would bring a salad or a sandwich from home. She'd try her best to get through at least the next payment. Would Chloe take money from her if she really needed it? Jenna didn't know but, just in case, she decided to try her best not to touch her savings.

The agency had said that she could expect to work on an

average of one or two days a week. "Of course, it might be an entire week and then nothing for a while, but as long as you're available we'll do the best we can." *I can always get a full-time job*, Jenna thought, then stopped herself. Chloe wasn't her responsibility. She was a big girl and well able to take care of herself.

She spent some time working on a budget, thinking of how Marcy would laugh. Budgeting? Jenna? When she'd juggled the numbers and made some conservative projections, she decided that things would be okay for a while. It was summer and she'd be filling in for lots of vacationing translators, but once fall came she was afraid her work days would dwindle and she might have to start digging into her meager savings.

Monday evening, she and Chloe disassembled the bed from the larger of the two remaining rooms on the second floor and wrestled it and the dresser to an upstairs room Chloe used for storage. "Holy shit," Jenna said, when she entered the small room. "It looks like the photos of King Tut's tomb." She wandered around, poking into stacks of boxes and jumbled piles of odds and ends. "If you don't mind," Jenna said, picking up a magazine rack, "I might move some of these things to my 'sitting room.' " She said the last two words in such a mock-snooty voice that Chloe had to giggle.

"Sure. Great. Aunt Elise was quite a collector and this was what was left over after we sold off the furniture. I was in such a state that I just dumped stuff up here." She tapped on a box of books. "I don't even know what all is up here, but I know that Aunt Elise would be glad to see some of this stuff being useful again."

"Collector?"

"Well, she shopped a lot on her travels, buying all kinds of things she just 'had to have' at the time." With a self-deprecating smile, Chloe said, "I guess that's where I get it from."

Jenna prowled. In addition to the boxes there were a few

small tables, one with a missing leg, four standing lamps, one particularly ugly one with a red-tasseled shade, a rolled-up throw rug, and a number of oil paintings that were balanced against one wall. An old-fashioned, full-length mirror, in a mahogany frame that allowed it to tilt, stood off to one side. She'd read about those in the occasional romance novel. *Pier glasses*, she thought they were called.

Tossed in one corner were a pile of pillows of all sizes, some with satin or velvet covers, others fringed, many embroidered with phrases like "Memories of the Catskills" and "April in Paris." One had a picture of the pyramids of Giza and another the Tower of London. "Phew. What an eclectic woman she must have been."

"Eclectic. That's a good word for it but let's be frank. Elise was a junk collector and she freely admitted it. She picked up nicknacks from anywhere and everywhere." Chloe pointed to several large cardboard boxes dumped haphazardly in one corner. "Those are filled with the contents of two large china cabinets we sold. Some of the stuff . . . well, you'll never believe it. From the beautiful to the unusual, to the just plain ugly."

"Can I rummage?"

"Anytime you want. And whatever you want for your sitting room, or anywhere else for that matter, use with Aunt Elise's blessing."

About a week later Jenna used her sitting room for the first time. She and Toby had had a second sexually charged dinner with a kiss as they parted that, as Chloe would have put it, curled her toes. The previous evening they had talked on the phone, a teasing conversation peppered with double-entendres and innuendoes. It had become clear to her that, after dinner that evening, she'd be dessert. Why the hell not, she told herself when she started to have second and third thoughts. Why the hell not! They were adults and could indulge in adult pleasures if they wanted to.

Toby picked her up at the house and they went to a trendy

East-Side restaurant that specialized in what they called nou-
velle fusion cuisine, whatever that meant. Knowing what was
to follow, Jenna found it difficult to eat her appetizer, some
concoction of crab and kiwi fruit, washing most mouthfuls
down with sauvignon blanc. She was concentrating so much
on her nervousness that she didn't notice that Toby wasn't
eating at all. "Jenna, this is silly," he said after the tenth long
silence. "I think we know what's happening here and we're
both nervous as hell. It's going to ruin what might be a great
meal. Let's get out of here."

Relieved, yet increasingly jittery, Jenna merely nodded.
The waiter looked disappointed when Toby asked for the
check before they ordered the main course, but he was quite
obviously pleased with the large tip Toby added to the credit-
card receipt. Silently, the couple left the restaurant and hur-
ried back to the brownstone.

Jenna led Toby to her new upstairs sitting room and the two
settled quickly on the sofa. Without much preamble, Toby's
arms were around her and his lips were pressed against hers.
Toby's mouth was soft, coaxing not expecting. His tongue re-
quested entry to her mouth and she granted it, reveling in the
emotions, the flaring heat, the excitement of something so
new. She slipped her hands beneath his jacket and pulled his
shirt from the waist of his pants so she could feel his skin,
drowning in a now frantic need for him.

It seemed to take only moments until their clothes were off
and his hands were on her naked breasts. They kissed and
fondled, driving her to the heights of arousal. All too quickly,
however, Toby unrolled a condom over his erection and thrust
deeply into her. It took only moments for him to climax.

Jenna was bitterly disappointed. She had expected all the
things she hadn't had with Glen and here she was having experienced the same kind of sex she'd had before. Quick, ordinary and unsatisfying. Later, as they lay stretched out on the
sofa, Toby sensed her feelings. "I'm so sorry, Jenna. I've been

anticipating this evening all day and I got a little ahead of you." His fingers idly played with her nipple as he talked. "You're so beautiful, so sexy that I got carried away."

"It was wonderful, Toby," Jenna said, trying to sound upbeat. "Anticipation got to me too."

He cupped her chin and turned her face so she couldn't help but gaze into his eyes. "Don't lie to me, Jenna," he said. "Don't ever lie to me like that. Just relax and let me see what I can do to make it up to you." He pinched her nipple until she gasped.

Jenna was used to Glen's style of lovemaking. He was never in the mood for more playing once he'd climaxed so she didn't want Toby to make promises that he wouldn't keep, either verbally or with his hands. She just wanted to drag her body down from its current excited state. "I'm fine, Toby."

He lifted himself onto one elbow. "I don't leave a lady unsatisfied," he announced, and he covered her mouth with his. Jenna wanted to hold back, keep herself from any additional disappointment, but his kisses were irresistible. She was already aroused so it took his hands and his mouth only moments to drive her upward. Colors whirled in her brain, bright reds and oranges, sulfurous yellows blending as she climbed.

She slid her hands around his waist, then up his sweat dampened back, the length of her naked body against the length of his, moving constantly so she could feel him. Firmly his knee pressed hers apart and his thigh pressed against her mound. She opened her legs and unashamedly thrust against his well-developed leg muscles.

As she rubbed, he slid down and closed his mouth on her breast. He suckled, then blew a stream of cool air on her wet skin. She felt her body responding and her legs parted further. Quickly his hand slipped between her thighs. "You're so wet," he said, "and so hot. Poor hungry, unsatisfied girl." God, she was so hungry. Would he know what to do?

He seemed to know exactly what she wanted. He found her

clit and started to stroke, creating a rhythm that she matched with her hips. "Yes, Jenna," he growled, his mouth still on her nipple. "Move with me." And she did, her hips writhing, trying to press his hands against all the places that itched with need. He bit lightly. "Tell me what you want."

"You," Jenna moaned as two of his fingers entered her swollen, slippery channel. "God. Do that."

"Good girl. Tell me. Show me."

She grabbed his wrist and held his hand against her as she rubbed her flesh against his fingers. Then he climbed off the sofa, knelt beside her, and pressed his cheek against her belly. "You smell of heat and sex. It's the strongest aphrodisiac I know." He grabbed her hand, put it between his legs so she could feel him, hard again. "See what you do to me?"

Then his face was between her thighs, his tongue caressing where his fingers had just been. Glen had never been interested in oral sex and she thought she didn't care about it either. What difference could it possibly make whether it was fingers or a tongue, but she was wrong. God, very wrong. The feel of Toby's mouth on her was electric, causing shafts of pleasure to rocket from her cunt to her nipples and back again. It was all she could do not to scream.

When she thought she'd had as much as she could take, he continued, adding his clever fingers to his mouth, filling her and driving her upward, only to relax and let her down so he could push her up again. "God, I can't stop it," she said, knowing she would climax in moments. Quickly he put on another condom and plunged into her again, his cock as hard as it had been before. His teeth pulled at her nipple and his fingers found her clit as she exploded and felt him join her.

Spasms rocked her for several minutes, then finally her body calmed. "That was unbelievable," she said, still panting. "No one ever—"

"Don't think about others. Just concentrate on enjoying what we did," he said, still playing with her cunt.

She'd had enough and gently pushed his hand away. "I'm sure I won't think of much else for quite a while."

Toby grinned. "I love playing like this. That's why I was so annoyed at myself for rushing before."

Jenna's grin was as self-satisfied as Toby's. "You certainly made up for it."

"I'm glad, but you have to promise me that you won't ever lie to me. If you need or want something, you have to tell me, or show me. Okay?"

"Okay." Could she actually tell a man what she wanted? Could she have told Glen? *Stop it,* she yelled in her brain. *Glen's several hundred miles and lots of time from here. Don't compare!*

"If you think that was the best ever I have a few surprises for you."

The phrase *I have a few surprises for you* echoed in her head until their next date a week later. Now she had no hesitation. She wanted to experience everything and anything Toby could think of. She wanted to learn and play and have fun with her new toy, sex.

She dressed carefully in a soft flowered, cotton skirt and co-ordinated soft rose, sleeveless top. It had been in the nineties all week so she left her legs bare and her sandals were easy to slip on and off. She had shopped for an especially sexy panty and bra set in pale pink lace. She was more than ready, wet and throbbing. Toby picked her up and she was slightly disappointed when he didn't suggest that they skip dinner and get right to dessert.

Instead, they arrived at the small Indian restaurant where they'd been on their first date and were shown to a banquette table along one wall. Instead of sitting across from her, Toby took the seat beside her, draping the long white table cloth over their laps. "Wine?" he asked.

"Whatever you'd like will be fine with me," she answered, already soaked, her nipples so tight they almost hurt. Toby ordered a bottle of cabernet and a sip of the deep ruby wine confirmed her previous admiration of his good taste. He ordered an assortment of appetizers and two main courses, bread and raita, the yogurt and cucumber savory she'd enjoyed on their previous visit. He seemed to remember everything she liked.

They chatted amiably, but it took all of Jenna's willpower to keep the conversation light. She was feeling itchy and impatient. When the appetizer combo arrived, Toby put a few bites on each of their plates, then picked up a piece of tandoori chicken in his fingers and offered it to her. As she opened her mouth she felt his hand squeeze her thigh beneath the linen tablecloth. He stuffed the bite into her mouth so she was unable to protest but, actually, she doubted she'd have said anything anyway with his fingers sliding up and down the inside of her leg.

"More?" he asked, not differentiating between the food and his fingers.

"Certainly," she said softly. Offering her another bite, his fingers slipped upward and found the crotch of her now soaked panties.

As she chewed, Toby said, "You seem quite hungry and I enjoy feeding you."

He offered her bite after bite, sweets and savories, continually rubbing her sodden crotch and now swollen clit with his other hand. Finally, the appetizers were gone and the main course arrived on the table. Toby placed portions of each dish on her plate. "Before you start, why don't you go into the ladies room and take off those panties?"

"Excuse me?"

"Don't play innocent with me, you heard what I said. Take off your panties. I want to feel you, play with you."

"Not here," she said, appearing scandalized but, secretly, incredibly aroused at the suggestion.

"Yes, here. I told you I had some surprises for you. Now go before things get cold—both you and your food."

Jenna gazed into Toby's deep brown eyes now filled with unabashed lust, hesitated, then threw caution to the wind. Without saying another word, she rose and made her way quickly to the bathroom. In a stall she removed her panties, placed them in her purse, then returned to the table. Toby was waiting, not having started his meal. As Jenna sat back down, Toby handed her a fork. "Just keep eating," he said, one hand again finding her thigh, the other picking up a fork full of chicken saag.

As his thumb found her pubic hair, she wondered how he could appear to be eating so calmly and be doing what he was doing. She put a fork full of lamb curry in her mouth but found herself unable to chew when his fingers slid onto her naked pussy. "Chew," he said with a deliciously evil leer, "and swallow. We wouldn't want you to choke, would we?"

She nodded and tried to concentrate on getting the mouthful past her throat. When his finger stopped moving she found she could swallow. She sipped her wine but as she put a bite of lamb into her mouth his index finger slipped inside her. "Just keep chewing," he said softly as his finger teased, withdrawing, then thrusting into her sopping body.

It was some kind of exquisite torture. She didn't want anyone else to know what was going on beneath the tablecloth yet she couldn't help her excitement. She was close to climaxing right there in the middle of the restaurant but somehow she managed to chew and swallow. "Are you close?" he whispered, when she paused again to sip her wine.

"Very, and you've got to stop," she said, not knowing whether she wanted him to stop or to push her over the edge.

"Not a chance. Put your glass down very carefully and come for me," he said, as a second finger joined the first and his thumb, stroking her clit.

"I can't, not here."

"You can. Right here, right now." He pinched her clit lightly. She plunged over the edge, swallowing hard to keep from crying out, unable to stop tiny whimpering sounds from escaping her throat. Trembling, she took several deep breaths and looked around. None of the other diners seemed to have noticed what had just happened, despite the fact that it should have registered on the Richter scale.

"Is everything all right here?" the waiter asked. Blushing, Jenna had no idea whether his was just a ritual visit or he suspected what was going on.

"Everything's just fine," Toby said, a smug grin on his face.

Regaining her composure, Jenna said, "Not for long." As he put a bite of chicken in his mouth, she reached over and unzipped Toby's pants. She found the slit in his shorts and pulled out his fully erect cock. "Just keep eating," she said, echoing his words and watching his eyes glaze over. "Chew and swallow."

Amazed at her boldness, she tented a linen napkin over his cock and stroked the length of him with one hand while calmly eating her meal and sipping her wine with the other. "Indian food's wonderful, isn't it?" she said with a twinkle in her eye. "Nothing you need a knife for." She was going to get him off in the middle of a busy restaurant. This wasn't her, part of her mind screamed. Oh, but it was.

Although he was obviously having trouble swallowing, Toby put a bit of bread into his mouth. "Take care. I wouldn't want you to choke," Jenna said, enjoying the turnabout. She thought about her sex life up to this point. *Dull, dull, dull.* This is how it was supposed to be. Adventurous and fun.

She continued to stroke until, with a grunt, Toby filled her hand with semen. She raised an eyebrow. "See?" she said, cleaning his cock and her hand with the napkin. "Two can play at that game."

Toby regained his breath. "And play is the operative word. I knew you'd be a treasure. Let's finish, then go back to your place and see what other games we can invent."

* * *

One afternoon several weeks later, Chloe and Jenna sat on lounge chairs in the tiny backyard. The early July sun was hot, the birds were twittering, and things were good. As the agency had predicted, her work was averaging about two days a week at a varied collection of translation projects, a few of which even allowed her to work at home. Home. She now considered the brownstone on Fifty-fifth Street home. Each time she walked down the block and turned to mount the steps she felt some kind of kinship with the inviting building. She totally understood Chloe and Aunt Elise's feelings about the place.

She missed her sister terribly and called her several times a week but Chloe filled the large hole. Jenna's sex life was becoming as varied as she had wanted it to be when she moved from Seneca Falls. Here were the activities she'd been dreaming of. There was more to sex than what she and Glen had been doing. So much more.

She and Toby had made love in her bedroom, in the back of a taxi, and on the Staten Island Ferry. She'd learned some of the things he most enjoyed, and loved to take him in her mouth. Once she'd done it for several seconds in the slow elevator of his building. God, sex was fun.

"I've got a favor to ask of you, Jen," Chloe said, "but it's a bit embarrassing and I want you to feel free to refuse."

Jenna put her iced-tea glass down on the small, white, wrought-iron table and turned toward her friend. She and Chloe could talk about anything, and had. What could it be that was causing the strange, awkward, embarrassed look on her face? "Anything; you know that. Is anything wrong?" Was her friend actually blushing?

"Oh, it's not anything like that." She smiled. "Don't get that 'big sister' look on your face. I'm fine. It's for Frank."

Frank Devins was one of Chloe's current boyfriends, a large man with giant hands that had thick, black hair on the backs, a sturdy body, and an almost ugly, craggy face that totally changed character when he smiled. Jenna had met him briefly several times during the past six weeks and had grown rather fond of him. When Chloe didn't continue Jenna said, "Give, Chloe."

"It's his birthday on the sixteenth and I want to give him something special."

Jenna wanted to suggest that she give something that didn't cost the earth, but she kept her mouth shut. Chloe's spending had calmed, at least for the moment. "I'm trying not to spend anything." She grinned her ingenuous grin. "See? I'm being good, and you can help."

"Me?"

"I want to give him something that will blow his mind and I've had a brilliant idea. I need you to help me. I want to act out his favorite fantasy and make a movie of it for him."

"Sounds pretty simple."

"Not that simple. I want to make a movie of us." After another pause she said, "Of me and him playing and eventually making love."

Jenna's jaw dropped. "A porno video?" She'd known Chloe was a free spirit but a porno video?

"Don't look so shocked. Lots of couples make videos of themselves in bed and I want to make one of us for Frank." Suddenly the words came rushing out. "I've got a video camera and a few months ago I bought a light set up." When Jenna's eyebrows rose, Chloe said, "Okay. I bought the lights to make a movie with another guy."

"So why can't you use it for Frank?"

"I made a movie of me stripping and that worked pretty well, but I stayed pretty much in one place so putting the camera on a tripod was okay. The one we made in bed didn't come out really well. Staying centered was almost impossible." She looked sheepish. "I'm not a very restrained lover and a good part of the time all the movie had was a picture of an empty bed and lots of grunts and heavy breathing. When we tried it again we were so conscious of the camera that we couldn't think of much else. This time I want to film Frank and me—and everything we do. I really want to do it right."

"You want me to help you set it all up?"

"Not just that, Jenna. I want you to take the pictures. Be the camera man. Camera person."

Jenna was totally taken aback. "You mean be there during . . ." She was rapidly expanding her sexual horizons but this was a bit much. Wasn't it? She was startled, but, if she were being honest, she was also a little titillated.

"That's what I want. Frank's enough of an exhibitionist that he'll go wild. Not only will it be an evening to remember but then we'll have the film to watch later." She lowered her lashes. "It will be a great present and it will be practically free."

"Don't get coy with me, Chloe. It won't affect my decision." She paused. "I really don't know about this." Did she want to get that involved in Chloe's love life? In Frank's?

"Please. You said you'd help. It will be so great."

"Are you sure you want something permanent like that? What will happen if you two break up?" *When* you two break up, she'd almost said. She knew that Chloe's relationships seldom lasted longer than a few months.

"I don't really care. If he wants to show it to his buddies, I think I'd be complimented. I'm pretty good in the sack and I want that to show."

Jenna felt herself weakening. "You really can't just set the camera up on the dresser?"

"I told you that it just doesn't work. I want someone to hold the camera, move around and get really good shots like those professional erotic movies. You know, zoom in? Pan around? I've already picked out the scene I want to act out and what I want to wear. Come on, Jen. Be a sport. Help me out here."

Jenna squirmed in her chair. "I don't know. It's very embarrassing. Are you sure Frank won't mind me watching?"

"He'll be fine with it. It's a fantasy of his, anyway, being watched. He thinks he's a stud—he is you know—and he's told me that he has dreamed about it."

"A fantasy of his?"

"Sure. We talked about it, and it excited him so much that we fucked our brains out just from that. Please, Jen. Do this for me."

Chloe had been such a good friend that Jenna felt she couldn't let her down. "What the hell. Let's figure this thing out. What's the scene?"

"He's going to pretend that he's in a hotel room away from home, and I'm going to be a hooker, hired by his friends to entertain him."

As the two women discussed the scenario, they talked about the things they could do to make a room in the house feel like a chain motel room. "Why don't we use some of that tacky furniture in the attic?" Jenna suggested. "There must be stuff there we can adapt."

"That's a fabulous idea," Chloe said, leaping to her feet, eyes glowing. "Let's go see what's up there that we can use."

Caught up in Chloe's enthusiasm, Jenna followed her friend up the stairs to the storeroom. In the jumble of boxes, furniture, and accessories they found an institutional-looking bedside table and three ugly lamps. Jenna grabbed several institutional-looking landscapes to hang on the wall. They lugged their treasures down to one of the third-floor bedrooms that had a double bed and dresser already in it. They pored through the linen closet and found an old flowered quilt and a set of plain white sheets and pillow cases. They hung a large, slightly cracked mirror on the wall and suddenly the room looked not unlike a cheap motel room. "He'll go wild," Chloe said. She pointed to one corner. "We can set the camera up over there with a tripod and everything, but some of the time you can hold it, move around and stuff. This is going to be so fabulous."

"You must really care for him. This is quite a bit of work for his birthday."

"He's a nice guy but this is actually mostly for me. I know he'll love it and I'll love making it come true. I've found, too, that it makes me really hot thinking about it. I guess it's sort of a fantasy of mine too. I'll make a copy of the video and keep it for those lonely nights when I don't have a date."

Jenna grinned and hugged her friend. "You're quite a liberated woman, Chloe. I admire you."

"With any luck you can grow up to be just like me," Chloe said with a wink.

"I'm trying. Lord knows I'm trying."

"Well, if this doesn't get your juices flowing, I don't know what will."

During the next few days Jenna found a video-rental store that had a large selection of XXX-rated films and watched about a dozen, noting the shots the camera man had concentrated on. She reasoned that what the film makers produced was what men wanted to see. Few of the films had any story and she was sure she could do just as well. Strange, she thought, she was doing more homework for this video than she'd done for some of her college courses.

The event, as the women called it, was arranged for the following Saturday evening. That afternoon they set up the camera equipment in the "motel" room." Sadly, the equipment wasn't invisible and the lights were quite bright, but the room was as natural as they could make it. Jenna practiced with the camera until she knew how quickly to pan, how to make the zoom work and how the lights should be arranged.

Now all she could do was wait.

Chapter
5

Jenna and Chloe had taped a note to the front door. "Dear Mr. Devins. As the proprietor of the hotel, I'm sorry I couldn't be there to greet you in person but something came up. Please, come right in. I've booked you on the third floor, the room on the left. I have you signed up for one night and I look forward to meeting you in the morning." The note was signed, "The Management."

At exactly eight o'clock Frank opened the door to the brightly-lit room the women had set up, and glanced around, smiling broadly. He looked like a typical tired businessman, dressed in a white, button-down, collar shirt and black slacks. A tie was threaded through the collar but not tied. Jenna, secreted in a closet, peeked out and saw him nod over and over again. Then he sat down on the edge of the bed and waited.

Jenna was a little nervous. This would be a one-time shot, one chance to make a video Chloe and Frank would enjoy for a long time to come. Could she do it right? Would she freak out watching her best friend and some guy she hardly knew make love? *Oh, well,* she thought, *only time will tell.* She rubbed her damp palms on her jeans and tried to calm her jittery stomach.

After only a few minutes a knock sounded on the door.

"What is it?" Frank called, sounding a bit exasperated. Jenna was amazed at how well he played his part.

"Hotel service," Chloe's voice said.

Slowly Frank got to his feet and crossed the room to the door. When he opened it Jenna was amazed at the sight that greeted both of them. Chloe was dressed in a figure-hugging, red dress, barely long enough to cover her panties, if indeed she was wearing any. The top was cut low in the front, showing a massive amount of cleavage and the lace edging of a bright red demi-bra. She wore thigh-high, red stockings topped with elastic lace, and strappy, red sandals with four-inch heels. A tiny, red pocketbook hung from her shoulder by a rhinestone strap and around her neck hung a glittering rhinestone necklace with a large drop that fell deep within her cleavage. Huge rhinestone earrings hung from her ears, long enough to brush her shoulders.

Chloe had deliberately overdone her hair and makeup so that, had Jenna not known, it would have taken her a moment to recognize her friend. Her short, curly hair was teased and swept high on her head. Heavy eye makeup and long false eyelashes changed her expression, and bright red lipstick accentuated her large, smiling mouth. "Hi, Sugar. My name's Candy. Want some?"

"Me?" Frank said, as Jenna slipped from the closet and turned on the camera which was, at that moment, pointed at the door. Fortunately the camera was completely silent.

"Sure. You're Frank, aren't you? I'm a gift from the boys at the office. Can I come in?" She was sucking a mint and swinging her purse from its long chain. Her entire body language said "hooker," hip thrust to one side, long, red fingernails stroking up and down her cleavage.

His jaw hanging slack, Frank backed up and allowed Chloe into the "motel" room. "Wow, you look great," he said, his voice a bit shaky. "I never expected—"

"Expected what, Sugar? I'm here for some fun. Got a drink for a girl?"

The two people were totally oblivious as Jenna pointed the camera and Frank turned to a bottle, a tray of glasses, and a tacky plastic ice bucket Jenna and Chloe had put on the bedside table earlier. "We seem to have some rum. I hope it's your favorite."

"Just right, Sugar. On the rocks."

Jenna heard the ice cubes clank into two glasses and Frank poured several fingers of rum into each. He handed one to Chloe who took a sip. "Mmm, dee-licious." Jenna quietly panned from Frank's face to Chloe's, then to the glasses.

"Yeah," Frank said, still obviously totally nonplused. "Nice." Jenna zoomed in on his face as his eyes roamed Chloe's body, then moved to Chloe's deeply shadowed cleavage. "Candy. Nice."

"Can I sit down?" Without waiting for an answer Chloe perched on the edge of the bed and patted the bedspread beside her. "Join me?" Slowly, Frank sat beside her. "So, what business are you in, Sugar?"

"I'm a floor broker on the stock exchange." Jenna knew that part of the scenario was true.

"Ooo," Chloe said. "You buy and sell all those stocks and bonds?"

"Something like that."

"You must be very rich."

"I do okay," he said. "You been in the business long?"

"The business?" She looked down a bit puzzled. "Oh, that. Yeah. I'm sort of new. I've been doing this for a few months. What do you want to do now?" she asked, sipping her drink. Jenna suddenly realized that, although Chloe appeared completely comfortable with her role, she was actually quite nervous. It added a sweetly vulnerable note to the film Jenna was shooting.

Frank set his drink on the bedside table and cupped the back of Chloe's head with his large palm. "This," he said and drove his mouth down on hers. Quietly, Jenna zoomed in on the scorching kiss. Barefoot, she moved around the room, angling in on the meeting of lips as they changed the position of their heads to deepen the kiss. "And this," Frank said as he placed his hand on Chloe's thigh and slid it up her stocking. Jenna tried to ignore the way the sight of Frank's large, dark hands against the red of Chloe's stockings made her nipples pucker.

"God, you're sexy," Frank groaned. "I'm going to get the guys' money's worth out of my whore for tonight." He guided her to a standing position. "Strip for me."

Looking a bit bemused, Chloe glanced over her shoulder at Jenna's camera, then back at Frank. "Sure, Sugar. Whatever you want." Spreading her thighs so Frank would be able to see her crotch, Chloe put her foot on the edge of the bed and unfastened the buckles on one sandal. Then she slowly rolled one stocking down her leg, her fingertips caressing her skin as it was revealed. When Frank reached out to stroke her, she playfully batted his hand away. "You wanted me to strip. Let me."

Frank nodded, his eyes never leaving Chloe's hands. When one leg was bare she placed her naked foot on the floor and repeated the performance with the other. At first Chloe had been glancing at the camera often, but as she got deeper and deeper into her role she seemed to become oblivious to Jenna's actions.

Frank grabbed the front of Chloe's dress and dragged her closer. "I want this gone," he said, his voice gravelly.

"You're sure in a hurry, Sugar," Chloe said as she slid her hands down the sides of the dress until she could grasp the hem. Then she wiggled her hips as she pulled the dress upward. Soon it was off and she stood dressed in only a tiny, strapless, brilliant crimson, satin and lace bra and thong panties. Jenna gradually zoomed out so she could get both Chloe and Frank in the same frame. The look on his face as his eyes roamed Chloe's body was something not to be missed. Jenna had never truly understood the word *smolder* until that moment.

"You like Candy, Sugar?" Chloe said, her voice breathy.

"Shit, baby," Frank said, licking his lips, "what's not to like?"

Jenna agreed. Although tiny, Chloe's body was beautifully proportioned with a flat abdomen and ample breasts. *Any man's fantasy*, Jenna thought.

Chloe rubbed her hands up her belly and cupped her fabric-covered breasts. Then, wordlessly, she reached behind her and unfastened the bra, allowing her flesh to fall from the cups. Jenna centered her camera on Chloe's nipples as Frank's dark hands reached for them. She watched through the lens as he kneaded, then dragged her close so he could fasten his lips on, first, one erect nipple, then the other.

Jenna was amazed at the way the scene made her body feel and she could now understand what people enjoyed about pornographic movies. It was as though she was experiencing what Chloe was. She could almost feel Frank's fingers squeezing and pinching her.

Seemingly unable to wait, Frank grabbed the front of Chloe's panties and Jenna could hear the sound of cloth ripping. Then the wisp of red was in his hand and he impatiently tossed it away, burying his face in the coarse hair between Chloe's legs.

The room now smelled of sex and the scent was intoxicating. Jenna moved around and watched Frank's tongue flick out and lick the swollen flesh between Chloe's legs. Then Chloe backed off. "You're still wearing all those clothes, Sugar," she said, reaching to unbutton his shirt.

When his torso was bare, Chloe leaned over and, growling, placed a line of bites along his shoulder. Then he stood and she quickly removed his slacks and briefs. It was all Jenna could do not to gasp. His erection was tremendous, thick and rigid, precum oozing from the tip.

Chloe fell to her knees and fondled Frank's engorged shaft. "Sugar, this is the best piece of meat I've ever seen."

"If you like it, suck it."

Chloe kissed the tip while she caressed his shaft. She stuck her tongue out and licked the length, as if it were an all-day sucker, while Jenna's camera zoomed in on her mouth. She flicked the tip with her tongue, and then her red-painted lips surrounded the head and agonizingly, slowly, took the entire length into her mouth. Jenna made sure that the recorder picked up both the sound of Frank's moaning and the slurping sounds made by Chloe's obviously talented mouth.

Jenna's camera moved with the rhythm of Chloe's mouth, suck and withdraw, until Frank was crazed with lust. Jenna moved the camera to his face, then back to Chloe's.

"Shit, baby. Now you're going to get the fuck you've been paid for," Frank said, pushing Chloe onto the bed and ramming his thick cock into her. Jenna focused on his buttocks and the play of muscles as he thrust and relaxed. She bent down at the foot of the bed and managed to get a shot of Frank's cock as it disappeared into Chloe's cunt. *Shit*, she thought, *if this comes out the way I think it will, it will be some video.* She thought they would want a cum shot like all the movies had, but she didn't want to break the spell so she let the action play out.

As she watched, her pussy became wet and itchy. She was so involved in the action that it almost felt as if Frank's cock was filling her. She was not aware of the little sounds of pleasure that her throat was making. She tried to keep her breathing even and hold the camera steady, despite her trembling knees and hands and her own heavy breathing.

Finally, with simultaneous shouts, both Frank and Chloe came and Frank collapsed on the bed beside his "hooker." Quietly, Jenna put the camera on the bureau and slipped out of the room, leaving the exhausted lovers entwined on the bed.

Jenna all but ran to her room and closed the door, pulling off her clothing as she dragged the bedclothes from the bed. She stretched out, marveling at how hot she was, so excited by what she'd watched that she would have joined Frank and Chloe/Candy if she had been invited. She'd never before even considered a threesome and certainly not with her best friend and her boyfriend. Naked, she undulated like a cat in heat, feeling the cool sheets against her buttocks and the backs of her thighs and calves.

She fondled her breasts as she imagined what it would have been like. She imagined that her hands were Frank's, or any man's. She wanted, needed, and used her hands to attempt to satisfy her unexpectedly raging fires. She filled her pussy with her fingers as Frank's cock had filled Chloe's. It was only a moment before Jenna felt the beginning of her climax growing in her belly. Only a few strokes of her practiced fingers brought her to a shattering orgasm.

The next morning, Chloe was up bright and early. She'd taken the day off so she wouldn't have to leap out of bed at the crack of dawn. Frank had left very early to change into work clothes at home so the two women brought their coffee out onto the lounge chairs and talked about the previous evening. "That was the best sex I've ever had," Chloe said.

"It was quite something," Jenna said, wondering whether it would be awkward talking with her best friend after an evening of watching her make love.

"Don't be embarrassed," Chloe said. "It was great and you were a big part of it. I can't wait until I see the tape."

"It was really weird for me to watch you two make love the way you did."

"Bizarre, but erotic, no?"

With a great intake of breath, Jenna admitted, "Erotic, yes."

Later that morning the two women stretched out in the living room and played the video. Jenna was amazed at how professional the film looked. Damn, she'd done a fabulous job if she did say so herself. Chloe was lavish in her praise. "That's the best," she squealed as she watched the shot of Frank's cock thrusting into her pussy. "I can't wait to watch it with him."

"How did the evening go after I left?" Jenna asked.

"We made love two more times. He was so hot just thinking about the movie and me as a hooker. He's never been a better lover."

Early one evening about a week later, Chloe found Jenna dressed in a pair of shorts and a light tee shirt in the brownstone's kitchen. While most of the bedrooms were air conditioned, the kitchen faced west and got hotter as the late July sun poured in through the open door. "What are you making?"

"I'm just opening a can of ravioli. It's too hot for cooking." Jenna unhooked the can and pushed the opener to the back of the counter.

"Got a date?"

"Not tonight. Tomorrow evening I'm seeing that new guy I met at that job I had last week. He's kind of cute, with great bedroom eyes and one of those beards that's not a beard. You know, the ones that are just a line along his jaw?" Jenna gently forked the contents of the can into a bowl.

After a moment's hesitation, Chloe asked, "Which nights later in the week are you busy?"

As she separated the little meat pies, Jenna said, "Okay. What's up? You don't usually beat around the bush like this."

Chloe dropped into one of the kitchen chairs. "I don't actually know how to ask this."

Jenna put the bowl into the microwave, pushed a few buttons and, as the fan hummed, sat down opposite Chloe. "The easiest way is to spit it out."

"Remember the movie you made?"

"How could I forget?"

"Well, Frank showed it to one of his friends."

"Is that bad? I worried that you'd become some kind of a porn star but the idea didn't seem to faze you."

Chloe held her hand up to interrupt Jenna's thought. "It's not that. Actually, I still kind of like the idea." As Jenna watched, Chloe actually preened a bit. "His friend liked the movie so much that he wants to make one of him and his girlfriend."

"It's not difficult. I could show him a few things about the camera and such if that's what you want."

"Not exactly." Chloe uncrossed and recrossed her legs, then tapped her fingers on the table. "It's a bit more complicated than that. He wants to use the room Frank and I used and he wants you to do the photography."

"Me?"

"He's got money to burn and is willing to pay three hundred dollars to rent your services. He wants some of the great shots you got. He specifically talked about the cock-sucking part and that fabulous between-the-legs-fucking one." Jenna tried not to wince at Chloe's blunt language. "Frank also told him that we could be trusted to give him the only copy of the movie."

"He's going to pay?"

"I thought we could split it. My house and your talent with the camera."

"I'm not sure I want to go into the dirty-movie business. Is it legal?"

"Sure. Why not? It's for private use only." Chloe hesitated and her finger-drumming continued at a slightly slower pace. "I could really use the money," she said softly. "I've got another tax bill due next month and I'm kind of strapped."

Jenna thought about her dwindling savings, but she'd still do whatever she could to help. "I could let you have a little more rent money if you're having problems." She looked around the kitchen, spotted her purse on the counter and reached for it. "I've got extra cash too. You don't have to go into the porno-movie business."

Chloe held out her hand. "I don't want a quick twenty, Jenna, but thanks for the offer. I just thought this might be a way for both of us to earn a little extra cash and have some fun doing it."

"I don't think so. Why don't you do it?"

"Take the pictures? Not me. I'm not good with a movie camera. I've tried and I pan too fast and things are never in the center of the picture. This guy specifically asked for the person who made our movie. You enjoyed making it, didn't you?"

Jenna remembered her excitement after the film was finished and the fantasies that had raced through her mind every evening since. "I guess."

"So what's the harm? Someone wants a movie and you can provide the means. It's not rocket science and it fulfills someone's fantasy."

Jenna considered, weakening. What was the harm, after all? She had to admit that she had really enjoyed making Chloe and Frank's movie. There was the money too, of course. "I'm busy tomorrow, you know."

"He can do it later in the week."

Jenna slowly shook her head. It sounded so simple, but was she beginning a slide down a slippery slope? To where? "Give me a day to think about it. And I don't want any of the money."

"Don't be silly. I couldn't take all of it. You're doing all the work."

"Of course you could. Put it all toward the taxes. After all I don't want to have to find someplace else to live."

"But you already pay enough rent."

"Think of it as a charitable foundation. The Society for the Fulfillment of Fantasies and Payment of Taxes. Agreed?" Jenna reached out to shake Chloe's hand.

Chloe burst out laughing. "I love it." She took Jenna's hand and gave it an exaggerated shake. "Okay. We'll keep a kitty toward the taxes. It sounds like you're agreeing to do it."

"Let me think about it until tomorrow." She'd consider, but in her heart Jenna knew her decision had already been made.

As the city suffered through the dog days of August, Jenna thought about the months since she had arrived in Manhattan and the ways her life had changed so dramatically. She was working a few days a week, moving from a large multinational corporation to a small law firm, from an advertising agency to a midsized publisher. She had contacts all over the city and had had dates with more than a half-dozen different, exciting and sensual men. She still saw Toby every few weeks for dinner and sex, which seemed sufficient for both of them and their busy schedules.

Two or three evenings a week she made videos for the dozens of cash-rich men and women who'd found out in one way or another about her little enterprise.

Couples had played out several different scenarios. One had arrived in wedding clothes to play out their wedding night. Another had shown up dressed as Robin Hood and Maid Marian. It had been enjoyable and arousing to make films, and she handed the couples the product immediately so there was no possibility of duplication, a worry for many.

In addition to her videography skills, Jenna became adept at both being invisible and helping the couples get over any initial nervousness. She reassured, complimented, and was generally supportive of whatever scene the couple had chosen.

Her only regret was that she hadn't told her sister about her enterprise, even when Marcy mentioned several times that she'd had disturbing dreams on nights which usually coincided with particularly arousing photo sessions. Although Marcy didn't want to discuss the nature of the dreams, Jenna was sure that her sister was somehow picking up on her excitement. She chuckled when she thought about it. She was becoming a master of amateur erotic videos and her sister was too prudish to discuss her erotic dreams.

One late August afternoon Jenna answered the doorbell to find a man with a large, gift-wrapped, deep gold chrysanthemum plant. "Ms. Jenna Bryant?"

"That's me."

"Sign here." The delivery man thrust a pad at her and she signed where he indicated.

In the kitchen Jenna set the plant on the table and found a card pinned to the bright yellow bow. "It's been three months and I hope things are going well. I miss you and hope we can chat soon. Remember above everything, I'm a friend." The note was signed "Glen."

Jenna sat down and stared at the card. Glen. Although she was busy, he was still in her thoughts. She didn't regret what she'd done at all, but she lamented the fact that such a great guy wasn't growing in the same way she was. Damn. I don't want to go back. I just wish he were here and part of this life.

Later, when Chloe spotted the flowers in the middle of the kitchen table, Jenna handed her the note. "He's really very sweet," Jenna said. "I wouldn't have talked to him on the phone, but this is a nice way for him to stay in touch."

"He sounds so sweet," Chloe said, gently.

"I want him to find someone else."

"But you're complimented too. It's great to have someone care about you."

Jenna's smile widened. "Yeah, it is."

Marcy visited for the Labor Day weekend and Jenna was delighted to see her after all their months apart. Although they talked almost every day on the phone, seeing her sister in person was so much better. They hugged and giggled at the airport and on the taxi ride into Manhattan.

Jenna and Chloe had removed the camera equipment and spruced up the "motel room" so that Marcy would be comfortable staying in it. Jenna had worried about how her conservative sister and free-speaking friend would get along but, although not immediately bosom buddies, the two seemed to hit it off better than Jenna had hoped.

For the next two days the two women showed Marcy around the city that Jenna was coming to love more and more each day. They did all the tourist things. They took a double-decker bus around Midtown, then spent the afternoon at the Bronx Zoo. On Sunday they joined the mobs and took the boat to the Statue of Liberty and Ellis Island, then walked around Battery Park. Chloe had plans on Monday, so the twins took the Circle Line, then walked north to the Intrepid Sea-Air-Space Museum.

Jenna introduced Marcy to more exotic ethnic foods than were available in their hometown. They ate everything from souvlakis to pad thai, from West Indian jerk chicken to Indonesian curry. The conversation ranged over all subjects except sex. Jenna told her sister about her male friends, both laughing about their foibles and extolling their virtues.

Monday afternoon, over a late lunch, Jenna told Marcy about Glen's flowers. "I thought it was such a nice thing to do," Jenna said. "Thoughtful but not intrusive."

"We have dinner occasionally. He's really trying to strike the right balance. He's not going to push but he's not ready to move on, either. How do you feel about him, now that you've had time apart?"

"I'm not sure at all," Jenna said. "I go days without thinking about him and then something happens, a phrase someone uses or the smell of the same after-shave he wears, and he jumps back into my mind and I remember all the good times."

"There were good times."

"There were. He's really a great guy."

"But you're dating lots of other men too."

"I don't know how to describe it. I feel like I need to taste everything before I settle down." She snorted. "I sound like some guy talking about being leg-shackled."

"Those feelings aren't limited to men, Jen. I'm not very experienced, either. I think I'd need to experience things before committing myself."

Jenna watched a slight sadness slip into Marcy's eyes. "I wish you'd date more. Maybe you should come down here for a few months, live it up."

Marcy's smile was forlorn. "You're the New York type, sexy, shapely." Skinny. Jenna heard the word her overweight sister didn't say. "I'm not the type for barhopping and going to clubs."

"Don't think everything here is like *Sex in the City*. There are normal people in New York too."

Marcy shook her head. "You're Manhattan, I'm Seneca Falls. I'm content with that. Envious, but content."

Jenna wanted to convince Marcy to emerge from her self-imposed house arrest and visit for a few weeks, but she also realized that it would get awkward. How would she explain to her superconservative sister about the movies she was making and the men Chloe entertained? "Promise me you'll say yes when any nice guy asks you out."

"Okay," she said with only a slight hesitation, "I promise."

It seemed that almost immediately after her arrival, Jenna was taking a cab with Marcy back to La Guardia Airport. "It doesn't seem like it's been three whole days," Jenna said.

"I know, and it's been wonderful. I think I'm beginning to see what you like about this city. It's so alive."

"Seneca Falls is alive too," Jenna said, defending their hometown, "but there is so much more here."

The cab crossed the Triboro Bridge and Marcy gazed at the skyline. "You're not coming back home, are you." It was a statement, not a question.

"I haven't made any long-term decisions yet. There's always the matter of a job."

"You seem to be doing okay," Marcy said.

In actuality she was barely making ends meet, but the last

quarterly tax payment had been made with a bit to spare. Maybe she could now keep a small part of the money from the movies. "I'm doing fine," she told her sister. "I might just look for a full-time job here, although from what I know of the market right now, that might not be too easy."

The cab pulled up in front of the departures entrance and Marcy opened the door. "It's been just wonderful, Jen. I love you and I think I'll miss you even more."

"And I'll miss you. We'll talk as often as we always have, promise."

"Promise." Marcy climbed out and the driver handed her her suitcase. She leaned in and kissed Jenna as each woman tried not to cry. "Talk to you soon."

The taxi took Jenna back to Manhattan.

"How was she? How did she look? Is she okay? Is she coming back?" Glen stood beside a small corner table in a steak restaurant in Seneca Falls the evening after Marcy's return from Manhattan.

"Slow down, Glen, and let me sit down at least." She slid into a chair and put her purse on the floor. "She's fine, happy, and working a few days a week."

Glen frowned. "A few days a week? That's not enough income to live on."

"Glen, let it go. She's fine. She's great. She's not paying a lot of rent and I'm sure she's eating regularly."

Glen's shoulders rose and dropped as he heaved a gigantic sigh and tried to calm his racing pulse. "I'm just worried about her."

"Here I thought you wanted to have dinner with me." There was a slightly acerbic tone to her voice so he reached for her hand across the table. There had never been any romantic relationship between them. They were just friends, with someone in common they both cared deeply about. Before he could defend himself, she grinned and said, "Don't get all defensive. I know why you wanted to see me, and I promise you Jenna's doing just great. She seems really happy."

"That's what I'm afraid of," Glen said, his excitement swiftly waning. "Is she coming back?"

"Glen, I'm going to be brutally honest with you. I don't think so. She's talking about getting a full-time job." She squeezed his hand. "You're a good friend and I'm very fond of you. You've got to let this go."

"I try, but I love her, Marcy. I had such beautiful plans for us, work for a year or two, build up a really big bank account so she could stay home and be a full-time mother to our kids."

"Did you ever discuss that with her?"

Glen hadn't wanted to scare Jenna off. "No, but I think she understood where it was all going." Hadn't she?

"We talked about you once, briefly, while I was there. She told me about the flowers you sent. She was touched. It was a nice thing to do."

Glen leaned forward, hoping for the best but bracing himself for the worst. "And . . . ?"

"She likes you and you two have a lot of history, but she still wants you to move on and I agree with her. It's been three months and it's time to let this all go." Marcy paused, then continued, "You're getting a bit obsessive."

Glen leaned back again. He wasn't obsessive, just hopeful. How often in your life do you find the perfect partner? Jenna was it. If she needed more time to realize it he'd continue to be patient. The flowers had been the first step in getting back into her life. Maybe in a few weeks he'd give her a call, just to chat. After all, he was a friend.

It was mid-September and Chloe had put Glen's chrysanthemums and several other pots in various colors around the tiny rear garden. Jenna was sitting out there eating a peanut butter sandwich when Chloe walked out and plopped into the chair beside her. "How was your day?" she asked.

"Boring, actually. I haven't had an assignment in almost a week and the next one I know about isn't until next Tuesday. It's getting tougher for Paula to keep me employed." Paula Jablonski was her contact at Languages, Inc., the employment agency she worked with.

"Summer vacations are over and there are fewer openings," Chloe said.

"Yeah. At this rate I'll have to either get a real job or flip burgers at McDonald's."

"Maybe not," Chloe said, a peculiar glint in her blue eyes.

"What's that supposed to mean?"

"I've got a proposition for you. And you can't say anything until I've finished. Okay?"

"Sure," Jenna said, puzzled. "Shoot."

"A man contacted me through Frank. He wants to use your services."

"Sure. Another movie? What scenario this time?"

"It's not exactly like that. He's got a scene in mind but he doesn't want just a movie."

Not completely confused, Jenna said, "So what does he want?"

"You."

"Me? He wants a date with me? He doesn't even know me."

"He wants to act out a fantasy with you and him in the starring roles. I talked to him at length and the scene he wants doesn't require you to move around, so we can set the camera on the tripod and just leave it running."

"Of course he wants sex."

Chloe winked. "He wants sex of a sort. He's willing to pay to have you help him fulfill his fantasy."

"I'd be a whore. No thanks."

"Why not?" Chloe said, a slight whine in her voice. "You have sex with guys all the time. Why not with this guy?"

"I don't even know him and I'm not going to be paid for the use of my body. No way. You do it."

"Too short."

"I beg your pardon?"

"I'm too short, and he already knows me. It wouldn't be the same."

Jenna had gotten so used to Chloe being a free spirit that this conversation didn't even seem bizarre. "No. And that's that. Next topic of conversation."

"There wouldn't necessarily be intercourse."

"What the hell does that mean?"

"The fantasy he wants would only require a good hand job."

"Come on, Chloe. I'm not going to be paid for a hand job. Period."

"I knew that would be your answer so I haggled a bit with him. He's willing to pay five hundred."

"Dollars?"

"He's got the money and he's hot to spend it. He wants his fantasy and his movie."

"Five hundred dollars?" Jenna's mind was blown. She had never anticipated that men would be willing to pay that kind of money for sex. Actually, not even really for sex. But the amount of money couldn't matter. She wasn't a whore. No way. "Why me? I make dirty movies. I don't participate. Why not hire a call girl?"

"Several people have commented on your ability to relax people, talk to them about their desires. He's really nervous about this whole thing and he thinks you'd help him stay calm."

"That's bullshit."

"Actually, it's not bullshit at all. I've listened to you with couples and you're great at finding out what they want to do and expanding their horizons, increasing their enjoyment. He's fastened on that. He says he wants a real person, not a hooker."

"But I'd *be* a hooker. And, anyway, I don't want my face in some porno movie."

"I talked to him about that and he agreed that he needn't be able to see your face in the film. From the neck down would be okay."

"No way. Sorry."

"Okay, I'll tell him no." She sounded disappointed, then added, "Maybe I could wait until tomorrow. Let you give it some thought. Will you agree not to say no until tomorrow?" Chloe wheedled. "Come on. It's not really prostitution."

"It's not? How did you come up with that thought?"

"Okay, maybe it is in a way, but what's the harm?"

"What's the harm?" That was the line that got her into the erotic videography business in the first place. "It's illegal and dangerous."

"It's fulfilling a need that men have. Instead of dinner and a movie, it's cash. I repeat, what's the harm?"

"God, Chloe. You're quite a piece of work."

"Think until tomorrow?"

"Okay. I won't say no until tomorrow."

Chapter
6

"Have you given the whole deal much thought?" Chloe asked the following evening as the two women settled in the kitchen when Chloe arrived home from work, her usual take-out bag from the local Chinese restaurant in her hand.

"Much thought? I've thought about little else." Jenna hadn't had an assignment that day, and it had been raining steadily so she'd had little to distract her. Her mind had been churning for twenty-four hours. Half of her was appalled, half titillated. She was proud of the former, horrified by the latter.

"Have you decided anything?"

"It should still be no," Jenna said.

"But?"

"Okay, I'm intrigued and the money is difficult to pass up."

Chloe's face brightened and she set the bag on the table. "So? Talk to me."

"First, tell me why this seems to be so important to you. Why do you want me to get involved in this—thing?" She couldn't find a word she liked for the activities she was contemplating.

"I think you'll enjoy it."

"Not enough reason for you to care."

Chloe batted her eyelashes. "You'll make a buck?"

"Don't pull the cutsie face on me, Babe. I won't be charmed. Why?"

Chloe's shoulders rose and fell. "Okay. Because I've already done it."

"Done what? Gotten paid for hand jobs?"

"Gotten paid for sex. Here, in this house."

"You're nuts."

"I'm broke, Jen. I can't seem to control my credit card and a guy offered me money to use me and the motel room."

Jenna couldn't focus. "When?"

"About a week ago. The night you had a date with the guy from the advertising agency."

Horrified, Jenna said, "You let some paying stranger into our house and fucked him for money?"

"You came home with that date and fucked him, didn't you?"

Jenna's voice sharpened. "It's not the same and you know it. Jeremy was a date, someone I knew. If we made love it was our business."

"Chris was a guy I knew," Chloe snapped, "and if we made love and I took cash, it was my business."

Jenna tried to calm herself. "In that you're right. What you do is none of my business. What I do is." She deliberately crushed her negative feelings. Some of what Chloe said made sense. For Chloe. But for her? "I'm sorry. I guess I'm yelling as much at myself for even considering this." Jenna, stalling for time, opened the refrigerator and pulled out a Sam Adams for each of them. She put the two bottles and two glasses on the table. "This whole thing confuses and worries me, even more now with what you just told me."

Chloe unpacked the plastic bag, spreading small white containers over the table. "Okay. What worries you? Last week was a spur of the moment thing and since then I've been thinking about it a lot too. Shoot."

"You were alone and that's really dumb."

Chloe had the good grace to look chagrined. "You're right and I realized it as we walked in. Fortunately, he was a nice guy, but I'll never do that again."

"Good. Where did he come from?"

"He's a friend of a friend of Frank's."

"Not good enough."

"True."

Chloe looked so apologetic that Jenna relented. "Doesn't Frank mind you making love to his friends—or friends of his friends? Or doesn't he know?"

"He knows and he doesn't seem to care. Neither of us is exclusive and it seems to be a boost for his ego to have others tell him how good I am." She winked. "And I'm dynamite."

Jenna couldn't suppress her grin. "I'm sure you are. But we have to be careful. If we do this thing, the scariest part is that people will know this address but we'll still be living here. It seems really dangerous."

"I don't think it is. These are all friends and acquaintances of Frank and his crowd. Think of it this way. To be able to spend that kind of money, they won't be rapists and druggies."

"I guess. Did you use condoms? The whole idea of AIDS and such scares the shit out of me. Can we insist that any guy use one? Can we make it mandatory?" She heard herself talking as though she was actually thinking about doing it, and was appalled.

"I don't see any reason why not. After all, we're making the rules here." She put four egg rolls on a plate in the middle of the table.

"I don't do drugs!"

Chloe looked horrified. "Of course not. Neither do I."

"If I entertain this guy, I can call it off at any time."

"I told him that and he says that's okay. Nothing kinky will happen unless previously agreed."

"You're talking like this is going to be some kind of an ongoing business. I'm only thinking of this one guy."

Chloe got plates and napkins, then sat down. "Why not make it a business? There must be lots of guys out there willing to pay for someone to fulfill fantasies and maybe having a film of it afterwards. Lord knows there are enough women making a living in the sex business. Why not us?" She pulled the paper wrapper off her chopsticks.

"Stop it, Chloe. I'm not a prostitute and neither are you."

"Okay. Call it what you will." She waved her chopsticks in the air to emphasize her points. "Call it the Society for the Fulfillment of Fantasies and Payment of Taxes. Here's how I see it. We do an interview beforehand and find out what the guy is like and exactly what he wants. That way we can decide whether or not to take the job. If we agree to do it, we set things up as close to his desires as we can. We'll make his fantasy real and he'll pay big bucks for it. If we can manage it and he's willing to pay extra, he can have a movie too. I would do this first one but he wants a tall brunette. I could do the brunette part with a wig, but I'll never manage tall."

Jenna's laugh was forced. "I don't know. You make it sound so reasonable but the taboo is really strong. I'm just a small-town girl at heart."

"Listen, Jenna. If you don't want to do this I can find someone else, do it somewhere else. I just want to do it for the guy and get a finder's fee. I don't want you to feel that you're being pressured into anything."

"Right," she said dryly. "You're not pressuring me."

"Okay. Just a bit." She picked up an egg roll and took a bite.

Jenna put a sparerib on her plate. "I'll admit I'm intrigued. I came to New York wanting some variation in my life, some sexual adventure. I needed to get away from Glen and boring sex. I just never considered anything like this."

Chloe grinned and took another bite of her egg roll. "I'm

sure you didn't. I told the guy I'd give him a call this evening, although he's got nowhere else to go for his fantasy."

"I know there must be other high-class call girls. Can't someone else do this?"

"I've asked around and there doesn't seem to be anyone else who specializes in fantasy fulfillment."

"Fantasy fulfillment. Beside tall and brunette, what does he want? The hooker in the motel room thing again?"

"No. He wants you to be a doctor and give him an exam and, eventually, a hand job." When Jenna looked a bit bewildered, Chloe continued, "It's a common men's fantasy. Going to the doctor and having someone fondle his penis and balls makes some men crazy. Since they can't do anything about it right then, it sticks with them and becomes the center of some wonderful nights of masturbation. Don't you read porn?"

Jenna felt herself weakening. "Not as much as I should if I'm going to do this, I guess."

Chloe jumped at her words. "Then you'll do it?"

"This one seems pretty harmless. All we have to do is set up one of the rooms upstairs to look like a doctor's exam room."

"It seemed a pretty good way to try this thing out. Are you willing?"

"I guess so," Jenna said.

Chloe raised her glass of beer. "To fantasies. To the Society for the Fulfillment of Fantasies and Payment of Taxes."

Jenna clinked her glass against Chloe's. "To Club Fantasy."

Jenna insisted on talking to Collin Shaw, the man whose fantasy they were going to fulfill, on the phone the following evening. She quickly discovered that he was sweet, a bit shy, unmarried, lonely and quite rich. He could certainly afford to have his fantasy fulfilled, which he outlined in amazing detail.

The two women began to work on an empty room. They rented a narrow massage table and placed it in the center, then papered the walls with medical diagrams they printed from the Internet. They took a small dresser and covered it with a white cloth, then topped it with jars, bottles and boxes, all containing items that resembled what one would find in a doctor's exam room. They moved a borrowed, standing scale into the corner and taped a height chart behind it.

After spending hours with the Yellow Pages, a book that was becoming like an old friend, Jenna found a wonderfully helpful man named Manny Grossman whose shop, MG Props and Costumes, rented or sold almost everything theatrical, specializing in satisfying the needs of the many off- and off-off-Broadway shows. She explained that she was going to fulfill a fantasy for her boyfriend and he gave her directions.

When she arrived at the two-story warehouse in Queens, she found a treasure trove of items, taking mental notes of the inventory for future fantasies. Future fantasies? Was she really thinking of doing this again as a business? *Well,* she reasoned, *it wouldn't hurt to be ready.* She'd made no decisions. Yet.

She puttered around the cavernous storage areas then, in a back room filled with pipe racks of costumes of every type, she found a short nurse's uniform that would certainly do for her doctor persona. After she stated her specific needs to Manny, he found a stethoscope and blood-pressure cuff, which he actually knew how to use. After he showed her how to wrap the cuff around the patient's arm, he suggested adding a hospital-type cover-up for her boyfriend. Somehow, the way he suggested it, she thought that he suspected something else. "You can get rubber gloves at any large drugstore and maybe a thermometer."

"Good idea," Jenna said. "Anything else you can think of to set the scene?"

"See whether you can find a roll of wide white paper. I'm afraid I don't have one I can sell you, but you can get them at big art stores or, if you have access, you can get roll ends from newspapers. Use it to cover the table. You can also pour some alcohol on a few cotton balls to create that doctor's office smell. Odors set the mood more than anything else."

"You seem to know a lot about fulfilling fantasies."

"That's what good theater is, creating a fantasy that the audience can climb into. If it's done well, of course. You look like the kind of woman who always wants to do it right."

"Thanks for the compliment and the help. I'll have all this stuff back by Friday."

"Oh, and don't worry about washing anything. I send everything out to be professionally cleaned or laundered before I put it back in stock." As she was leaving with her props, Manny yelled, "Have fun."

"I will," Jenna yelled back. And, amazingly enough, she thought she probably would.

Collin was scheduled to arrive at eight that evening and by seven-thirty Jenna was dressed. She wore the stark white uniform with white, thigh-high stockings and white shoes with heels so high that no real doctor would be able to stand on them for more than a few minutes. Following Manny's advice, instead of perfume, she dabbed rubbing alcohol behind each ear. She had pulled her hair back in a tight chignon and fastened it with only three pins, which she could remove to let her hair fall loose when and if she wanted.

She had discussed her makeup with Chloe and the two women had agreed that it should be professional yet sexy. She'd used a soft shade of lipstick, but lots of eyeliner and mascara. She'd even found an old pair of sunglasses, removed the plastic lenses, then perched the empty frames on the bridge of her nose. She'd looked at herself in the full-length mirror on the back of her bathroom door. *Not bad,* she thought. *Very well done if I do say so myself.* To complete the look, she picked up the stethoscope and draped it around her neck the way she'd seen doctors do on TV.

They'd set up the camera in the corner of the "doctor's office" where it would focus on the table. She would make every effort to keep her back to it.

She had just wandered into the hall when she heard the doorbell ring and the front door open. "Yes?" Chloe said, her voice very professional.

"I'm Collin," a soft voice said. "Collin Shaw."

"Of course, Mr. Shaw. The Doctor is almost ready for you. Why don't you sit down?" Jenna and Chloe had agreed that anticipating the "appointment" would only make it more delicious, so Jenna knew that Chloe would seat him in the living room and hand him a magazine. Several minutes later, Chloe said, "I'm sure it will only be another few minutes."

"Of course," Jenna heard Collin say, his voice obviously trembling.

Finally, about fifteen minutes after Collin had arrived, Jenna called down, "You can send in the next patient, Ms. Mallory."

"Of course, Doctor. Mr. Shaw, you may go up now."

Jenna heard rustling, then footsteps as Collin climbed the stairs. When he arrived at the third-floor landing, Jenna got her first look at him. He was about forty, average height, with glasses and a small moustache. He wasn't handsome, but he had a friendly, open face with a dimple in his chin. He wasn't at all what she had expected, even after their phone conversation, but then what had she expected? Some degenerate with rotting teeth and dirty fingernails? She mentally slapped herself. "Mr. Shaw?" The man nodded. "Go into the exam room and remove all your clothes. You'll find a gown on the exam table. Put it on with the opening in the front. I'll be with you in a moment." She motioned him toward a door, on which she had hung a sign saying *Exam Room 1*.

Collin looked her over thoroughly, from her high-heeled shoes to her slicked down hair, to her long, red fingernails. "Yes, of course," he said, his face flushed and his breathing raspy.

Jenna waited two minutes, and then followed Collin into "Exam Room 1." He was sitting on the edge of the narrow table, his naked legs hanging out from under his short, blue-patterned gown. She modulated her voice so it sounded lower and more businesslike than her usual speech. "Good evening, Mr. Shaw. I'm sorry, but Dr. McCoy had an emergency," she said, remembering the name of Collin Shaw's regular doctor. "I'm Dr. Oakes and I'll be doing your exam today." Jenna had chosen the name Hillary Oakes for her sexual persona. It tickled her that if you said H. Oakes together it sounded like hoax. "If you'll just lie back, I'll try to make this as easy for you as possible. I understand this is just a routine checkup. Have you been having any problems?"

Collin took a breath as if to actually answer her question, then sighed and stretched out on the table, pulling the gown closed over his belly and half-erect cock. "Nothing special."

"That's fine. Let me take your blood pressure." She wrapped the cuff around his upper arm and placed the bell over the inside of his elbow. She'd practiced what Manny had showed her on Chloe, and had actually been able to hear her friend's heart beating. She knew it didn't matter what she heard but it made everything all the more real. "That's just fine," she said, taking a clipboard from a side table and scrawling something on a sheet of paper. She took his temperature, listened to his breathing with her stethoscope, then said, "I'll need to do a full body exam. Don't be embarrassed. I won't see anything I've never seen before." She parted the gown and saw that Collin's erection had hardened. "Just relax," she said, trying not to smile.

She palpated his abdomen, then cupped his testicles as if to weigh them. "That's fine," she said, watching his hard cock bob and a small drop of precum ooze from the tip. "I'll need to check your prostate."

She had tried to mention a rectal exam to him on the phone but he had been too embarrassed for her to consider saying anything about it. She had told him that he could refuse anything she wanted to do by just asking her to stop. Barring that, she'd use her radar to try to ascertain exactly what he wanted most. "Is that really necessary?" he asked. He sounded worried, but aroused, and she could see his cock twitch.

"I certainly think so. We can't be too careful."

Collin sighed, then said, "Okay. Anything you say." She almost smiled.

Jenna made a big show of putting on a pair of rubber gloves, and then took a tube of KY Jelly from the table behind her. She watched Collin's eyes open wider as he watched her spread a big dollop of gel on her finger and a pool in her other palm. "Put your knees up and just relax," she said, again, trying not to grin. After he placed his feet close to his buttocks she parted his cheeks and reached between them to thoroughly lubricate his anal area. She gently pressed her finger against the tight opening until it slipped inside. She pulled it out and pushed it in a few times, watching his entire body tremble and his eyes close.

She knew enough about anatomy to be able to find his dome-shaped prostate and, with her slippery other hand, she grasped the base of his rock hard cock. "Take a few deep breaths," she said, as she rubbed deep in his sensitive ass, holding his penis tightly enough to prevent ejaculation.

When she thought he'd had enough, she rubbed his cock from base to tip, while still rubbing her other middle finger over his prostate. He came in a rush, grunting and saying, "Oh, God, Oh, God," over and over again.

Finally, when she sensed that he was completely exhausted she removed her gloves and said, "There's a shower behind that door if you want one. I hope that lived up to your expectations."

"God, I didn't last nearly as long as I had hoped but that's not your fault. It was so real and so like my dreams. It was fabulous. What's your first name so I can include it in my fantasies from now on."

"Hillary," she said, smiling.

"Can I ask for you again?"

Ask for me? Again? She'd have thought that, at five hundred dollars, this experience was some kind of special occasion, a one-time thing. Trying not to sound too hopeful, she said, "Of course."

His smile was wide. "That's great. Thanks for the best hand job I've ever had."

"You're welcome. Make yourself comfortable for a while, but you know that your time here is limited to two hours." She and Chloe had made that a condition. "The videotape will be here on the table for you on the way out."

"I'll take a quick shower and be out of here in a jiffy. Thanks, again."

"I'll look forward to next time," she said as she closed the door behind her.

As she tidied up the "exam room," Jenna thought about her adventure. It had been delightful. She'd given a man something really first-rate that he'd obviously appreciated. She gazed at the bills lying on her dresser. Five hundred dollars. Cash. Amazingly enough, she didn't feel at all demeaned. Of course she hadn't had intercourse, either. She heard Collin singing in the shower, and smiled.

"How was it?" Chloe asked when Jenna had changed into jeans and come downstairs after Collin's departure. "If it was awful I promise not to suggest that you do it again."

"Actually, it wasn't as awful as I thought it would be."

"But it was pretty bad?" The delicious way she licked her lips and waited for details almost made Jenna laugh out loud.

"You're such a devil," Jenna said, stifling a smile. "Okay, it was sort of fun."

Chloe's eyes opened wide. "He looked happy as he dashed past me and out the front door. Did you fuck? Tell me everything."

"I won't tell you much. This guy paid for privacy in addition to everything else. I will tell you, however, that we didn't fuck but he left here one satisfied guy. And he said he'd ask for me next time."

Chloe let out a little whoop. "Good going, Jen. So you're willing to do it again?"

"For him, sure."

"For other guys?"

Jenna bristled. "Have you got guys lined up? Did you assume I'd go along?"

"Not at all, and relax. It's just that this fantasy fulfillment stuff is dynamite. There's nothing like it around. The word's gotten around on the floor of the exchange and several guys have asked Frank about doing something like this. It would involve fucking though."

Jenna shook her head slowly. "How can you sit there and discuss this so calmly?"

"Because now we've both done it," Chloe said, softly, "and I, for one, want to do more."

She was so conflicted that the more comfortable Chloe seemed with it, the more she pulled back. "Okay, you do it and leave me out. Except for Collin, of course. I promised I'd be here for him next time."

"Okay, if that's what you want, but it would mean you wouldn't have to get a full-time job or go back to Seneca Falls." Her voice held temptation.

"I don't know, Chloe. Maybe. No. Not a chance. I don't know."

Chloe's impatience was starting to show. "Stop worrying about what you're supposed to think. If you don't want to do it, that's fine. Do what you want to do and stop waffling. Make the decision and stick to it; stop making it over and over again. You've changed since you moved here. You're not the small-town girl you pretend to be, shocked at a little casual sex, with or without money involved."

"I know." She closed her eyes and shook her head. "I can just hear Marcy's reaction."

"So don't tell her. You haven't shared anything about it up to now so why tell her anything."

"But we tell each other everything."

"Like about Collin?"

"What about Glen? This isn't the way he thinks of me at all."

"Why do you care what he thinks? I thought he was in your past."

"He is, of course. It's just that . . ."

"I would like to do this fantasy thing as a business. The money's too good to pass up and it would be doing things I enjoy anyway. If you want to do it with me, great. If not, make movies, entertain Collin, and that's that. I hope you won't be angry with me if I go ahead."

Jenna thought about what Chloe had said. She had kept deciding to do it, but then she would think about what everyone would say if they knew and what she thought she *should* want. Wasn't it time to do what she wanted and to hell with what others would think? She slowly nodded her head. "I want to do it too."

"That's great," Chloe said, squeezing Jenna's hand. "I'm glad you've decided."

"Me, too. It's just—"

"Stop. Right now. No more second thoughts. We're in this together. Think about the money. If we can entertain in one of the upstairs rooms, oh, let's say three times a week, at a thousand dollars a pop, that's quite a bit of cash."

"A thousand?"

"I've raised the price," Chloe said. "If they can't afford it, they can do without. We're the only ones out there doing this."

"That certainly takes care of Aunt Elise's taxes."

"We could put some in the kitty and keep the rest. It should mount up really quickly and we'd pay no income taxes."

"That bothers me. I know that selling sex is illegal, but most of the high-profile cases of madams—phew, I just said that word, didn't I—getting caught and tried, it's for tax evasion. Isn't there any way around that?"

Chloe shrugged. "Good point, and I haven't a clue. Maybe we need some way to protect ourselves too. I'm not the type to organize things. I'm just the graphic designer."

"Don't look at me. How the hell do we cover all the bases?"

Several days later Jenna and Chloe were again sitting over a Chinese dinner. "Frank was talking to me about Club Fantasy today and he made a suggestion."

"Club Fantasy?"

"That's what we've begun to call it. The name you suggested sort of stuck and it's perfect. Anyway, Frank knows a woman who runs a very high-priced, call-girl operation. She's really nice and would be willing to give us some pointers."

"A madam?"

"I guess that's what she would be. Some of Frank's friends and business associates have used her women for parties and such, and have been pleased, not only with the women but with Erika's professionalism. Her business is called Courtesans, Inc., and he suggested that we could call her."

"Interview a madam. I feel like a talk show, but I guess we could give it a try."

"Not we, Jen," Chloe said. "You. I'm electing you to handle the business end of this thing we're considering."

"Why me?"

"Because I haven't the foggiest idea about business."

"You're copping out," Jenna said. "You were a stockbroker after all. Don't play dumb with me."

Chloe lowered her gaze. "Okay, you got me, but the whole idea of keeping records and filling out forms gives me the shakes. Please? Just talk to her. See how she answers some of our questions."

Jenna sighed. Chloe's "cute act" didn't endear her to Jenna, but she was right about one thing. If they were going to make a business out of Club Fantasy it would have to be her who made it happen. Did she want to create a business out of fulfilling fantasies? It seemed immoral somehow, and she shuddered at that thought. However, she'd made the decision and, as Chloe had pointed out, she couldn't keep making it over and over. She was having fun, and could call it off at any time if it got too complicated in any way. And the money was quite an added incentive for both women. "Okay. I'll talk to her."

"Great. I'll call Frank and have him set it up."

Chapter
7

The following afternoon Jenna sat in a trendy East-Side, Italian restaurant waiting for Erika. She'd debated about what to wear for a meeting with a madam, and she finally settled on a soft rose, short-sleeved blouse and a narrow, black skirt. She'd kept her makeup light and her hair loose around her shoulders. She sipped a glass of sauvignon blanc and tried to picture what a two-thousand-dollar-a-night madam looked like. When she spotted the woman who was making her way to her table she realized she had been completely off base.

Instead of seeming slightly seedy, this woman reeked of class. Tall, slender, shapely, with shoulder-length, medium brown hair lightly streaked with dark blond, a confident walk, and a charming smile. She wore a pair of silver-gray, linen slacks and a navy blue, silk blouse, navy blue, flat-heeled shoes, and carried a matching handbag. Her makeup was soft and natural, making guessing her age difficult. Jenna glanced down at the woman's hands, usually a giveaway to age, but saw only well-manicured mauve nails and a pair of rings, one a classic diamond solitaire, the other a plain gold band. The fact that the woman was married surprised Jenna. She stood and took the woman's extended hand. "I'm Erika Dunlop," the woman said, her voice softly modulated, "and you must be Jenna. That's such a pretty name."

"Thanks. I've no idea where my parents got it, or *Marcy* for my sister."

"You've got a sister? How wonderful. Guaranteed playmates. I wasn't so lucky. I'm an only."

"She's actually my twin and that's both good news and bad news. We always had someone to play with as kids, but it got a bit tiresome living as half of a unit as we became adults."

The waiter arrived and Erika ordered a glass of the same wine that Jenna was drinking. "I'm starving," she said as the waiter hustled off to get her drink. "Do you mind if we order?"

"Not a problem," Jenna said, and the two women quickly decided to share an antipasto and an order of veal piccata with roasted potatoes instead of spaghetti.

During a leisurely meal the two women got to know each other. Jenna told Erika about her life in Seneca Falls, Marcy, Chloe, and even touched on Glen. She was amazed at how easy the other woman was to talk to. When she mentioned it, Erika said, "It's part of my job. I'm a courtesan, and a superior one has to be able to bring out the best in a man, and to do that you have to be able to understand his wishes, his deepest desires. How? By talking with him. I try to have dinner with a man before I go to bed with him for the first time. That way I can ferret out all the little things that matter to him. It's sort of like a job interview, although the man must never realize it."

"I see your point. Before we get to the reason I wanted to meet you," Jenna said, "tell me a little about you. How did you get into all this?"

"Frankly, I needed the money. My husband decamped to Switzerland with every cent my daughter and I had in the world and refused to send any alimony or child support. So one thing led to another and I began to entertain men for money. I joined a wonderful woman named Valerie and the rest, as they say, is history."

"I know you run a business. Do you still entertain men yourself?"

"From time to time. I still have a few of my old clients, and a few of my employees are still around, but I don't take on anyone new on either side. I'm trying to phase the whole thing out but I'm like a fire horse. The bell rings and I can't resist throwing oil on the fire, if you'll pardon a very mixed metaphor."

Jenna glanced down at the engagement and wedding rings Erika wore. "You're married. What about him?"

"My husband is very tolerant." Her eyes got soft and gentle. "Stuart's a wonderful man. We've known each other forever and been married for almost three years. It's still as great as it always was."

"Does he know about your business?" Jenna asked softly.

"He's the one responsible for it. It's a long story and I'll tell you all about it some time if you're really interested. However, you didn't meet me to hear my life history. I know about your movies and I've even seen one. An ex-client showed me the one he and his wife made after he got brave enough to share his desires with her. It was amazingly professionally done. You're very talented and, to use his word, simpatico. That's why I want to hear more about Club Fantasy."

"You know that name? Chloe and I kid about it but I didn't think anyone else knew."

"One of my regulars told me about it. Word has gotten around and people are excited about it. They think that if you do it as professionally as the films it will be wonderful. Personally, I think it's a great idea. My employees fulfill fantasies all the time, but not with props, costumes, and such. It could be quite a business."

"Can I ask you a question?"

"Of course. You can ask me anything but I reserve the right not to answer if I want. Shoot."

There were so many things that she wondered about that Jenna was at a loss where to begin. She finally asked, "Why are men willing to pay so much money when they could get a plain hooker for a lot less?"

"A serious question with a serious answer. In my case, they get someone cultured, classy, someone to decorate their arm at a social function with fringe benefits afterward. In your case, a man, or woman for that matter, would pay quite a bit for someone, or someones, who would do the things with him that he's been dreaming about and masturbating to for years."

Erika sipped her wine, her long fingers gracefully cupping the glass. "There's more too. They want anonymity, the knowledge that, unless they say something, no word of what they've done will get back to family, friends, or job. We have famous clients too, men and woman who want to have great sex with cultured partners who will keep their mouths shut and not go running to the nearest tabloid. Think for a moment about poor Kobe Bryant. He had sex with a groupie, or whatever she was, and look at the mess he got into. It seems unimportant to ascertain exactly what occurred. If he'd employed a professional, none of that would have happened."

"I guess I never thought about it that way. If you'll pardon me for asking, what do you charge?"

"We charge anywhere from a thousand to two thousand an evening. Most goes to the employee and the rest to Courtesans, Inc. In return for the money they give up, the men and women who work for me get health insurance, vacation pay, and, most important, the vetting of all the clients."

"Vetting?"

"We make doubly and triply sure that the people we entertain are on the up and up. No cops, no weirdos."

"You said you employ men. Do women use your services too?"

Erika looked startled. "Of course. Men aren't the only ones

who get lonely and needy. Women have fantasies just like men do."

"I never thought of that. I guess I'm not thinking about employing anyone else, just Chloe and me, having some fun with men who are willing to pay."

"You don't have to go any further than that, of course, but if you want to expand your horizons, there's a lot more you can do with a business like the one you're considering. You have to be willing to go all the way, of course."

"All the way?"

Erika leaned forward and placed her hand over Jenna's on the white tablecloth. "Let's be perfectly frank. If you want to consider entertaining men and playing with their deepest sexual fantasies, you will have to be willing to do some pretty unusual things."

Obviously, Erika didn't realize that she hadn't actually had intercourse with a man for money yet. Wasn't she really just splitting hairs? "Like?"

"Like oral sex, anal sex, threesomes, spanking, bondage, all the more esoteric things that men dream about. They can do ordinary things with their wives or girlfriends. They will want to do the more unusual with you. They might want to rape you, or be raped, tie you down or be tied. They might want you to become an experienced older woman or a child, and you'll have to be all those things and more."

Discouraged, Jenna said, "You're probably right."

"Darling, been there, done that, and you can too if you want to. It's a very lucrative business but it has its downside. Days when all you want to do is stay in bed, alone, but you have to be up, on, understanding, without a care in the world. Days when you have your period or a belly ache or a head cold. You can't disappoint a client or you'll lose him and all the men he talks to."

Jenna sat back, deep in thought. "I guess you're right. What

Chloe and I have done so far has been a lark. You're talking about a business."

"I certainly am. If you want to continue on a lark, as you put it, that's fine and it can work for you. But, if you want to make real money, hire employees, and in every way expand Club Fantasy to something larger, that means records, bookkeeping, taxes, health plans if you want that, schedules, and lots of psychology. It's not easy and it takes lots of time and energy."

She had both, but did she want to spend them on a major business? "I gather." She thought about Marcy and her lists. Could Jenna become as organized as her sister? It was obvious that, if she and Chloe wanted to make Club Fantasy a success on a bigger scale, Chloe couldn't take on the responsibility. She could.

Erika spent the next hour explaining the intricacies of the business to Jenna. She offered to demonstrate her computer programs for scheduling, tracking employee hours, and, most important, collecting and cataloging customer preferences. "I'll give you copies of anything you need. I'll even show you how to dial into my system from your home phone and check on whether a particular man has been my client and what his specific tastes are."

"Why are you being so generous? We've just met, after all."

"Many years ago someone I cared about very much was as generous to me in similar circumstances. Valerie's in Dallas now and I'm trying to close my business."

"I can't believe you're quitting. You're a legend." When she watched Erika's eyes widen, she realized what she'd said. "I didn't mean it like that."

Erika's chuckle was warm and friendly. "I'm not at all insulted. I'm a happy woman now. Stuart's the love of my life and my daughter's pregnant with my first grandchild. I'm ready to be a plain old housewife, in the best sense of the word."

Her voice filled with her surprise as Jenna said, "You're going to be a grandmother?"

"Yup. After lots of years of estrangement, Rena and her husband Alex are living in Westchester, and we're very close. I'm trying to resist buying every piece of baby stuff I see, but I've already got a few things put away."

"That's wonderful. Congratulations."

"It's good news for you too. I'm more than glad to help you get started but you have to want it. Consider what you expected when we met. I'm a madam, although I prefer courtesan, and with that label comes lots of negatives."

"I've thought about that. I don't think I could even tell my sister what I'd be doing."

"That's the problem. I had a hell of a time when my daughter found out about Courtesans, Inc."

"It obviously all worked out."

Erika shook her head sadly. "Not without lots of problems."

"Why do men do it?"

"Pay? Because they want something they can't get at home. It's just that simple. Either they don't have anyone, or they think their partner isn't interested in what they want. Sadly, many times the husband or wife would be more than willing to play but the couple just can't communicate. However, that's not our responsibility."

"Any more advice?"

"Lots." Erika took a sip of her wine and signaled the waiter. She looked at Jenna. "Coffee?"

"Sure."

Erika waggled two fingers and the waiter hustled off. "Okay. If you're going to entertain as a professional, there are lots of things I can tell you. From the business end, I suggest that you never entertain anyone you don't know either personally or through someone you trust. There are too many weirdos and cops out there."

"Cops. That's scares the shit out of me."

"It should, if only to make you wary. I've never had a problem. Courtesans, Inc., identifies itself as an entertainment corporation. We take clients to dinner and entertain them. If there's sex afterwards, that's not part of the package, and it's difficult for the cops to get their teeth into that unless they've been 'entertained.'

"I pay my employees properly, with all taxes taken out, and I file all the forms with the IRS.

"From the personal side, be charming, interested, and get to know your client and all his desires. The more you know the happier he'll be. I say he, but, as I said, don't overlook female clients. Eventually you might want to employ men as entertainers for women."

"Do you?"

"Of course. Actually my son-in-law worked for me several years ago. That's where he met my daughter."

Jenna was having a hard time taking it all in. Prostitutes of both sexes with families and private lives just like real people. "Shit. It's all incestuous."

The corners of Erika's mouth turned up. "It is a bit, isn't it. Cleanliness, sweet breath, deodorant and diaphragms for those days of the month are all important." The two women talked for another hour, consuming several cups of wonderful hazelnut coffee.

"You haven't done it yet, have you," Erika said suddenly.

Unable to deny it, Jenna shook her head and told her about her evening playing doctor.

"How wonderful. I'll bet the guy was in heaven. Making the final jump into intercourse for money is like crossing the Rubicon. After that, it's all fun and games, with the emphasis on the games. You've obviously decided to do it."

"I still vacillate but I think I've made the decision."

"Just thinking isn't enough. As I said, it's a gigantic step, at least it was for me. Some woman can do it without much soul searching but for us—pardon me for assuming I know you but I think I do—it's not just doing it. It's an entire change of attitude and you have to be sure. Once you're sure, go for it in every way and don't second guess yourself."

"You sound just like Chloe."

"When and if you are sure, straighten your backbone and give whoever the guy turns out to be the best fuck he's ever had. Then continue to do that every time."

Early that evening the phone rang. "Hi, Jenna, it's Glen."

Jenna dropped into a kitchen chair. "Hello, Glen," she said, schooling her voice to be cheerful and impersonal. "It's good to hear from you."

"I thought it would be okay to call. After all, it's been four months."

"Has it been that long?" Jenna said, knowing full well how long it had been. "I got the flowers. Thanks so much. They are lovely."

"I know. Marcy told me. How are things in the big city?"

Keeping her voice light, Jenna told Glen about her life in New York, carefully omitting any reference to the topic at the front of her mind. It was difficult to keep the two sides of her brain clearly separated, one steeped in sex and the future of Club Fantasy, the other a small-town girl with an old lover back home. Home? No. Her home was here now.

"So you're enjoying yourself," Glen said.

"I really am. I just love New York. I know I must sound like a commercial, but I'm happy here."

She heard his hesitation. *He's not going to ask whether I'm coming back. He doesn't want to hear my answer.* "I'm glad you're happy."

"How are things back in the Gateway to the Finger Lakes?"

"Things here are great." He spent five minutes filling her in on office gossip and the goings on at AAJ, much of which she already knew from her sister but she let him ramble.

"Sounds like things there are about the same," Jenna said, when he'd wound down.

"The same, but really quite interesting."

"I'm sure they are," Jenna said politely. It sounded as exciting as a church social.

"Well, I guess I'll be going now. Can I call from time to time, just as a friend?"

She put all the warmth she could into her voice. "Of course you can, Glen. As a friend."

Chloe walked in as she hung up the phone. "You don't look so good. Bad news?"

"Not really," Jenna said. "That was Glen."

"The old boyfriend?"

"Yeah. He called as a friend, he says, to say hello."

"And?"

She propped an elbow on the table, chin resting on her palm. "Lots of old stuff. I feel guilty, as if I led him on, then dropped him. He still sounds lost and I couldn't seem to tell him straight out to give it up."

"Did you love him, way back when?"

Jenna shook her head slowly, then said, "I don't really know, Chloe. I thought I did, but when he asked me to marry him I freaked. Now that I'm here I can't imagine going back to the kind of life I had there."

"You don't have to if you don't want to. Ever." Chloe sat across from Jenna. "Did you talk to Erika?"

"We had quite a lunch. She's an amazing woman."

"I'm sorry I couldn't join you."

Chloe's work schedule made weekday daytime plans impossible, and Erika couldn't make it any other time. "I'm sorry too. You would have liked her a lot. She's a real person, and I don't use that term lightly." Jenna relayed most of Erika's conversation, then said, "Sometime during the conversation I think I made my decision. I'm ready to go through with this nutty idea. The whole Club Fantasy thing."

"Did you tell Erika about it? She might be competition."

"Yes, I did, and no, she's not. She loved the idea and even suggested that we set up a few rooms in the house as specialty areas. Keep the doctor's office and the motel room, maybe make a Western room, and even create a dungeon." Jenna vividly remembered that part of their discussion:

"If you're really going to fulfill fantasies," Erika had said, "you need a room for dominant and submissive games and someone who knows how to use it."

"Like what?"

"Let me suggest that you rent some videos about bondage, discipline, and such. Then you can set up a room, a basement if you have one, for folks who want to play with darker fantasies."

"There are men who want that?"

"You are really new to this." Erika had smiled indulgently. "Lots and lots of men either want to be dominated or want to dominate. You need to read a few books on the subject and watch lots of movies. Your education is sorely lacking."

"I guess so."

"One important thing. If you're going to play with BDSM fantasies, you need to screen your clients extra carefully. You can't afford to make a mistake. One error in judgement might be one too many. Trust your stomach, then check everything once more. If you have any doubts, say no. It never hurts to turn down a customer. There are always more."

"Phew," Chloe said in the kitchen. "I never thought about it like that."

Jenna glanced at the counter. "I picked up a few books Erika recommended, then went to the video store and rented lots of movies. We really should watch a bunch, then consider what she said about a dungeon. We could use the basement."

"You're really getting into this. It'll take a lot of time and muscle to get it cleaned up but I think it's a great idea." Chloe pulled a movie called *Bondage Sluts* from the plastic bag on the table. "You said she's phasing out her business. Are you sure she won't be competition?"

"Not only is she ending Courtesans, Inc.," Jenna said, staring at the cover of another video, one that showed a shapely woman in a leather bathing suit and thigh-high boots, a whip in one hand, standing over a man with his hands and feet bound, his smooth, white ass covered with red welts, "but she'll even let us use her computer system and employ some of her people if we want."

"Whoa. Computer system?" She made an X of her fingers. "Not me. That will be your department. I'm hopeless. The Erika thing sounds too good to be true."

"She seems to be a happily married woman, ready to get out of the business. I think she's just hanging on for the people who depend on her, both employees and customers."

"That's fantastic. Okay. Let me grab a bite of dinner, and then we can watch some of these films on the big-screen TV."

While the two women ate, Jenna thumbed through one of the sex books, this one based on the joys of the BDSM lifestyle. As she flipped pages, she realized that she'd already begun to think of this as a business, not prostitution. Certainly she'd be selling her body. No, she corrected herself, renting her body. But what was the harm? Erika seemed to have come out of it all a happy, together person. Why not her? Why not indeed?

Together, Chloe and Jenna watched four videos trying not to laugh at the poor quality of the acting and the visibly faked whippings. But the atmosphere was real and it was obvious that lots of men did get off being tied, spanked, humiliated, and possibly even wounded. "I don't think I could really hurt someone," Jenna said with a sigh.

"I don't know," Chloe said. "I think I could. I might be dynamite as a midget power wielder."

"You're right," Jenna said, brightening. "I hadn't thought about that but someone with your lush body and small stature would be a knock out—pardon the pun. Have you ever tried it?"

Chloe actually blushed. "Yes, with one guy I knew."

When she didn't continue, Jenna asked, "Did you have fun? Did you dress up?" When Chloe nodded, sheepishly, she continued. "Do you still have the costume?"

"Oh, yeah," she said, looking slightly sheepish, "and lots more."

"You never told me about that side of you."

"Actually, it never came up and it's not something you drag into a conversation by its heels."

"I guess not," Jenna said. "I don't think I could do any of that, money or no money."

"You'd be amazed at what you'd do if it turned someone on. It's like being drugged. You see his excitement and you'd do anything to make it even better. Before I first spanked a man I didn't think I'd like it either but when push came to shove, if you'll pardon the pun, it was wonderful. He got so excited that he came without my even touching him, except where he lay across my thighs."

"I'd love to hear about it. Was it like the movies we just watched?"

"Not at all. Rick was here from Oregon and I met him through work. We had dinner together and finished a wonderful bottle of cabernet. Needless to say, I was loose and horny. When he suggested we go back to his hotel room I was more than ready."

Chloe and Rick walked into his hotel room and Rick ordered a bottle of champagne from room service. The room was actually a suite, and they settled in the living area, Rick on a straight chair and Chloe on the sofa. While they waited they continued a conversation they'd been having in the taxi, getting into a heated argument about the way a current court case should be prosecuted. "He's just a kid," Chloe said. "He should be treated like a kid and his parents should be horse-whipped."

Suddenly, Rick seemed to get flustered and, as he cleared his throat and squirmed in his chair, the waiter knocked at the door. Rick let him in and signed the room-service check while the white-jacketed server opened the bottle and filled two glasses.

After the waiter left, Rick and Chloe clinked glasses and, while she sipped, he downed the entire glass. He poured another, cleared his throat again and said, "You really think so? About the kid's parents, I mean."

"Sorry," Chloe said, wondering why the guy was suddenly so flustered. "I forgot what I said."

Again Rick coughed. "You said the parents should be horse-whipped."

"Right. It's really their fault that the kid got into so much trouble."

He cleared his throat again. "Would you horsewhip anyone whose kids got into trouble?" he asked, his voice hoarse and low.

"I guess so," Chloe said, confused and disappointed. She had thought they had come to his room to have sex. Her panties were wet and she was anxious to get to it. Now he wouldn't stop talking about this court case.

"What if one of my kids, uh, did something like that?"

Slowly the light dawned. "I guess I'd have to horsewhip you," she said, a coy smile now spreading over her face. She'd never actually hurt anyone, but she had dated a man several months before who had liked to be swatted on the ass as he was about to come. She was starting to get the message Rick was sending.

"Would you? What if you didn't have a horsewhip?"

Chloe looked at Rick carefully. His hands were trembling, his chest heaving as if he'd run several miles, and his eyes downcast. She didn't have to be a rocket scientist to know what was going on. "I guess my hand would have to do."

"Oh," he said.

"It would be even worse if you'd been bad yourself. Have you?"

Chloe watched his body shrink, his shoulders droop, and his chin fall against his chest. "Maybe."

Making her voice sound stern, she said, "Don't give me any maybes, have you been bad?"

"Yes, ma'am."

Shit. She could feel her pussy twitch and fluids sop the crotch of her panties. This game was raising her temperature as much as Rick's. "I might just have to horsewhip you," she said, and watched his body jerk.

"Yes, ma'am."

"I might let you off with a spanking if you do a good job." She sipped her champagne. This was getting to be fun.

"At what, ma'am?" he said, his voice barely above a whisper.

Chloe stood and slid her slender skirt down. She was not wearing stockings, merely a tiny wisp of lacy panties. She pulled them down as well, then sat on the edge of the sofa, knees spread. She crooked her finger for him to approach. "Crawl over here and see what you can do with my pussy," she said. "Then we'll decide on your punishment for being bad."

"Oh, yes, ma'am," he said, scuttling across the brown tweed carpet on his hands and knees. Somehow it was even more exciting for Chloe since he was still wearing a three-piece suit, white shirt and tie. As he approached, she grabbed the back of his head and pressed his face into her crotch.

He had a wonderfully talented mouth. He alternately flicked her engorged clit and stuck his pointed tongue into her canal, exploring every fold, licking and delving. After a few moments, he pressed his lips around her clit and sucked, rubbing the tip with the flat of his tongue. "Shit," she said as she

came in a rush, straining against his face. "Shit." He didn't
stop pleasuring her pussy until she pushed his face away, totally replete.

"You did that very well," Chloe said, having trouble breathing. "Therefore, you will only need five swats." When he
looked disappointed, she said, "I mean ten."

"I couldn't take ten, ma'am."

"I don't really care," she said, standing and heading for the
bathroom. "Remove your pants and briefs and wait for me."
In the bathroom she cleaned up, then returned to the living-
room area where Rick waited. He still wore his vest, shirt and
tie, and his shoes and socks. His pants were discarded on the
floor, his erection hard and thrusting straight out from his
groin.

Chloe sat on the edge of the sofa and patted her bare thighs.
Panting, trembling, he stumbled, then stretched out across
her lap. "P-p-please don't hurt me."

"It's necessary." To prolong the excitement, she caressed
his pale ass cheeks, making large circles with the tips of her fingers. "I'll try not to hurt you too much," she crooned. Suddenly,
she raised her hand and brought it down across Rick's buttocks.

"That's one," he said. "Two," he continued as Chloe's hand
landed again. "Three, four," he said. Then his entire body
shuddered and she felt his hard cock twitch against her thigh
and semen dribbled down between her legs. "Oh, God," he
said.

Chloe took a deep breath. "He was scheduled to return to
the West Coast the following day, but he calls me occasionally
to make sure I'll be around if he ever returns to New York."

"I never considered all that stuff until I talked to Erika.
Now I find out that you're a practicing sadist."

"No, I'm not really. I just get so high out of giving pleasure
and he certainly enjoyed it."

"It's going to take a while for me to get used to all this." *There's so much,* she thought. *So much.*

"Eventually, we can look over the basement and see what we have to do?"

"Sure. This is really strange. I haven't actually done anything yet, with a guy for pay, I mean, and here I am planning a business, complete with bondage room. It's sure happening fast.

"One more thing. In my talk with Erika, she mentioned that you'd been talking it up and word about Club Fantasy had been getting around. You've got to get serious about this. What we're considering doing is illegal as hell and really dangerous."

"How dangerous?" Chloe said, her eyes widening. "It's just folks Frank knows."

"And folks those folks know and on and on. Chloe, there are lots of guys out there who get their jollies out of hurting women or taking things we aren't willing to give. We've been talking about bondage. What if you let someone you didn't know tie you up, then he got nasty?"

Chloe's face quickly registered her shock. "I never thought about that. I'm really sorry. You're right."

It was important to Jenna to make sure Chloe was careful, yet not to scare the daylights out of her. "Chloe, it's okay. Just keep your mouth shut. Enough folks know about this for the moment. We'll have to have some rules about who does what to whom. Remember that this is our house and the guys will know that it's a brothel of sorts. We don't want anyone hanging around outside thinking they can get stuff for nothing."

Chloe looked concerned. "Will we have to move?"

"Certainly not yet. We'll play it by ear for the moment but one wrong vibe and I, for one, will be out of here."

"I guess that's fair. God, I never thought of all that."

Jenna knew her friend well enough to know that Chloe seldom thought about anything too deeply, but she was Jenna's best friend so she reached out and wrapped her arms around the tiny woman. "I know. Let's just pretend that it's all right for now. Maybe it's playing ostrich but it's either that or not doing it at all."

"You're right, of course."

"You said there's a guy who wants to play out a fantasy with me. Like what, exactly?"

"Actually, it's pretty simple. He wants to watch."

"Watch what?" Jenna asked.

"You know those films where women masturbate? He wants a live show and he's willing to pay a thousand bucks for it, and for the ability to fuck you after he's seen enough."

"Oh," Jenna said, considering how she'd feel playing with herself while some slobbering guy sat there and stared at her. "I'm not sure I'd know what to do."

"Back to the video-rental store," Chloe said, regaining her composure.

"When does he want to do it?"

"He wants to do it yesterday but he's willing to abide by your schedule. Maybe one evening next week."

Jenna felt like she was standing on a diving board about to jump into the deep end. It was terrifying. Now she wasn't worried about letting some guy make love to her, but rather about making sure the man got his money's worth. A thousand dollars was a lot to spend so she'd have to give him lots in return. Well, if he wasn't satisfied he could have his money back. "You said he wants to fuck me when he's seen enough. He might want to stay all night and that's not an option. Like we did with the guy who played doctor, we have to agree on a time limit. There have to be rules to protect both parties. We need to list some of the dos and don'ts." She thought about Marcy and her lists.

"Like what?"

"It can't be open-ended—like, until he's satisfied. So, let's say he gets two hours like Collin did. And, for anyone, if he isn't satisfied he can get his money back."

"I won't give the money back if he's fucked me. I mean, what's to prevent someone from getting it all, then wanting a refund?"

"Good point. Okay, up to but not including orgasm, they can ask for their money back."

Jenna watched the wheels turning. Between the two of them they should be able to make this work. "That makes sense," Chloe said thoughtfully.

"Who pays expenses?"

"Expenses?" Chloe asked.

"We can do lots of stuff with what's in the attic and some easy additional things, but what if someone wants us to rent costumes, for example."

"You're right. We'll have to discuss that with a client before-hand. I'm the one who took all those psych courses in college and you seem to know people instinctively," Chloe said. "Finding out exactly what the client wants and what he needs to pay to make his fantasy real shouldn't be too difficult."

"It seems we've started something here. Club Fantasy might just become a reality."

Chapter

8

Jenna wasn't as confident about her own ability to satisfy the fantasy desires of a client as she wanted to be. Inside she was a wreck during the days before the big event, arranged for the following Tuesday evening. She rented numerous videos and found masturbation stories on the Web. She'd been masturbating since she was in her midteens, but this was very different. This wasn't a quick satisfaction for her. Rather, it was a show she would put on for a man. It was scary as hell.

Jenna found a small erotic boutique in the East Village and bought a split crotch, black teddy trimmed with ivory lace and a matching negligee and several new dildos and vibrators she could play with. When it came right down to it this was just a matter of doing what felt right and gauging the guy's reactions, right?

As planned, Chloe met the man at the door, collected his money, explained the rules, then guided him up to the "motel room." The ambiance had been completely altered with the simple addition of a few green plants, an urn filled with dried wheat, softer pictures on the walls, and a satin coverlet with a few matching pillows on the bed.

"This is Juan," Chloe said as the man entered the room. It was all Jenna could do not to grin as Chloe surreptitiously waved a check behind Juan's back. "And this is Hillary. Would you care for a drink?"

The man shook his head as Chloe left, seemingly unable to take his eyes off of Jenna's body. Juan was about forty, a swarthy, olive-skinned Hispanic with a thick neck and wide shoulders. He wore his hair long, hanging to his shoulders, and had his facial hair trimmed into a neat moustache and goatee that surrounded his wide-lipped, sensual mouth. He was dressed in a simple light blue polo shirt and khaki slacks.

As he stared, his blunt-fingered hands clenched and unclenched. Jenna had to admit that she looked stunning in her teddy and peignoir, black stockings attached to the teddy's long garters, and black sling-backed pumps with four-inch heels. She'd played down her makeup, not wanting to look like an overblown hooker, but rather a model ready for a photo shoot. "I'm glad you came to watch my rehearsal," she said, slipping into character. "I'm going to be doing this for a movie tomorrow and I thought you'd like to see me rehearse."

"Movie?"

"I'm going to be filming one of those erotic videos tomorrow. When I'm facing a camera I can't judge how men might be receiving my performance so I thought I could use you as my test case. Is that okay?"

"Test case?"

Jenna wanted to smile. He was almost speechless, looking her over, knowing what was to come. "If that's okay? I have all sorts of toys here that I could play with and you could watch and let me know what you like."

"Sure," he said as she motioned him to a spot on the end of the bed.

Her heart pounding with a combination of excitement and terror, Jenna slowly removed her negligee and draped it over the dresser. She opened a drawer and pulled out three dildos of varying lengths and thicknesses, two vibrators, and several kinds of massage oil, placing them on a side table within easy reach. "I can't thank you enough for helping me. For example, I'm never sure," she said, her voice soft and breathy, "whether I should leave my shoes on or take them off. What do you think?"

"Leave them on," Juan growled.

"Of course." She stretched out on the bed. "Want to see my tits?"

When Juan nodded enthusiastically, she pulled down the straps of the teddy, baring her ample breasts. "I love touching my tits," she said. "My nipples are so sensitive. When I pull on them they make my pussy really hot." Juan's eyes never left her hands as she twisted one nipple in each hand. She took a bottle of oil from the table, dribbled some on each breast, then slowly rubbed the shiny fluid all over her flesh. She was never much for breast play but, watching Juan's eyes, she realized that he was delighted with what he saw. His rapt expression told her that she was doing everything he wanted. As Erika had said, his satisfaction was her goal.

"My pussy gets so hungry when I do this. Would you mind if I touched it?" She took his silence for acquiescence, so she slid one hand down her belly and buried her middle finger in her crotch.

"I want to see," Juan growled, so she obligingly spread her legs. He watched for a few moments, then said, "Got a scissors? I want to see more."

What does he want? she wondered. He'd paid for the evening and she wasn't worried about her safety. She thought for a moment, then remembered that there was a pair of scissors in the top dresser drawer. He quickly got them, bent over the bed, and with a quick snip, cut the crotch from her teddy. The outfit had cost a small fortune but Jenna considered it a learning experience. The split crotch hadn't let him see enough. "Next time shave your pussy, too," Juan said.

Shave? She'd clipped the hair short but she should have thought of actually shaving. She loved the phrase "next time."

It was the best indication that he was enjoying the show. "Of course." She'd had false nails put on and she knew that her bright red polish stood out in her deep brown pubic hair. "Which dildo should I use?" she asked, motioning to the collection on the table.

Juan picked up the largest one and handed it to her. It was probably eight inches long and several inches around. "Ooo, you picked my favorite one," she purred. Then she held it to her lips and sensuously licked the head. "I want it to be really slippery." She sucked on the tip, then snaked her tongue up and down the shaft. She rubbed it over her oily breasts, then down to her pussy. She pressed the tip against her opening, then, inch by inch, pushed it into her cunt. "It's soooo big, I just love the way it fills me up." Amazingly enough, "in the midst" of all the phony words and actions she found she was getting genuinely turned on. She watched Juan's eyes, moving as her hands moved. For long minutes she continued to stroke herself, seeing her pleasure reflected in Juan's eyes.

Finally she reached over and picked up a vibrator, turned it on and stroked her clit with it. "I'm afraid I'm going to make myself come," she said. "Would that be okay?"

"I want to see you fuck yourself until you come," he said, "then I'm going to fuck those luscious tits of yours."

Fuck my tits? Okay, she thought. *Whatever he wants. After all, he's paying for it.* She rubbed all the right places until she felt her orgasm build. "Hold this," she said, gesturing to the dildo, disappearing and reappearing between her inner lips. Eagerly, Juan grabbed the dildo and rammed it in and out, while Jenna played with her clit. "Oh God," she hissed as her orgasm overtook her. He pulled the dildo out and watched her juices drip from the large phallus.

With almost lightning speed, he pulled off his clothes and straddled Jenna's chest, his large erection resting in the valley between her breasts. "Hold them," he roared, pressing her hands against the sides of her globes so that they surrounded his cock. Still slippery from the oil, the cleft was smooth and slick so his engorged cock slid through easily. She raised her head and flicked her tongue over his cockhead as it emerged at the depth of his stroke.

As she watched, he shuddered, screamed, semen splattering her chin and chest. Panting, Juan climbed off the bed and collapsed on a side chair. For several minutes the only sound in the room was their hoarse breathing. When they had finally calmed, Juan dressed. He opened his wallet and pulled out a handful of bills. "For the black thing I cut up," he said, "and for the best show I've ever seen." He opened the door and, as he was leaving, he added, "I'll be back."

As the door closed behind him, Jenna chuckled. She'd done this sort of thing twice and she still hadn't been fucked. Amazing.

Jenna had to admit that she was a prostitute. She'd rented her body, although to date not her vagina, to eager men. She'd done it. For the next several nights it was Chloe who entertained in the motel room, and they both watched the bank account they'd set up for Club Fantasy begin to grow.

Erika was a godsend. She met with Jenna twice more at the Courtesans, Inc., office and showed her the basics of the computer system. "Why are you shutting the business down?" Jenna asked one afternoon. "Isn't there someone to pass it off too?"

"My long-time business partner and best friend, a wonderful woman named Barbara, just got married to a doctor she met when I was in the hospital a few years ago. She's 'gone straight' and is happy as a clam, however happy that is."

"That's wonderful." Happily ever after. Two women who'd been the classiest of high-priced hookers had moved on to happily-ever-after lives. Three if you counted the woman named Valerie whom Jenna had never met.

"Are you having second thoughts?" Erika asked, when Jenna was silent for a long time.

"No, of course not." She fiddled with the computer keyboard. "Maybe just a little. To take money occasionally is one thing, but to run Club Fantasy as a business is another."

"This business isn't for everyone. It isn't for most people. You need a strong self-image that won't be tarnished by what some folks think and a good head for business. Do you think you're ready for me to give people your phone number when I don't have anything to satisfy their needs?"

One last slight hesitation, then she said, "I'm as ready as I'll ever be."

"Good, because if I send someone to you, I have to know you won't let him down. It's my reputation too." She squeezed Jenna's hand. "I, for one, think you'll be great. Do you have a special phone for your business?"

"We're going to get a separate cell phone for the Club this week," she said. "It'll be pretty much untraceable. I'll give you the number as soon as I get it."

"How about an easy introduction?" Erika said, a slow smile spreading over her lightly glossed lips. "I have a client, he's such a wonderful man. He wants something a little out of my line. Shall I have him call you?"

Without hesitation, Jenna said, "Do it."

Now sitting in the backyard, she was a bit nervous. She wondered what "out of my line" meant. Well, she could always turn someone down if his desires were too bizarre. When the cell phone rang she anxiously picked it up.

A soft voice with a slight British accent said, "Is this Club Fantasy?"

"Yes," she said. "Can I help you?"

"My name is Howard Klein and Erika Holland suggested I could call." Holland, Erika's business persona.

"I'm Hillary Oakes. What can I do for you?"

"I want a fantasy and Erika said you do that sort of thing." He cleared his throat. "This is a bit embarrassing for me."

"I can certainly understand. Why don't we meet some-where for coffee? We can talk better in person I think."

There was a long pause. "I guess if you are going to trust me, I have to trust you. How about meeting at Anna's Diner?" He gave Jenna the address. "This afternoon at two?"

"Great. I'll see you there."

Jenna was already sitting at a small table by a window that looked out on to a damp, cold, October afternoon, when a man of about fifty walked in furling his umbrella. He was about five feet six, almost painfully thin, with curling, nut-brown hair and a dimple in his chin. She waved and he made his way through the maze of mostly empty tables. "Ms. Oakes?" His voice was slightly high pitched, yet breathy.

Jenna smiled at the use of her cover name. "Yes. It's nice to meet you, Mr. Klein," she said as he slid into the chair oppo-site her. Through the windows they could see Eighty-third Street and a few pedestrians hustling toward their destina-tions, pushing groaning umbrellas in front of them. "Terrible day," Jenna said, trying to appear as if she met men to discuss sex every day.

"I know," he said. "It seems we're going to have autumn, whether we like it or not." He signaled the waitress. "I need some coffee," he said. "You?"

"Make it two," Jenna said. She pushed the sleeves of her royal blue sweater up to her elbows and clasped her hands on the table. "What can we do for you, Mr. Klein?"

"Call me Howard," he said, clearing his throat. "This is a bit awkward."

Jenna called upon every bit of her charm. "I can understand that, Howard. It's a highly embarrassing topic, but I need to know what you have in mind." She tried to sound experi-enced, knowing and trustworthy.

"You see my wife's been ill for almost a year. I'm a very, oh, let's just say, active man. I'm also very private and I can't satisfy my needs easily, that's why I frequented Courtesans, Inc. If word ever got out . . ."

"No need for you to worry. Like Courtesans, Inc., everything we do at Club Fantasy will be strictly confidential. Exactly what did you have in mind?"

"Ms. Oakes, I'm a small man, with lot of money and a business that practically runs itself, both left to me by my father. I want—" He slammed his mouth shut as the waitress approached, placed a mug of coffee in front of each of them, then disappeared into the back of the restaurant. The two were silent as they poured milk and sugar into their cups. "Ms. Oakes, I want to become a powerful man, if only in my fantasies. I want to rescue the lady in distress and have her generously bestow her favors on me. I know that sounds corny and my language comes right out of a cheap novel, but that's what I've dreamed of for as long as I can remember."

"It's not corny at all," Jenna said, exuding confidence, although she had no idea what he was getting at.

"You're so like Erika. She didn't make me feel stupid when we talked about this, and you're being so understanding."

"Thanks for the compliment." Comparing her to Erika made Jenna feel wonderful. "Exactly what kind of situation are you thinking of?"

After a silence, he said, "This will sound silly but I want to be a John Wayne type, who just won a gun fight and now gets the girl. Can you imagine something like that? Can you provide something like that?"

She gazed deeply into his eyes, her brain running a mile a minute. It certainly could be done. Maybe this was why Erika had suggested a Western room. "We can make that happen for you, but would you mind very much if I were the girl? I'd really like that. Would I ruin the illusion?"

He stared at her as if unable to believe what he was hearing. "You can do it?"

"We can."

"I would like for you to be part of it very much. Can you really do the rest? The Western part?"

"It can be arranged."

She watch the tension flow from his body. "That's wonderful. You've made this easier than I thought it would be. It's so difficult talking about something like this. When I say it, it sounds so juvenile."

"It isn't at all." She tried to sound as if she heard this kind of request every day and maybe one day she might. She trusted Erika's assessment of the man, so she wrote the address of the brownstone on a slip of paper and handed it to him. He took it with an amazement that spoke to his delight. "What evening next week would work for you?" Jenna asked.

"Can we do it on Wednesday?"

"Of course. Be there at eight."

"What should I wear?"

"Do you have a Western-style shirt? Jeans and boots?"

"Yes, of course. And thank you. Thank you, so much."

When Chloe arrived home that evening, Jenna related the meeting to her. "I thought we might set up a sheriff's office in one of the upstairs rooms."

"Fabulous," Chloe said. "A Western room. Maybe there are others who would love to get the girl that way." Chloe grabbed the Yellow Pages. "Costumes shouldn't be a problem. We can go back to the place you got the doctor stuff."

"I thought we could get a tape of that old-time, tinny piano music that's in movies. Maybe it comes in from the dance hall next door. I'll bet they have something at that CD and tape warehouse store I've passed a few times over on the West Side."

Chloe was busy rapidly turning pages. "Here's another prop rental place just in case Manny's doesn't have what we want," she said, tapping her long nail on a large display ad, reeling off a list of items she thought they'd need.

"I guess that's why you're the artist and designer," Jenna said, intrigued by Chloe's imagination and tenacity.

"I don't think this was what my design teachers had in mind," she said with a twinkle, "but it sure works."

Jenna and Chloe planned to devote their entire Saturday to prowling through rental shops, second-hand stores, and music shops to set up their first complicated fantasy room. Once it was established, they'd subtly suggest it to men who wanted power fantasies.

They started at MG Props and Costumes. They quickly found an Old-West-style, rough-hewn wooden desk with several chairs, a fringed, leather vest, a Stetson, and a pair of very realistic guns with gun belt. In another place they located a sweet, old-fashioned, checked dress with tiny pearl buttons up the front in Jenna's size. She would wear it with a pair of patent-leather pumps and white, high socks. The music CD proved most difficult but they finally found one that would suffice in a small, esoteric music store on Eighth Avenue.

On Wednesday, Jenna stood in front of the mirror fastening her hair at the nape of her neck with an easily removable clip. Then she added the poke bonnet she'd found in a consignment shop the previous afternoon. She'd been so caught up in fulfilling Howard's fantasy that she actually found herself enjoying the quest for the perfect items.

Lightly made-up and perfumed as she imagined a lady of the Old West might be, she climbed to the third floor and entered "the Western room." If you didn't look too closely, it came off pretty well, if she did say so herself. Chloe had created several wanted posters on the computer and hung them on the walls next to a gun rack they'd found at a prop rental place in Soho. Jenna had even cut up a pair of old white sheets and created curtains to cover the window, then hung a large mirror they'd found in the attic beside it. Chloe added several ashtrays, an old, crystal inkwell, and a few small nicknacks. Jenna had pawed through boxes in the storeroom and found an old-fashioned pendulum clock with roman numerals denoting the hours. It didn't keep time but she didn't think that would matter to Howard. As they'd looked around earlier, each had been impressed by the other's ingenuity.

"There's no bed," Chloe had said.

"There wouldn't be a bed in a sheriff's office," Jenna answered.

"Where will you do it?"

"On the desk or the floor if he wants. Otherwise, we can go into the motel room, which is sufficiently plain that it probably can become whatever is in his mind."

She sat on an uncomfortable wooden chair now, waiting for Howard. Then she heard footsteps on the stairs. Chloe should have already given him his hat, vest and guns, and explained that he was the sheriff who'd just returned from shooting it out with the man who'd killed Hillary's father. The door opened and Jenna stood. Howard walked in looking uncomfortable, like the middle-aged businessman he was, only now dressed in Western garb. Illusion was everything, she thought. She needed to create this one quickly. She affected a slight Western accent. "Oh, Sheriff, how can I thank you for what you did?"

Howard looked around and Jenna watched his eyes widen and his mouth fall open in a silent *Wow.* "It's nothing, little lady," he said, making a nervously poor attempt at a John Wayne drawl.

"You were so brave to face him like that, at high noon on the street in front of the saloon."

"It's my job."

"I know, but you're so brave." She untied her bonnet and put it on the desk. "So brave. He's such a fast draw that I was sure you'd be killed, but you were faster."

"It wasn't anything." Actually, it came out as *twerent nothin*, and she noted that he sounded a bit more confident in his role.

Slowly, Jenna unbuttoned the top button of her dress. "Oh,

but it was." She crossed the room and placed a kiss on the sheriff's cheek. "I can't thank you enough." She stepped back and unbuttoned several more tiny buttons.

"I don't know what to say," he mumbled, his hands shaking.

"You don't have to say anything," Jenna said, her hand finding the swollen ridge beneath the zipper of his jeans. "Let me show you how grateful I am." She unbuttoned the remaining buttons and let the upper half of the dress fall to her waist. Beneath she wore a plain white cotton bra which she removed and dropped. Then she snaked her arms around his neck and kissed him full on the mouth, undulating her body against his so her nipples rubbed against the rough fabric of his shirt.

His hands found her naked back and pulled her still closer. With her eyes closed and the sound of the dance-hall music, she could almost believe her own scenario. She took his hands and placed them on her breasts, cupping her flesh so she filled his palms. His eyes closed and he kneaded her, rocking his hips against hers. For long moments the only sound in the room was the music and the hoarse sound of Howard's heavy breathing.

Becoming accustomed to her own arousal, Jenna kissed his cupped hands, then dropped to her knees and released his already hardened cock from his pants. "Oh yes, you're so powerful," she said. It was obviously what he wanted to hear and she watched his cock stiffen and twitch.

She cradled him in her hands, fondling his testicles and stroking his shaft. "Mmm," she purred, caressing him with both her hands and her voice.

"Oh, Lord," he said, pushing her away. "Not yet."

"Of course not," she said, stepping back and smoothly removing her dress. As he watched, she pulled down her petticoat until she stood in only her white cotton pantaloons, socks and shoes. "I want to thank you," she said, "my way."

She guided his hands to the drawstring of her drawers and

he quickly opened the bow knots and she dropped them on the floor with the rest of her clothing. Now, clad in only knee-high, sheer, white socks and shoes, she stood proudly while he looked her over. "Now you," she crooned, and she quickly removed all of his clothing. Then she perched on the edge of the desk and showed his fingers where to touch until she was wet and ready. "Yes, like that. It's so good," she moaned. "I want you, and not just to show you how grateful I am."

"I want you too," he groaned.

She reached into a desk drawer and pulled out a small foil packet, unrolled a condom over his cock and pressed his buttocks until his erection slid easily into her. It was fast, but she sensed that he was more than ready.

She'd done it. She was actually having intercourse for money and she felt great—no regrets, just exhilaration. It was a fabulous feeling to be able to give such obvious pleasure. She wrapped her legs around his waist and hooked her ankles together. Then she pumped him in and out until he came with a soft expelling of breath.

He stood for several moments, then stepped back. She handed him a small towel from the drawer and he wiped himself clean, then dressed quickly. "That was perfect," he said, his back to her. "It was so real and I came so quickly. You make the most wonderful magic."

"I hope so," she said, still seated on the edge of the desk.

"I know so. Don't change this room. It will play a big part in my fantasies from now on and I'll be back often."

She smiled; relieved and excited, she spoke in her real voice. "I'm glad, Howard."

He placed his fingers over her lips. "Don't destroy it, little lady. I'm glad I could help with the desperado."

"I'm glad you could too—sheriff," she said, western drawl back in place.

Grinning, he left.

She'd done it. As she sat on the chair beside the desk in the sheriff's office, pulling on her underwear, she accepted that she'd enjoyed the whole thing. She thought about the look on Howard's face and couldn't suppress a smile. He'd been delighted and she'd done it. Three times she'd made men happy, given them tremendous sexual satisfaction. And gotten paid for it. Life was wonderful!

Jenna spoke to Marcy several times a week, swapping stories of work and friends, but she didn't tell her sister about the business. Every time she thought she'd worked up the courage to broach the subject, she chickened out at the last minute.

Jenna had talked to Toby on the phone several times in the past month. They'd been to a few movies but, much to her regret, they hadn't been able to find much time to be together. She hadn't told him about the business, either. Rather, she'd made one excuse after another for not being able to see him. Finally, one cold, rainy, Monday evening toward the end of October, she met Toby in a steak restaurant in Midtown.

Over medium-rare sirloins and an excellent cabernet, they caught up on each other's activities in the weeks they'd been apart. "I've been disappointed at how seldom we've been able to get together," Toby said as they finished large slabs of "death by chocolate" cake.

"Me, too. I've just been so busy."

"What in the world keeps you so occupied in the evenings? I've imagined that you have a bevy of boyfriends."

Jenna considered. She'd debated telling him about Club Fantasy, even inviting him to play with her in the Western or motel room, but decided against it. Now she wasn't so sure. She wasn't by nature a secretive person and here she was keeping a large part of her life from two of the three people she considered herself closest to: Marcy and Toby. The business had become such an important part of her life that not being able to share it, to have to watch every word, was becoming more and more difficult. She would never violate the confidences of her clients, but there were funny stories she'd like to share with someone besides Chloe and Erika.

She wanted to be able to tell stories about some of the strange folks they had dealt with. Like the man who had filled her pussy with oysters, then eaten them one by one. Or the man who'd played with her toes for over an hour. Or the man who'd covered her pussy with lipstick, then kissed her "luscious red lips" over and over.

She wouldn't have dreamed of telling some guy on a first date, of course, but she and Toby were more than just casual. She had high hopes of the relationship becoming something more. "It's not quite like that," she said, watching his eyes across the table.

"Not quite?" Toby said, his eyebrows rising to meet the hair that fell across his forehead. "What does that mean?"

How was she going to say it? "I've sort of gotten into a business that takes up a lot of my evenings."

"That's great. I hope it's helping your finances." She'd once mentioned her money worries to Toby.

"Oh, it certainly has."

Toby leaned forward on his elbows and said, "So tell me about it."

Still stalling for time, she opened a packet of sugar and dumped the contents in her coffee, then added cream. "Chloe and I are doing some entertaining?"

"You mean like parties?"

"Not quite. We're entertaining men." She stirred her coffee.

"Entertaining how?"

She could see the wheels turning in Toby's head. "The obvious way, I guess."

Toby leaned further forward and hissed, "You can't mean that the way I'm thinking."

"I guess I do."

"You've become a prostitute?"

"I don't think of it that way," she said, watching his body tighten and his elbows draw closer to his sides. "We're providing a much-needed service." It sounded suddenly hollow.

"A service. Right." He was now talking through gritted teeth. "You told me Chloe was a free spirit so I guess she suckered you into something. You should really pick your friends better."

Jenna was annoyed at his characterization of her best friend. "Chloe didn't sucker me into anything," she said, her face tightening. "We're doing this together and I'm enjoying it."

"Enjoying it?" he said, his voice now bitter. "You've got to be kidding."

"Toby," she said, reaching across the table and placing her hands over his clenched fists. "It's not as bad as you think. These are nice men who need—"

"A whore," he spat. "And you're it."

"I didn't have to tell you but I wanted to share with you what's become a large part of my life."

He pulled his hands away. With a rueful smile, he said, "I thought we had something going for us."

"We did—do."

She watched as he stood, his back rigid, and dropped several bills on the table. "No, we don't." He turned on his heel and stalked out of the restaurant.

Jenna watched his back disappear through the front door. Could she blame him? If she were being honest, she didn't. Not really. What if the situations had been reversed? How would she have felt if he'd told her he entertained women for money? Now she might understand, but three months ago? Before any of this had started? She probably would have walked out the same way Toby had.

Well, she thought, as she gathered up her purse and sweater, *that certainly means I'm not going to tell Marcy.* If that was how Toby reacted, she wouldn't risk telling her sister. She might hate subterfuge, but she'd hate this kind of reaction from her sister so very much more.

Deeply saddened, and resigned to her silence, she headed home.

Most of the evenings at Club Fantasy were pretty routine. The motel room was still the most popular location for acting out erotic dreams, but the Western room appealed to several men when it was suggested. They had a call for something unusual a few days later and they didn't have to create a new room for it.

Jeff Marcus had always dreamt about women and water. He'd bought X-rated films in which large-breasted women stood under waterfalls, in heavy rain, or played with hoses. His favorites, however, were movies in which women showered, lathering their bodies until they were slick with soap, and then sluicing water over their naked breasts, bellies and legs. He wasn't obsessed, but it was close. He thought about finding a way to peek into women's bathrooms but he wouldn't have dared. Then he heard about Club Fantasy from a business associate. "I was flabbergasted," his friend Mark had said. "They had a room all set up like a Western sheriff's office and this sweet Western woman thanked me in every way possible for killing the man who'd shot her father. And I do mean every way possible."

"That's sounds interesting," Jeff responded, trying not to sound too eager. "How did it all work?"

"First, over coffee with this really understanding woman, I talked about what I wanted, and she set it all up. She said they can do lots of different fantasies. It's pretty pricey but it's really worth it. You thinking of doing it?"

Jeff quickly jumped in. "Not a chance. It's an interesting concept, though. A fantasy brothel."

That was when it took root in his mind. His own fantasy. He

began to embellish it, only minimally concerned that he was building it up so much that it could never live up to his expectations. Who cared? The long-term creation was the pleasure, the acting out only the momentary interlude.

Once he'd decided on the details he used the phone number he'd gotten from his friend's address book and called. "My friend Mark Hoskins recommended you folks," he said to the friendly voice on the other end of the phone. "Could we meet and talk about things?" He had no doubts, no hesitation. He knew what he wanted and hoped that Club Fantasy could get it for him.

Jenna listened, clearly remembering Mark and their hours in the Western room. She'd initially checked Mark up in Erika's database and found him listed as a valued client with enough money to afford whatever he wanted. He was now in Jenna's PDA with a similar code.

Chloe met with Jeff at a small bar in the East Fifties and later related the conversation to Jenna.

"I want to watch a woman shower through a clear shower curtain. Actually, without a curtain would be even better," he'd said to Chloe, who'd introduced herself as Melissa Mallory, her business name. "She should be medium height with brown hair and big breasts."

"As you can imagine it's difficult to satisfy physical requirements, especially since you've created someone so specific. We can provide a woman who meets your general requirements, but she might not be exactly the woman you're dreaming of."

"Is she built? I want someone who's built."

"Jeff, you've obviously given this a lot of thought and I worry that we won't be able to create a fantasy that will live up to what you've already imagined."

"Of course," he snapped. "I understand all that. I want you to come as close as you can."

"We give you a money-back guarantee up to a point but you understand that we can't be responsible for making everything live up to your very high expectations."

He paused, then seemed to relax. "I guess I seem pretty sure of myself and in ways I am. I thought it would impress you that I knew exactly what I wanted. Frankly, I'm a little nervous about all this as well." His small smile made him much more likeable. "I know you have limitations and I know too that you'll do your best. You really do come highly recommended."

"With that understood," Chloe said, opening a personal digital assistant and tapping a few spots with the stylus, "how's next Thursday at seven."

"That would be fine."

"So it seems you've got a client Thursday evening," she said to Jenna. "It will certainly be the cleanest encounter you've had." The two women laughed.

At seven, Chloe ushered Jeff in and led him upstairs. She showed him into the upstairs bathroom and guided him to a canvas director's chair they'd set up beside the beige plastic, molded shower stall with its clear plastic shower curtain. She watched him settle in, kick off his shoes, and wait for the show to begin. She slipped out and closed the door behind her.

It was only a few moments until Jenna walked in, dressed in a tight, black, cropped shirt and skin-tight jeans. She watched him look her over and, from his expression, knew that he admired her flat stomach and lightly tanned skin. He grinned when his gaze settled on her bare feet. "Hi," she said. "I'm Hillary. I'm ready for a nice long shower."

"Right," he said, but it came out more like a grunt.

While he watched, Hillary began to remove her clothes. Since he had such a clear idea of what he wanted, she asked, "Shirt first?"

"Please."

Revealing her skin only an inch at a time, she sensuously raised her top. She had great tits, spilling out over the tops of her bra cups. The bra was a medley of bright red lace and black flowers, the flowers carefully arranged so that her nipples were hidden. He squirmed waiting for them to be revealed.

"Which would you like next?" Jenna asked. "Jeans or this," she said, stroking the sides of her bra.

He cleared his throat. "Jeans," he said, and she pulled them off. Color rose in his cheeks. "Panties," he said. As Jenna pulled the tiny wisp of lace and flowers down her long legs, she had an idea. She handed the panties to Jeff. "You can keep them." She loved the way he trembled as he cradled the silk in his hands.

Before removing the last of her clothing Jenna reached into the shower and turned on the water, carefully adjusting the temperature. Then she reached behind her and unclipped her bra, allowing her generous breasts to spill out. "I love to use one of those scrunchy bath things. Is that okay with you?"

"Fine," he managed to say, running the panties through his fingers.

Jenna pulled the curtain to one side and climbed inside. She poured bath gel onto a pure white bath latherer and started to soap her body. She thought that the white of the scrubby would contrast wonderfully with her tanned skin. She threw her head back and lathered her chest, swirling around her size-C tits and now erect nipples. Water poured down her body, running into all the sexy places as he watched.

"Wash your cunt," he said.

"Of course," Jenna said, and slid the scrunchy between her thighs.

"More." She washed again and again. "Use your hands on your tits and your cunt."

Suddenly he leaped to his feet. He ripped of his clothes, pulled back the curtain, climbed into the shower, and knelt between Jenna's thighs. Her bush was just at the height of his mouth and he dove in, licking and sucking, water pouring over both of them. Jenna leaned against the shower wall and braced Jeff's head with her hands as he licked.

Without stopping his tongue and lips he reached down, wrapped his hand around his cock and, with only one or two strokes, came. He continued to suck until he got hard again and then came a second time, sliding down the wall until he was sitting on the shower floor.

Jenna turned off the water, climbed out of the shower, handed him a thick white bath towel, and dropped several more in the puddles on the floor. With Jenna now wrapped in a large bath sheet, Jeff dried and dressed. In a sort of daze, he walked down the stairs and out of the building.

Suddenly, as if flood gates had opened, Club Fantasy had more clients than they could manage. Friends of previous customers were calling and Erika was suggesting their services to many of her customers. Several of her employees were using the rooms as well and giving part of their fees to Club Fantasy. Men were arriving and departing at all hours and, since Jenna had more time during the day, she was doing a lot of the leg work, finding props and costumes for the fantasies they were acting out. In addition to the motel room, a very popular spot for hooker fantasies, they also used that room for the "burglar and victim" and for several superhero playlets. The tax fund was now bulging and they decided that each woman would keep half, then quickly changed it to three quarters, of the money she received.

Chloe was popular with men who wanted to play with a tiny, cuddly woman. She played Southern belle and virginal bride. Jenna, on the other hand, played the sophisticated neighbor's wife, the strong business woman who conducted erotic "job interviews," and the society matron picked up in a bar. Many of the encounters were filmed, for a hefty, extra fee.

By mid-November, Jenna and Chloe found they had little time for their own dates. They had decided that they would never be alone in the house with a client, just in case, so one of them let the man in and guided him to the appropriate room, then just stayed around or, on rare occasions, had their own client. It soon became both necessary and possible to carve time out for themselves, so they made a house rule that Mondays and Tuesdays were off-limits so that they had a few evenings for themselves.

Club Fantasy had become a thriving business.

Chapter
9

A few weeks before Thanksgiving, Erika called and asked to pay a visit to the brownstone. "I'm dying of curiosity to see your place and I've got someone I want you to meet. What time would be good for you two?"

At five the following afternoon the doorbell rang. Chloe had gotten out of work early and, when she opened the door, Erika walked in, clutching her heavy, black coat around herself to keep out the freezing drizzle that had begun several hours earlier. As Jenna leaned forward to buss Erika's cheek, a man filled the doorway. He was well over six feet tall, with a completely shaved head and heavy, angular features that would have looked ridiculous on a smaller man but made him, if not exactly handsome, arrestingly masculine. Although his skin was dark, his eyes were piercing blue, and his lips were full and sensual. A large diamond stud winked in his right ear. He was wearing a heavy, black trench coat and Jenna thought he'd look right at home in a James Bond movie. She wasn't sure which side he'd be working for.

"This is Martin Rockford—his friends call him Rock. He's someone I want you two to get to know and I'll explain why later." She turned to the huge man and said, "Rock, this is Jenna and Chloe."

"It's nice to meet you two," he said, his voice surprisingly soft, with a slight Southern accent, a strange contrast to his hard features. Jenna took his coat and, as he stuffed his gloves and knit hat in the pocket, she noticed that his hands were wide-palmed with long, blunt fingers. He looked like a professional wrestler, a look compounded by the form-fitting, long-sleeved, black sweater and black slacks he wore. Below his left sleeve he wore a watch that had more dials than the cockpit of a 747, and encircling the other wrist she saw the tattoo of a thick-linked chain. Jenna thought that should have made him look like a gang member or a high-level mafioso, but it all looked somehow proper on Rock.

"Nice to meet you too."

"Now show me around," Erika said, dropping her coat on a living-room chair. "I'm so envious of you, having a place like this for entertaining. Everything Courtesans, Inc., does is either in a small apartment I have on the West Side or in someone's hotel room. This is so fabulous."

For the next half-hour, the four wandered around the brownstone. Jenna and Chloe showed off the sheriff's office, the motel room which, she explained, with a few changes could become a bridal suite, a European hotel during World War II where spies hid, or the recently added British drawing room where the master of the house was entertained by the chambermaid.

They climbed to the top floor and entered a new addition, a desert retreat. Chloe and Jenna had covered the floor with heavy plastic sheeting and poured a hundred pounds of sand over it. They had draped the ceiling and walls with canvas and hung ropes here and there, all rigged up to look like a Bedouin's tent. They'd added satin fringe, attached a few poles to the walls with one central one, well braced and anchored to the floor. They'd covered everything with the sand, then topped it with a small carpet and added lots of pillows from the attic.

As she looked at the room, Jenna remembered her interview with the man who inspired the desert room.

* * *

Jenna had met with Leo Martin, a man recommended by Chloe's old boyfriend Frank. She assumed that at least the Martin part was a pseudonym since he'd stumbled over it when he'd introduced himself. Many of Club Fantasy's clients, she realized early on, gave phony names but good references. Leo was of medium height and build with a head full of short, tight-blond curls. *How many women*, Jenna wondered, *would give how much money to have hair like that?* He was in his early thirties, with soft hazel eyes and very white skin. He had a slight gap between his two front teeth that showed when he spoke about his desire to ravish a woman.

At first, Jenna had wondered whether being the one to talk to the customer at their first meeting and then being the central character in a fantasy would interfere with a man's ability to lose himself in the moment, but she quickly found out that it didn't matter to most customers.

When she asked Leo whether he minded if she played in his fantasy, he said he didn't mind at all. He actually looked flushed and delighted, as if having Jenna play with him was a stroke of luck. He did, however, mention at one point that he wanted his woman to have long blond hair but that was easily handled. She'd just have to find a good theatrical-wig store. If Dolly Parton could do all her on-stage gymnastics in the fantastic wigs she wore, Jenna could certainly manage.

Jenna and Leo talked for an hour as he explained his desires. He wanted to be a sheik from a desert clan who'd just captured a beautiful woman from a neighboring tribe. It quickly became obvious to Jenna that she'd be playing her first submissive fantasy. From all the reading she'd done she knew that many men fantasized about being in complete charge of lovemaking, so she wasn't surprised by Leo's request. She was confident that she could trust him and setting up for his fantasy should be fun. Every new dream gave her fresh outlets for creativity in the construction of the scene and increased depths of understanding of the way men's minds worked. She also learned more about herself with every encounter.

As she set up the sheik's tent, she included a wooden post, well anchored to the floor, for her to be tied to. She scattered lots of scarfs and silk cords around the room for binding if Leo wanted, but it sounded like he wanted his force of will to subdue her. Something new was being added to her repertoire of sexual activities and she was eager to see how she'd react to being controlled. Of course, Leo would never know whether she really enjoyed their scene or not, since Jenna would be sure he was completely satisfied.

She entered MG Props and Costumes the morning of the appointment. Manny greeted her like an old friend. "Jenna, it's so good to see you. You're becoming my best customer."

She extended her hand and found it enclosed in both of Manny's. Manny Grossman was the stereotypical small Jewish man with a hooked nose, and a full beard and moustache. "It's nice to see you again, Manny."

"What do you need today? And don't tell me it's for a surprise for your boyfriend. You can't be surprising him that often."

"Let's not talk about why. I need a harem outfit for me with lots of bangles and a sheik sort of thing for my husband." She maintained the illusion that she was partying in private.

Manny shook his head. "Come on, Jenna, this can't be for partying with your husband. You must be running some kind of theatrical business to be here so often, but you just keep most of my stuff for a few days. A repertory company?"

As good a cover story as any. "You guessed it," Jenna said, trying not to giggle. "It's a private sort of thing. Can I just go in the back and see what I can find?"

"Of course. You know your way around here almost as well as I do. Help yourself."

When she returned to the front of the warehouse with the

items she needed, Manny stroked his beard and said, "If you ever need a little Jewish guy for your company, let me know."

Jenna couldn't help laughing. "I'll certainly keep you in mind." She leaned across the counter and kissed him on the cheek. "I think you'd be perfect."

Just before Leo arrived, Jenna sat down on one of the pillows beneath the tent. She had dressed in Manny's gauzy, harem costume, a jeweled bolero top that ended just below her breasts and a pair of harem pants, held around her hips with a sequined girdle, that revealed more than it hid. She wore no jewelry and her feet were bare, her toes unpolished. The hair of her long, blond wig was straight and hung almost to her waist. She flipped it forward so it covered her breasts. When she finally heard footsteps, she slipped her arm into a circle of rope attached to the center pole, pulled it tight, lowered her head, and waited.

Chloe had showed Leo where to change into the costume Jenna had rented and, as he walked into the room, his desert robes swirled around his ankles. Jenna tightened her muscles so her body quivered and kept her head down. Playing a scene like this one brought out all her theatrical skills. As she did with every customer, she wanted to give Leo an experience as close to his dreams as she could, so she immersed herself in the scene. Maybe Manny wasn't far off. Club Fantasy was a repertory company of sorts.

"I see they dressed you and left you here for my pleasure," Leo said as he strode around the room. Although his step was sure, his voice was trembling.

Jenna raised her head defiantly and thrust out her chin. "I don't belong to you."

"You do now. You were trespassing on my kingdom," he said. "I am the ruler of everything you see, as far as you can see. Since you intruded on my land you are now mine to do with as I choose."

Jenna recognized the opening lines of a short script she'd written for Leo. He'd had a definite idea of what he wanted, but since he was unsure about how to begin she'd suggested that she write a few opening lines for him to use as a jumping-off point. She relaxed her body and lowered her head. "I'm sorry, sir," she said, "I didn't know. If you'll just have one of your men set me on the right road, I'll never bother you again."

"How do you happen to be out here alone?" he asked, his voice a bit steadier.

"I was foolish," she said, "and ran away from my caravan when my father threatened to beat me."

"Then no one knows where you are?"

"No, sir," she said, her voice soft and timid.

She sensed his smile and the strengthening of his tone. "Then you are mine. If you please me, I might let you live."

"Let me live?" She sounded shocked and indignant. "I have done nothing." She pulled at the rope that bound her wrist to the center pole of the "tent." "Let me go."

"Silence!" he snapped, adjusting his stance so that his feet were spread, his hands resting on his hips.

Jenna smiled inwardly. He had reached the end of the lines Jenna had written and now seemed more confident. She wondered what he'd choose to do with her now.

He unfastened her wrist, then said, "Stand up and let me look at you."

Slowly she got to her feet, her toes digging into the layer of sand on the floor and finding the carpet beneath. He used the crook of his index finger to raise her chin. "You're not too bad to look at," he said, turning her face first right, then left. "I might enjoy you."

Her voice quavered as she slipped more deeply into the part she was playing. "Enjoy me? What are you going to do?"

"You're a woman with a vivid imagination. I'm sure you can think of something to convince me not to just send you out into the desert to be food for the buzzards."

When she remained silent, he barked, "Bare your breasts. I want to see what I've captured." She deliberately didn't move so Leo snapped, "When I tell you to do something, do it immediately! This is the last time I will tell you to do something twice. Bare your breasts!"

With fumbling fingers she unhooked the top of her outfit and let it fall to the ground. Her shoulders remained hunched, her hair hiding her skin as she cowered before "her master." She had covered an old beanbag chair with a length of red satin fabric and Leo now settled into it, stretching his legs in front of him. "Stand up straight!"

Slowly she straightened her spine. It wasn't unusual that, as they got deeper and deeper into a scenario, Jenna would lose more and more of herself to it. She actually felt trapped by this powerful desert prince.

"Dance for me."

"Dance?" she said. "I don't know how."

"Do you want me to tell you twice?" He slapped her lightly on her thigh. "Say, no, sir."

"No, sir."

"Good. Then dance, and you'd better please me."

Awkwardly at first, then with increasing confidence, she undulated her body, closing her eyes and letting her long blond hair drape over her now bare breasts. She loved the tickling of the wig-hair over her swelling nipples. Hips swiveling, shoulders rising and falling, she danced for several minutes watching Leo's eyes as he watched her. Slowly a smile spread over his face. Feeling bold, she used her hands to lift her breasts and teasingly offer them to him, then she backed away.

"Ah. You've decided to play with me, my lovely one," he said. When she kept her silence, he continued, "Take off the rest."

As gracefully as she could, she removed the girdle and harem pants until she was naked. He gasped. To enhance the illusion, she'd used a temporary bleach to lighten her pubic hair. "Fabulous. Come here."

Now naked, she walked hesitantly toward him as he sat, his body relaxed, his expression softening. With every movement of his, she assessed his enjoyment level, trying in every way to make the fantasy as rewarding as she could. She wondered how he wanted her to play this next part. Should she be submissive or should she fight him. She was confident that he'd let her know.

"It's good that you don't try to resist me," he said. "It would be of no use. Since you have no choice, nowhere to go, I will have you."

When he reached out to grab her wrist, she pulled away. Often, what a man told you *not* to do was exactly what he most desired. "Don't," she said. "I did what you asked."

"Now I want more and you are in no position to resist. You will do as you're told." He leaned forward and, with a quick catlike strike, grabbed her wrists and pulled her down on top of him. His hands were all over her as she struggled to get up from her awkward position. Fingers pulled at her nipples, a palm cupped one ass cheek; then he grabbed her legs and pulled them apart until she straddled his thighs, facing him. "Sit still and don't move," he snarled. "Don't move a muscle!"

She considered fighting, then decided that she would do as she'd been told. She sat quietly with her legs splayed across his lap as his hands fondled her body. He pushed one index finger into her mouth, then took the wet tip and rubbed it over one nipple. He squeezed her buttocks and kneaded her breasts. His hands were everywhere and she held completely still as he explored.

Finally his fingers combed through her pubic hair, finding her wetness. "Ah, you're aroused. That's good. You are still forbidden to move. Do you understand?"

"Yes," she whispered, her voice flat, appearing as if all the fight had gone out of her.

Her found her opening and thrust one finger into her. "Not a virgin. That's unfortunate."

"Please," she said, her voice almost whining, "Don't do that. I'm a good girl. I've only done it once or twice with the man who would be my husband. Please don't."

His leer warmed Jenna's heart. "As you see, I can do whatever I want and you can do nothing to stop me." He sawed his finger in and out of her sopping channel. "You're being a very bad girl. You're enjoying what I'm doing." He rubbed her clit with his thumb.

"No. I'm not."

"Your body tells me different. Wet and hot. I like that. You don't want to be aroused, but you are. By my hands."

"Please," she begged, but his fingers continued to tempt and excite her. Mentally she stepped back and realized that she was enjoying the play, and enjoying his mastery of her. So far there hadn't been any form of sex she hadn't found arousing.

"I love a woman who begs for me. Beg me to fuck you."

"No. Don't. My betrothed will never take me back if you do that."

He leered again. "You won't be going back to him, anyway. If you beg me to fuck you, I might go easy with you."

Jenna hesitated; then her shoulders slumped and her chin touched her chest in surrender. "Please," she whispered.

"Not nearly good enough. I want to hear you say it loudly. Say, please master, fuck me."

Still softly, she said, "Please, master, do it."

"Say fuck me and say it loudly."

At about half-voice, she said, "Please master, f-f-fuck me."

"Louder."

Finally she acquiesced, and said strongly, "Please, master, fuck me." His fingers were still playing with her pussy and she found she really did want him to fuck her.

He stood up so quickly that he dumped her onto the floor. Then he parted his robes to reveal his naked groin, his thick cock sticking straight out. "Make me wet first."

She scrambled to her knees and cradled his testicles in her hands. "Like this?" she asked, licking the tip of his erection.

"Be a good little cock sucker and do it."

Jenna had become an expert at knowing exactly what strokes and licks a man wanted. She used all her tricks to please him. She held his cock in her fist as she sucked the head into her mouth. She gently squeezed his balls with the other hand and listened to his harsh intake of breath. She tightened her fingers one at a time, moving up and then down his cock as she drew his cock head into her mouth, then released it.

Jenna tried to figure out where he wanted to come, in her mouth, in her hand, or in her body. Many men had told her that, since a condom was mandatory at Club Fantasy, they preferred oral sex or hand jobs. It wasn't long before Leo grabbed her long blond hair in his hand and held her mouth against him, as his hips bucked and he bellowed his climax.

"You ladies have created something amazing here," Rock said, bringing Jenna back from the desert sheikdom. "I'm really impressed with your ingenuity. I love the binding pole in the tent. Have you used it yet?" His eyes were sparkling.

"Once," Jenna said.

"But you haven't created a dungeon yet, I gather," Erika said.

"We've got a great basement for it, but we've been so busy that we haven't had time to do much of anything," Chloe said. "Within the next few weeks we'll get that done too."

"Then the real fun begins," Erika said, "and that's what I wanted to talk to you two about. Got time for some serious conversation?"

"Sure," Jenna said. "We haven't got anyone coming until after eight." There was a slight pause, and then everyone caught her accidental double-entendre and laughed.

The four settled in the living room, Rock filling an uphol-

stered chair, legs stretched in front of him, crossed at the ankles, arms folded. It took no time for Erika to get to the point
of her visit. "I wanted you to meet Rock for lots of reasons."

"Erika, let me give Jenna and Chloe a little background,"
Rock said. "Believe it or not, I was a scrawny kid, all elbows
and knees and shoulder blades. At fourteen, I was the shortest
in my class and, if you know anything about teenagers, I was
the butt of all the jokes. As you can imagine, I was miserable."

Jenna stared at the huge man with the body-builder physique
who filled the chair he sat in. "You obviously grew."

He chuckled and continued, "I grew. I worked at it. My father found a gym and a personal trainer who specialized in
skinny kids like me. He not only worked on my body, but on
my self-esteem. He made me assertive without being aggres-
sive. He taught me to defend myself without having to prove
anything to anyone. In addition to working with weights and
machines, I learned tae kwon do, which taught me to move
gracefully despite my increasing size. It took me thousands of
hours but I finally became a third-degree black belt. If you
ever want to see me break wood with my feet, let me know."
His lifted eyebrow and little boy grin softened his face until
he was almost handsome. "He also suggested that I call myself Rock instead of Marty and cultivate a persona to match. It
worked. The new name and the fact that I grew almost a foot
and a half during high school created a new me."

"That personal trainer sounds like quite a guy. I wish I
could find someone like that for my sister."

"Marcy's her twin," Chloe said.

"Two like you? How delicious. You two could fulfill many a
man's twin fantasy if you wanted to."

"Not Marcy. She's about as different from me as could be:
overweight, quiet, shy and not very attractive, at least from
the outside. Inside she's wonderful, but if you didn't know we
were twins you'd never guess."

"Too bad. Maybe we could get her to meet with my trainer. He's still working with insecure people like I was twenty years ago."

"Sadly, she lives upstate." It would be great, she thought, to give Marcy some of the same self-confidence Rock seemed to have. Jenna did some quick addition. It was impossible to tell Rock's age, but now she placed him in his midthirties.

"Actually, I'm thirty-eight," he said with a twinkle in his eye, which softened his face and gave him almost a pixieish look, despite his size. "As years passed, I cultivated this image. When I graduated from high school, I became a corrections officer and this look you see helped me out of some tight spots. I don't look like a guy to be messed with."

Erika picked up the story. "I met Rock through a friend about three years ago. He was looking for a way out of the policing business and I was told he was pretty good in bed. At the time I had several female clients who were looking for someone of Rock's type, big yet gentle. He's been working with me ever since."

Grinning, Rock continued, "Two years ago I quit the department and now I work with Erika exclusively. I've developed a specialty that might come in handy for you two."

"That's one of the reasons I wanted Rock to meet you," Erika said. When Jenna looked puzzled, Erika continued, "He's the guy to show you ladies how to run your dungeon. He's wonderful at power games and has played with dozens of my clients. They've been delighted."

"I love power," Rock said. "For me it's the strongest aphrodisiac there is. The feeling that a woman is completely submissive to me hardens my cock. If I have to use force, so much the better."

Jenna felt her pussy twitch with excitement listening to Rock talk. This dungeon business was going to be more fun than she'd imagined. She'd enjoyed her scene with Leo and now she'd be getting tips from a professional. Maybe she'd even try her hand at the other side of dominant/submissive games. There was so much to play with.

"You're right," Chloe said, a coy, little-girl tone in her voice. "He's perfect. I don't know whether we'll have female clients, but he can teach me any time."

"Jenna?" Erika said.

"Sure. Sounds like someone we need."

"I'd love to help you design your basement to maximize the pleasures available, but there's more," Rock said.

"Jenna, Chloe," Erika said, leaning forward in her chair, "I've been giving this setup a lot of thought. I don't think you can continue to live here. It's rapidly getting too dangerous."

"Come on, Erika," Jenna said. "Aren't you getting a bit carried away? After all, Chloe and I have discussed it and taken precautions. We've got a state-of-the-art alarm system with a panic button in every room. We never work in the house alone and we've never had a problem."

"You may never have a problem and that would be terrific. However, once is too many times," Rock said. "That's where I come in. I want to move in here."

"Excuse me? Didn't Erika just say *we* couldn't live here?" Jenna said.

"It's not the same problem for me. Here's what Erika and I thought we could do. I have a nice little apartment in a very quiet neighborhood in Queens and I'd love to switch with one of you two."

Erika quickly said, "And I've got an unused apartment on the West Side for the other. It used to be used by my employees and their clients, but hasn't been needed for several months so I can declare it off-limits from now on. I'm suggesting that you two move, one into Rock's apartment and one into mine. Club Fantasy can pick up the rent for my apartment and Rock would continue to pay for his apartment but he'd be living here rent-free. That way you don't have to worry about anyone getting any funny ideas about this building and thinking he can take something without paying for it. Of course, this can all be temporary until you find your own places if you want it that way."

"Move out?" Chloe said, leaping to her feet. "Not a chance. That's why I started all this in the first place. This is Aunt Elise's house and she wanted me to have it, to keep it, to live here."

"Relax, Chloe," Jenna said, and Chloe sat back on the sofa. "We won't do anything we all don't agree to."

"You think this is a good idea, Jenna?"

Jenna sighed, as unhappy about the prospect of moving out of the brownstone as Chloe was. She did, however, see the wisdom of it. "I think it's worth some thought. Consider this: from all you've told me about your Aunt Elise she was quite the free spirit. How do you think she'd really feel about what we're doing?"

Chloe's face softened and her shoulders rose and fell. She huffed out a breath. Ruefully, she said, "Actually, I think she'd be delighted, especially about my role in it. She always told me to loosen up." Her pixie grin reappeared. "This is about as loose as it gets, but if I move out I feel like I'm deserting her memory."

"I think Erika and Rock are right about us living here. I've been feeling increasingly uneasy. We really have two choices. We can move out, and what they suggest would work out perfectly, or we can call all this off, cancel the phone and go out of business."

"It's a big decision," Erika echoed, "and I understand your feelings about your aunt, Chloe. You certainly don't have to decide today, but you've got to do something pretty soon. You can't continue to have men here for the kind of sex you ladies sell, then close the doors and pretend it's just a residence."

"I know." Chloe paused. "I'm having so much fun and the money's not to sneeze at, either."

"So you think you might take Erika and Rock up on their offer?" Jenna asked.

"I need a day or two to convince myself. What about you, Jen?"

"I'm still not sure how long I'm going to be here," Jenna said. "I could decide to go back to Seneca Falls at some point."

Chloe winked. "But not quite yet?"

"But not quite yet. I guess, like you, I'm having too much fun. I'm for taking Erika and Rock up on their idea."

"So you'll give it serious thought, Chloe?" Rock asked.

"I don't know. What about you?" Chloe said to Rock. "You'd be living here. Wouldn't that be just as dangerous as us being here?"

"Come on, be real. Look at me. What kind of lunatic would mess with this?" He spread his arms, displaying his massive chest and arms beneath his tight sweater. "One more thing that this arrangement does. I'd also to be here most of the time when you ladies are entertaining, just to be on the safe side."

"What's in it for you?" Chloe asked. "You'd be living in a bordello. No privacy. No room for dates. Nothing."

"I don't date much and when I do I'll do whatever I need to do. What's in it for me? I want to be able to use your rooms, especially the basement, to entertain my clients when it's convenient for all of us."

"How many clients do you have?"

"Dozens, of both sexes."

Erika chimed in, "There's lots of money in bondage and domination."

"I guess there must be," Jenna said. "There's even a place in Las Vegas that does it right out in the open." Chloe looked at Jenna. "I saw it on *CSI*."

"If either of you want to play, I can certainly show you lots of tricks." Rock looked from Jenna to Chloe. "With your size, you'd be dynamite, Chloe. And Jenna, with the right outfit, men will grovel at your feet and love it. But don't overlook women. I have many—let's call them lady-friends—who love to spend long hours tied, gagged, and forced to do unspeakable things, which, of course, we speak of at great length. A few have asked for a mistress."

"I'm certainly ready to learn, but it's a little out of my league," Jenna said.

"I gather. Try this." His voice became soft, low, and almost hypnotic. "Picture yourself with your hands tied and fastened to a hook above your head. Your ankles are fastened to a spreader bar so your legs are wide apart. I can touch anywhere, kiss anywhere, slap anywhere, and you're helpless to prevent it. Does that wet your pussy?"

Jenna nodded slightly. The crotch of her panties was soaked. She knew why he was such a success with his women friends.

Erika said, "If it does, you're not alone by a lot. Lots of women agree with you. And Chloe, picture yourself with a whip in your hand, some man crawling toward your high-heeled shoes, ready, willing, even anxious to lick your boots, or your cunt, or wherever you want him to put his mouth for as long as you want."

Chloe's "Yeah" sounded like a long sigh.

"What do you think of the whole idea?" Erika asked. "We can solve lots of problems at the same time. You gals get safety, Rock gets a nice place to live and play, and you all get a dungeon to be filled every night at a hefty fee."

Jenna considered, listing problems and their easy solutions. Their mail could still come to the brownstone, and since she and Marcy kept in touch by cell phone her sister wouldn't have to know she'd moved. For now, she couldn't see herself discussing any of this with her sister. She was planning to go back to Seneca Falls for Thanksgiving. Maybe she'd tell her then. No! She vividly recalled Toby's reaction. She couldn't tell Marcy anything, but, with a bit of care, she wouldn't have to. "I think Chloe and I need to talk, but it sounds like a good deal to me," she said finally.

"I guess I do too," Chloe said, turning to Jenna. "You, Rock, and Erika need to work out the numbers, of course, but the dungeon sounds like fun." Jenna almost laughed out loud. Chloe, professionally helpless when she didn't want to do something, was now interested in becoming a dominatrix. Oh, well, that was Chloe.

"I think we've got a deal," Jenna said. She found a bottle of champagne in the refrigerator and they all toasted the new arrangement. Then everyone hustled out since Club Fantasy was booked for the evening: Chloe in the Western room, Jenna in the desert room, and one of Erika's employees in the motel room, now set up to be a newlywed's bedroom.

As she walked up the stairs to get ready for her "date," she thought about the way the business had grown. The numbers were staggering. The previous week, they had taken in almost nine thousand dollars from Chloe's customers and hers, in addition to several visits by Erika's people. They could easily cover the rent for Erika's apartment and that way Jenna would be living rent-free. The cost of redoing the basement would be small in comparison to the amount they'd charge. The numbers kept getting larger and larger.

Jenna had just about stopped accepting any translation assignments and Chloe had cut her time at the advertising agency to three days a week. Actually, there was no need for either of them to work at all, but Chloe felt more comfortable with that stability.

Rock moved in two days later. He welcomed guests like the concierge in the finest hotel, while providing an imposing presence that no one could ignore. A sort of combination of maitre d' and bouncer. It quickly made both women feel much more secure. Chloe was delighted with Rock's apartment in Queens.

It was just a quick subway ride from Midtown, but Chloe seldom used public transportation. She was rapidly becoming a taxi-only woman.

Jenna loved Erika's small apartment, one Erika said she'd lived in when she first moved to New York City from Long Island. It took Jenna two buses to get there, but it was worth the slight inconvenience. It was comfortable and secure. The furniture had been changed several times and, when she'd stopped using it for business, Erika had bought a new bed. Jenna was glad not to be sleeping where so many others had frolicked.

Rock took over Chloe's room and, with the addition of new bedding and some of Rock's personal things, the room became his.

Rock was scheduled to entertain his first client the Tuesday before Thanksgiving. Since Chloe and Jenna had declared Monday and Tuesday their off days, Rock could use the empty rooms without the need to be available for security. He and Jenna sat over coffee Monday afternoon. "I know you've wanted to learn about what I do. I thought, since you've got that motel room set up with cameras, I could film our session and you and I could watch later together. Would you like to do that?"

"We have a policy here about never taping an encounter without the complete consent of everyone involved."

"A sensible idea and I will certainly abide by it. What about watching from another room through your TV-and-VCR system?"

"I'm sorry," Jenna said, although she was dying of curiosity to see Rock in action. "Not without the client's permission."

"Good girl. I like the way you handle things here. Let me see what Eleanor has to say. I don't think she'd object."

"Rock talked to me about taping our evening together," the woman said to Jenna when she arrived at eight the following Tuesday. Eleanor was an ordinary-looking woman in her mid-forties, with a slight potbelly and a double chin. "I like your rules about cameras and I trust you since I trust Rock. If I didn't, I couldn't play with him. I don't object to being taped. Rock will make sure that my face isn't visible. Anyway, I rather like the idea of being the subject of a lesson in this stuff. My only demand is that after you watch the tape, you destroy it."

Jenna was excited that they had been able to come to an agreement. After the discussion the previous evening, she had set up the camera so it had a wide view of the bed in the motel room just in case Eleanor agreed. She had also shown Rock how to use all the equipment. Now Rock whispered something in Eleanor's ear and she stepped aside so Rock could climb the stairs. Carrying a small tote bag, she followed meekly behind.

Chapter

10

Two hours later, Jenna sat curled up on the corner of the sofa and Rock, in what Jenna viewed as his typical position, filled a side chair, legs stretched out in front of him, ankles crossed, his arms folded. Although Jenna knew he was harmless, dressed in his usual unrelieved black, Rock exuded an air of arrogant menace. No, maybe danger was more like it.

"I'm sorry that Chloe couldn't be here," he said. Since it was an off day, Chloe had a date with a new man she was very excited about. With Eleanor gone, Jenna and Rock were alone in the building. If she were honest with herself, Jenna had to admit that she found that fact deliciously threatening.

Rock pressed the play button on the remote and the video showed Eleanor, fully dressed, being led into the motel room, a hood over her head. "For Eleanor, a blindfold is a deeply sensual experience," Rock said to Jenna, his voice low and a bit gravelly. "The hood makes her completely dependent on me." He pressed the pause button. "I know very little about Eleanor, except that she's been widowed for about three years and her late husband left her very well provided for. They had a dominant/submissive relationship throughout their ten-year marriage and she found she needed to continue that for the sexual release it provided. She found me through Erika and, as they say, the rest is history."

Jenna turned to Rock. "What exactly do you mean by the release? You mean orgasm?"

"Not totally. It's sexual of course, but it's more than that. When she's totally under my control she doesn't have to think about anything, make any decisions. She does only what she's told and speaks only to answer questions."

"I played with a guy in the desert room a few weeks ago and he spent quite a bit of time giving me instructions on exactly what he wanted." She recalled how freeing it felt not to have to worry about what to do. "I can understand how Eleanor feels."

"You enjoyed it?"

Jenna thought about it seriously as she hadn't done previously. After a long pause, she admitted, "Actually, I did."

"Did you two have a safe word?"

"What's that?"

"A way for you to say I don't want to do that."

"We didn't talk about that. If he did something I didn't want, I would just say stop, I guess."

"What if part of the scenario involved you screaming 'No! No!' How would he know when it was real?"

"I never thought of that."

"If you ever play like that again, you need to do more than think about it. Eleanor and I have agreed on *Desist*. If she says that word I stop whatever I'm doing."

Jenna considered. "That means she really has the control."

Rock grinned and said, "You understand what most people don't. Eleanor doesn't really, probably because she doesn't want to. It would ruin some of the fun for her, I think, if she knew that the ultimate power was hers."

"Safe word. Interesting. I'll have to remember that."

"It's something you need to agree on with anyone who plays in the dungeon. If I gag someone I give them a small object to hold. If they drop it, it means stop, just like the safe word."

A picture flashed through Jenna's mind of herself tied to the pole in the desert room or in the as-yet-to-be-completed dungeon, blindfolded and gagged, with Rock's hands all over her. She felt herself moisten and quickly returned her attention to the TV. The video came back to life. Silently, Rock lay Eleanor out on the bed, then tied her wrists to the headboard. "I'll bet you never considered how perfect that motel room is," Rock said to Jenna. "The head and foot boards work really well for what I'm doing now."

As Jenna watched, Rock pulled Eleanor's legs apart and tied one to each post at the sides of the footboard. "You must tie someone with just the right degree of discomfort," Rock continued as the video rolled on. "If she's too comfortable it ruins the illusion and too uncomfortable ruins the mood."

Eleanor's hips were squirming as she pulled at the restraints. What was Rock going to do with her clothing, her lightweight denim pants and a yellow, button-down, men's shirt? *Always the problem solver,* Jenna said to herself, laughing inwardly. Rock would obviously deal with it.

In the film, Rock opened a dresser drawer and pulled out a pair of scissors. He pressed the cold metal against Eleanor's cheek and she made a tiny squeak. "Notice, Jenna," Rock said, "I say very little. The silence makes her anxious, wondering what will happen next. In addition, being deprived of sight and sound allows her to concentrate all her senses on her skin and erogenous areas."

As Jenna watched, Rock made cutting motions with the scissors near Eleanor's ear. With each snip, Eleanor jumped. Then he moved to the foot of the bed and slowly cut up the front of one leg of her jeans until he reached her belt. He did the same with the other side, then cut across, between the two legs and, while the jeans remained belted around her waist, the lower parts fell open. He then made a few more cuts and fileted her panties the same way. "If you're wondering, Jenna, she brought a change of clothes as she always does. She never knows what I might decide to do."

Jenna expected him to cut away her shirt next, but he didn't. "I think Eleanor likes this next part best," Rock said, as he combed his fingers through her pubic hair in the video. "Sometimes it's only a slight trim, but this time we hadn't been together for several weeks so it took quite a while." Then, scissors snipping loudly, he began to work carefully. "First, I clip the long hairs, then I make it neat and close to her skin." Although she couldn't see much since the camera was aimed at Rock's back while he trimmed Eleanor's bush, she could hear the scissors and almost feel his fingers on her own crotch.

"Ever trimmed your hair, Jenna?"

"I try to keep it neat, but from the sound of it you're doing more."

"Maybe you'll let me play barber for you sometime."

Jenna remained silent as she wondered how close she and Rock were going to get this evening. How close did she want them to get? He was certainly an intriguing man.

They watched the film for several more minutes while Rock ministered to Eleanor's pussy hair. Finally, when he had it clipped to his satisfaction, he sat back to admire his handiwork. "You should really keep this beauty visible," he said to Eleanor. "You know how good it is to feel so exposed, even under your panties." Jenna noticed that when he purred like he was doing, his Southern accent got thicker. Was it an act or did he get so far into his pleasuring that he became more genuinely himself?

"I know," Eleanor said, her voice slightly muffled by the hood, "but I do so like it when you take care of me."

Rock chuckled. "So you do." He ran his finger through her now exposed slit. "You're sopping wet. Do you want to touch yourself?" he asked.

"Oh yes, but I know you won't let me."

His voice was like warm honey, sweet but firm as well. "Of course not. You know that eventually I will be watching you on film."

"Yes. I hope it will excite you even though I'm not there."

"It will."

"It does," Rock said to Jenna, then returned his concentration to the film.

"I want a close-up shot of your neatly clipped, little pussy," Rock said to Eleanor. "I'm going to play photographer." He picked up the camera from the dresser and walked toward the bed. "I'm going in for a close-up of your cunt. Closer and closer," he crooned as he moved to the bureau and picked up a high-intensity light that had been aimed at the bed. "I want more light so now you'll be able to feel the heat of the lamp on your flesh."

As Jenna watched, Rock shined the lamp on Eleanor's almost naked skin. She watched the tissues swell and moisten and found her pussy doing the same thing. "I can tell," Rock said to Eleanor, "that you're enjoying this. The camera will show just how hot this makes you." He kept the camera aimed at Eleanor's groin for several more moments, then replaced the equipment on the dresser. "Now for your top."

For several minutes there was only the sound of the snipping scissors, and Jenna moved on the sofa to take some of the pressure of her jeans off her groin. "Getting hot yourself, Jenna?" Rock asked. "Why don't you admit how hungry this makes you? I'd love to satisfy that hunger and you know that I know just how to do it."

What could she say? Yes, she wanted it. Jenna had watched lots of X-rated films to prepare herself for her customers, but this was an entirely different experience. The film was real. Real people and real hot sex. Real excitement, not the phony stuff she'd seen on the professionally made videos. And, of course, the man in the film was sitting beside her, offering to pleasure her.

She remained silent as she focused on the TV screen. Rock now had Eleanor's clothing completely off but she was still tied, spread eagled on the bed. From a dresser drawer he took a piece of fur and began to slowly stroke her with it. He began with her arms and lower legs, then moved on to her breasts, the insides of her thighs, stroking one spot then quickly moving to another.

"It's particularly sensual for her," Rock whispered to Jenna, "since she can't see where I'm going to touch next."

He repeated the stroking with a piece of nubby fabric, then held both and alternated as she undulated beneath his hands. He took an ice cube from an ice bucket on the bedside table and slowly stroked her heated flesh with it, her arms, legs, the palms of her hands, and soles of her feet, eventually lightly touching her overheated cunt. As the camera watched, he rubbed the shrinking cube through every fold. "You know what I'm going to do now, don't you Eleanor?"

"Yes," she whispered.

He pushed the ice cube into her pussy and again focused the camera on her. Jenna watched the melted water trickle from her, obviously teasing her hot flesh. "How long are you going to tease her?" Jenna asked, now almost unable to breathe.

"As long as it's pleasure, and not one second past the moment that it becomes discomfort."

"How do you know when that moment comes?"

"I know," he said softly, a slight chuckle in his voice. "I always know."

"I'll bet you do."

Rock put the camera back on the dresser and took a large dildo from the drawer. "You know what's next," he said to Eleanor, "and that you can't stop it or make it go any faster."

"I know. And I know that begging does no good, but please. I need it so much."

"I know you do," Rock said, holding the dildo against her

opening but not pushing it into her. Jenna could see Eleanor's hips reaching for the thick plastic phallus and watched Rock's amusement at her struggles. "You really want this, don't you?"

As Eleanor said, "God, yes," Rock rammed the dildo into her. Jenna watched the flesh colored staff disappear into her body, then reappear as Rock pulled it out. In and out, over and over, until Eleanor was writhing with pleasure and need.

"She's ready right now," Rock whispered into Jenna's ear. When had he moved to sit on the floor beside the sofa on which she was sitting? "You are too, aren't you?"

Why deny it? She turned and gazed at his chiseled profile as he watched the video, diamond stud winking in his ear. Handsome? Not really. Sexy? You bet. And she wanted him. "Yes."

"Good," Rock said. "We'll play when this is done."

While Jenna watched, Rock used his finger to stroke Eleanor's clit, bringing her to a screaming climax. She should stop this thing right now, she thought. He's playing with me and he knows it. He's teasing and tempting me to do things. *Why am I so reluctant?* she wondered. *I'm supposed to be a professional at this yet I'm playing the ingénue. Why not just let nature take its course? Consider it a learning experience.*

On the screen, Rock kept thrusting and rubbing until Eleanor had come several times; she finally moved a limp hand and, panting, said, "Desist." With Eleanor lying semiconscious on the bed, Jenna watched Rock get up and turn off the camera, still completely dressed. In the living room, Rock stopped the VCR.

Jenna marveled at the way he wove an erotic web over himself in the same way that he put on his black clothing to enhance his macho image. Somehow both seemed to become part of him. Were they real? She had no idea what the real Rock was like but that didn't change her feelings. She wanted him. It was lust, pure and simple. But was anything with Rock simple?

Pulse pounding in her ears, she tried to lighten the mood. "You didn't make love. You didn't come," she said, "or even fake something."

"It's not what Eleanor wanted. I would have fucked her if it had been what she desired but the ending was just what she craved, all for her. And we did make love. Everything we did was making love. It just wasn't fucking."

"You're right, of course."

"That scene really got to you, didn't it?" Rock said, his mouth only an inch from her ear, his breath warm, tickling and teasing.

"I'm being totally silly here and it's not like me. I want to deny it, tell you it didn't make me incredibly hungry, but it did." She turned and gazed into his deep, almost black eyes, barely able to function for the wanting.

"You're right. You're being silly. Let's play together."

"I've never done anything like what you did on the film."

"All the better. I'll teach you. I don't mean to brag or anything but I'm damned good at what I do. Ladies, and men too I might add, pay big bucks for me to do what I'm going to do with you for nothing. Well, not for nothing. I'm going to do it for fun, and, Jenna, it's been a long time since I've done this for fun and I'm looking forward to it tremendously." He stood and reached out to her. "Shall we go upstairs?"

She hesitated only a moment, then took his hand.

After making her trembling legs climb the stairs, Jenna stood in the middle of the motel room, the same room in which Eleanor had been given so much pleasure just a few hours before. By someone so accomplished. That was the word she'd been groping for. Accomplished, like a virtuoso whose natural talent had been honed by years of training and practice. She found she was both hungry and nervous, jumpy as a cat, eager yet reticent. She was beginning to empathize with the nervous men she'd been with. Yes, it was a learning experience. She'd be so much better at understanding her clients now.

Stop rationalizing! she told herself. *You're tremendously turned on and you crave what Rock's offering. He's obviously a very good lover and you want what he can give.* Deep in her mind she wondered what she could give him. Later, she thought, or maybe some other time she'd be the one to give to him, and it would be explosive because she, too, had become good at what she did. She was a bit daunted at the prospect of pleasing him. He was so much better at the game than she was, but she was learning.

"Have you ever watched yourself make love?" he asked, his voice thick with an elemental drawl.

"No," she whispered.

Without a word, he left, then returned a little while later carrying the standing mirror she'd seen in the storage room. Mahogany trimmed, it stood about five feet tall and could be tilted so the viewer could see his or her entire reflection. "I rummaged—I hope you don't mind—and put this in my room. I knew it would come in handy one day." He stood the mirror on the floor at one side of the bed and returned to stand before Jenna. "You're wearing too many clothes," he said, turning her to face the mirror across the expanse of the double bed.

Standing behind her, he reached around and slowly removed her shirt. Sliding his hands over her shoulders, he purred, "Lovely. Look at yourself, your skin so soft and white with my heavy, dark hands against it. Watch my hands, Jenna. Watch what they do to you."

He unhooked her bra and let it fall to the floor. "Look at your breasts. See how your nipples are already hard?" He rubbed the palms of his hands over her tight buds. "They tease my hands, making me itch to surround your flesh with my fingers." He curved his hands over her full breasts, just brushing her skin. "I'm teasing both of us," he whispered against her hair. When Jenna leaned her head against his shoulder and closed her eyes, surrendering to the sensations, he said, "Open your eyes. I want you to see everything."

She obeyed, then watched both his hands and the expression on his face. His look was one of almost rapture. He loved women, she realized with a start. He loved giving and experiencing. In that way they were kindred spirits. She loved men.

Finally, her breasts aching with the need for him to embrace them, he dug his fingertips into her and kneaded her fullness, her swollen nipples searing his palms. He filled his hands with her, weighing, scratching, stroking, and all the time she watched. She thought these were the most erotic moments she'd ever spent.

Finally his hands slipped down her belly to the waistband of her jeans, unsnapping and unzipping until the pants were at her feet and she stepped out of them. "Your body is wonderful," Rock said. "Lovely but not so perfect that I'm afraid to touch it. So responsive."

Through his slacks Jenna felt the hard ridge of his erection against the crack between her buttocks, so she pressed backward, rubbing him. As she did, his hand slipped beneath the top of her bikini panties to comb through her hair. "Can you see my hand disappear beneath the silk?" he asked. "See where my fingers are? Feel them entering your most vital place? Ummm," he purred against her cheek, the vibrations echoing in his chest and through her entire body. "You're so wet, so hot." He touched her clit. "So swollen. I love a woman who's so hungry."

He pulled off her panties, then sat her on the side of the bed facing the mirror. "Spread your legs wide," he said, and she did. "See your sweet pussy. See how open it is for me." He climbed between her knees, keeping low so she could see herself and his fingers as they explored her every fold, every crease, slipping through the juices that now soaked her cunt. "If I rub right here," he said, touching her clit, "I can give you climax right now, but I want to play. Can you wait?"

He was right. One touch in the right place and she'd explode. When she nodded, he pressed her clit gently and the throbbing abated slightly. When she'd calmed a bit, he inserted one finger into her. "Have you ever watched a man make love to your beautiful pussy before?"

"No," she whispered, barely able to make a sound. She wanted to lay down, but she propped her hands on the bed behind her and remained upright, unable to take her eyes off herself and Rock's hands.

"Don't look away," he said, before leaving her for a moment, only to return with a large dildo. "Watch yourself being fucked." He pressed the tip of the dildo against her opening. She watched it slowly disappear into her body, filling her. He left it there, quiet, motionless, as he turned to watch her in the mirror. She could see herself, his hand splayed on her belly, his eyes gazing at her pussy. They both watched him pull the dildo out slightly, then press it in as deep as it could go. Over and over he pulled and pushed.

It was as though she was on a plateau just below climax, able to revel in the ecstasy of near-orgasm. He seemed to know when she finally decided she could wait no longer and he pressed a small button on some kind of remote control and the dildo started to hum inside of her. He leaned over and, with a flick of his tongue over her clit, she came. Hard. Long. So long. The spasms felt as though they lasted for hours.

Panting, then slowly descending, she was eventually able to sort her thoughts. It had been amazing, a perfect demonstration of sexual control and talent. But he hadn't been really involved. He was teacher and she was student. "I want to do to you what you did to Eleanor," she said without thinking.

"If you like," he said calmly, still appearing relatively uninvolved. He undressed and stretched out on the bed, while she found the restraints he'd used and fastened his ankles and wrists to the bed. He was beautiful, his skin smooth and deeply tanned, his chest hairless. He obviously still worked out and took pride in his physique. He should. He was a pleasure to look at.

"It's your turn to watch," she said, adjusting the mirror so he could see his crotch, his cock now only semierect. *Damn him for being so in control,* she thought. He'd experience his own deep need if she had anything to do with it. From the bathroom she got a bottle of water-based massage oil and poured herself a palmful. She rubbed her hands together until it was warm. Then she started on his chest and upper arms. She knew that most men didn't particularly enjoy long massages the way women did, so she tuned in to his excitement to find the parts that aroused him. Then she moved swiftly over his body, avoiding his groin.

She discovered that he found his fingers erotic so she concentrated on them. As she massaged each as though it were a miniature cock, she watched his penis twitch. He might appear uninvolved, but his cock gave him away.

Watching his penis harden, she separated his fingers and pushed her thumb between them, in essence fucking his hand. Oh, yes, she realized, he was involved. "You want me to think you're neutral on all this. You want me to think you're the giver of pleasures but are immune to them yourself. I guess it makes it easier to do what you do when everyone thinks you're above it all. Well, you're not. Look at your cock."

She again fucked his fingers and they both watched his cock twitch and swell. "Not fair," he said, chuckling.

"Very fair." She refilled her palm and worked on his inner thighs, pressing deeply at the top, near, but not touching, his testicles. "Very fair." More oil and she cupped his sac, weighing the heavy globes within as he had weighed her breasts. His cock was erect now but she wanted so much more for him. As she played with his balls she watched the arrogant look leave his face and pleasure glaze his eyes. "I'm also good at what I do," she said. Her hands now found his long, thick shaft, both hands wrapping around it, squeezing, milking him. She listened to his rapid, raspy breathing and saw his fists clench and unclench as they hung impotently from the headboard.

"Watch my hands as they play with you," she said and saw his eyes open and stare at the mirror. "My white hands on your dark skin makes a beautiful contrast, doesn't it?" she said, an imitation of the words he'd spoken to her.

He merely smiled. She saw his glance flick to her breasts so she took more oil and rubbed it in her cleavage. Then she crouched over his cock and surrounded it with her hot flesh, sliding along his erection, pleasuring him between her breasts.

When his cock was as hard as she thought it could get, she quickly unrolled a condom over it and straddled his hips. "Have you ever watched your cock disappear into a woman's cunt before? You probably have, but not into mine."

Using her thigh muscles she slowly lowered herself onto the head of his shaft. When only an inch of his cock was inside her, she said, ""Maybe I'll just stay here, keep you right where you are."

He bucked and grabbed her waist, ramming himself into her. "You need a few lessons in knot tying," he said, banging into her hard and fast.

"And you need some lessons in staying uninvolved."

"Not with you doing what you do, witch," he said, laughing as he thrust over and over until he bellowed and emptied himself into her.

In their joy they laughed loudly for a long time, then settled against each other, sweat cooling on their bodies. "Lady," Rock said, "you're the best, almost as good as I am."

"Let's agree that you're an expert on ladies and I'm pretty damn good with men."

"Agreed."

Chapter
11

The following afternoon Jenna was on a plane to Syracuse on her way home for the long holiday weekend. Thanksgiving. Boy, did she have things to be thankful for. The sad part was they were things she couldn't discuss with her sister. The previous evening had been a revelation on two fronts. She'd learned a lot about herself and she'd given Rock something to think about.

After their post-coital collapse, Rock had kissed her good night lightly on the lips, then moved to his own room. Jenna had decided to sleep in the motel room, then dash to her temporary apartment in the morning to pack and grab a cab to the airport. She'd wanted to gauge Rock's reaction to the previous evening's fun and games, but when she had gotten up in the morning, he'd already left the brownstone.

What was he thinking? she wondered. Was the kind of explosion he'd experienced normal for him or was she, as she'd said so herself, pretty damn good at what she did? Had it been more than merely a lesson for him as it had been for her?

During the night she had accepted the fact that this wasn't anything serious. He wasn't the man for her in the long run. The evening had been just a wonderful sharing of intense pleasures. She'd have to wait until she came back to the city

Sunday, or after, to find out how he felt. For the long run she still thought about Glen. Too bad it couldn't work out.

LaGuardia Airport had been a zoo and the airport in Syracuse was even more chaotic. It seemed that every person in New York state was flying somewhere, but suddenly, as she walked toward baggage claim, there she was. Marcy. Although they talked several times a week they hadn't seen each other in almost three months, the longest time they'd ever been apart. She opened her arms and Marcy's tears mingled with hers as the twins hugged. "I'm so glad you're home," Marcy said.

Home? Manhattan was home now, wasn't it? This was just a visit with her sister and some friends. Then she'd return to the city and play with her new toy. Rock. She couldn't wait to work on the dungeon. It would open an entire new realm for Club Fantasy, although with the business they had now they didn't really need new customers. What if they took on some of Erika's staff on a more permanent basis? Maybe she'd talk to Erika about that when she got back. She snapped back to her sister. "I'm so glad to be here."

Although Marcy was wearing a heavy, black peacoat and her usually oversized black jeans, Jenna thought she felt a bit thinner. "Have you lost weight, Sis?"

"I wish. Actually, I've gained a few pounds." Jenna quickly let the subject drop. Weaving their way through the milling crowd, Marcy asked, "Did you check any bags?"

"Nope. I'm making do with what I've got on my shoulder," she said, patting her small overnight case, "and what's in my dresser drawers in my bedroom. It is still my bedroom, isn't it?"

Marcy smiled through her tears. "It'll always be here for you, Sis." Arm in arm they made their way to Marcy's car, the same blue Toyota that she'd been driving for four years, with the same dent in the passenger side door where an errant shopping cart had crashed in the ShopRite parking lot several months before she'd left. Jenna climbed in, moving Marcy's bag of Jelly Belly's to the back seat.

On the trip to Seneca Falls, the two women couldn't stop talking, often interrupting each other and talking simultaneously. The fall colors were gone and Jenna felt a loss when she realized that she'd missed them. In years past she'd crunched over fallen leaves on long walks, admiring nature's brilliance for hours, alone and with friends and family. In Manhattan she had seen the leaves turn in Central Park as she commuted between the brownstone in the East Fifties and her apartment in the West Eighties, but somehow she'd never walked in them. The colors had slipped passed her. It just wasn't the same.

They arrived at the small split-level and Marcy pulled the car into the driveway. Home. Jenna climbed out of the car and stood, gazing at the house. It hadn't snowed yet, but the leaves were all gone from the big oak in the front yard. Strange. Except for the change from short sleeves to jackets and coats, seasons in Manhattan passed pretty much unnoticed. Of course there were big fall rainstorms with weather forecasters' warnings to drivers about freezing conditions on the roads. It got dark earlier and earlier too, and she and Chloe had had to give up sitting in the backyard.

Here, winter felt closer. Trees without leaves and piles of brown crispy ones underfoot. Puddles had turned to ice that melted only late in the afternoon, only to freeze again at night. It wouldn't be long before snow covered the ground, heavy and white. "Have you gotten in touch with Phil, yet, to have him plow the driveway?"

"Hey, I'm the organized one," Marcy said. "I had that done by the end of September."

As Jenna stood beside the car, a school bus lumbered by and stopped at the corner. Several middle-schoolers got out, yelling to each other, celebrating the beginning of a four-day weekend. Jenna took in a deep breath of cold air. It smelled cleaner, fresher than the air in Manhattan. Life was different here. Better? Worse? Maybe just different. All at once she was unsure of where she belonged. Club Fantasy and bright lights were back in the big city. Marcy and comfort were here.

Jenna grabbed her shoulder bag from the back seat and, arm in arm, she and her twin walked up the front walk.

Back in the house that they'd shared for most of their lives, Jenna sipped freshly brewed coffee while Marcy munched jelly beans. Marcy and her jelly beans. It felt so familiar watching her work around the black ones. She could never actually take them out. By the time she got to the bottom of the bag, only black ones were left. Then she'd put the bag in the closet until they were all stale before she could finally throw them out.

Home. Manhattan was home, wasn't it? But it felt so good to be here as well.

The twins talked for hours. Jenna told Marcy about the milder parts of her sex life, describing clients as dates, not customers. Lying? Yes, but it was necessary. Marcy would never understand.

Marcy shared tales of AAJ Technologies and the people with whom she worked. The contrasts between their lives hit Jenna very hard. How had it felt to be normal, without scenarios, without men using her body? *Stop it*, she told herself. *It's not like that at all. You really enjoy what you* do. *Yeah*, she argued, *but you shouldn't*.

They had a familiar dinner at the local spaghetti joint and, as they sipped cups of cappuccino, Marcy was silent for several moments, then asked, "Did something happen to you last evening?"

The image of Rock's hand on her body flashed through her mind. Something had certainly happened. "What kind of something?" she asked, trying not to reveal anything.

"This is going to sound really odd but I had one of those experiences that we used to have. That twin connection thing. I sensed something. Felt something. I can't really explain it."

Explain it? Not a chance. Marcy was suddenly uncomfortable. How could she explain what had happened? Not to her sister, close though they were.

In the past few months, Marcy been having sudden rushes of erotic images but the previous night had been the most vivid. Some nights she was awakened by the sensation of her breasts being fondled. She could feel it. On occasion, she'd even reached down to embrace the hands but nothing was there. But her nipples hardened as though . . .

The previous evening she'd changed into a cotton nightgown and climbed into bed about ten o'clock to read for a while. Too excited by Jenna's impending visit to settle down, she got out of bed and went down to the kitchen to fuss over her special cranberry sauce for Thanksgiving dinner. *I might as well do it tonight*, she thought, *then I can refrigerate it until I need it*. She added sugar to the pot of water and berries and started to chop walnuts, when she was suddenly overwhelmed by a wave of erotic pleasure that forced her to drop into a kitchen chair.

She had flashes, visions, snapshots. Dark hands on white skin. Bare breasts. Whose? A man's face smiling in ecstasy above a smooth, muscular, hairless chest. A diamond stud in an ear. Piercing blue eyes. A fully erect penis and white hands on it. She had almost felt a large cock sliding into her. Almost.

Marcy had had several boyfriends and one year-long serious relationship that had finally dissolved with both parties on relatively good terms. She wasn't a virgin, but she'd never experienced anything like what she'd felt. Hesitantly, she reached down and cupped her bare breasts, touching her hardened nipples. She'd masturbated occasionally, but in the past touching herself always had made her feel incredibly guilty. Now the guilt was totally overshadowed by the need to relieve the waves of almost painful need. She let her head fall back and rubbed her breasts, waiting for the sensations to subside. They only got more powerful.

Unable to stop herself, she pulled up her nightgown and touched her bare flesh. Soaking wet and quaking, she found her clit and rubbed gently, knowing in some basic way, just where to touch. She came quickly, trembling and totally mystified by the enormity of what had just happened. It had been so fast, so violent. It had been wonderful.

Now she looked at her sister. How could she explain what she'd felt? "Never mind," she said shaking her head. "It was nothing."

"Are you sure? You went a bit pale for a moment. Is everything okay?" Jenna's face looked so concerned.

"Everything's fine." She changed the subject.

Thanksgiving dinner for just the two of them consisted of enough food to feed half the population of Seneca Falls. Groaning, the two women eventually stored the leftovers and made themselves comfortable in the living room. "Tell me about New York," Marcy said.

"You know about New York," Jenna said, obviously puzzled. "You were there."

"Are you staying there permanently? I keep hoping you've made some kind of decision."

"I haven't."

Until she had arrived at the Syracuse airport, Jenna had been sure she understood her life. Manhattan. Fast-paced, ever alive, busy Manhattan. Everything that Seneca Falls wasn't, New York City was. It was where she belonged. Now, she wasn't as sure. On the trip from the airport Marcy had driven through familiar streets. Past the elementary and high schools they had attended. Past the pizza parlor and the diner, the bowling alley and the multiplex. They'd made a stop at the mall for

some candles for the holiday table and Jenna had watched ordinary people hurry by.

It wasn't New York City, but it felt good. It felt like home.
Too. She was now totally confused. How could she describe it
all to Marcy? "I thought I had decided to make New York my
permanent home, but here, well, it feels comfortable. I love
you and I love this house. As much as I might complain about
'The Gateway to the Finger Lakes,' I love Seneca Falls. I
guess I need some more time."

"AAJ's open tomorrow," Marcy said. "Maybe you should
see about lengthening your leave. Everyone complained when
you left and I know they haven't been able to replace you.
They've hired two different people in the months since you
left and each lasted about a week. Too high pressure, I guess.
So, for the moment, they just farm most of the work out and
they've stuck me with some of the simultaneous translations
at meetings too. I've actually gotten pretty good at it, but I'm
not you."

"Thanks for the vote of confidence. Maybe I'll do that."

"What about Glen?"

Yes, she thought, *what about Glen?* "He calls once a week or
so and we talk like friends. I'm not sure that it's a good idea to
encourage him, but I like him and I let him know during each
conversation that I'm not moving back here any time soon."

Marcy hesitated, then said softly, "He asked me to suggest
that the two of you have dinner together Saturday night."

"He didn't say anything about that when we talked last
week."

"He was afraid to mention it so he's using me as a go-
between. He thought you'd say no."

"I don't know, Marcy. He needs to cut the cord and move
on."

"You don't care for him any more?"

"I don't know what I feel. I never have. Part of me cares
deeply for him and part of me needs something he can't give

me right now. I'm really torn but I can't lead him on. It's not fair to either of us."

"Why don't you have dinner with him and see what happens?"

"I'm terrified that the same thing will happen with him as happened with this town. I thought I understood that New York City was my future but when I felt the comfort here I got all confused again. I can't push Glen away with one hand and pull him toward me with the other."

"You're probably right. He's really a great guy and I guess I hope we'll all live happily ever after."

Hopeful, Jenna said, "You sound like you have feelings for him." Getting Marcy and Glen together would solve so many problems. Or would it?

Marcy shook her head. "It's not like that, Jen. I love him like a brother. I want good things for all of us and I keep hoping that means you and Glen. You'll move back, marry him, and we'll all be together again. I miss you like crazy."

The two women clasped hands. "I miss you too, Sis. I wish I could live that happily-ever-after life you see, but things are much more mixed up inside of me than you can imagine."

"Is there someone else? One of those guys you've been dating?"

"There are lots of guys but no one in particular." Rock? No. He's lust and heat and new pleasures, not a relationship.

"Okay. Maybe you need to get Glen out of your system once and for all and you're not going to do it from a distance."

"Why are you pushing, Marcy?"

Marcy sat back on the sofa and popped a blueberry jelly bean into her mouth. "I love both you and Glen. I think he's a great guy who needs to see you to get past you. I think you need to see him too. Have a fight or kiss and make up or just agree to disagree, but make it clean. It's too messy now."

"Messy. That's a good way to put it, and I'm afraid you're

right. I need to piss or get off the pot and I don't think I've done a very good job of either."

"Good. Now tell me more about your social life in the big city."

Jenna steeled herself to lie to her sister, and she hated it. But how could she tell Marcy about Club Fantasy? She'd become something totally unlike the person who'd left to go to New York. Was she ashamed of what she was? Was "she wouldn't understand" just another way of saying that she'd be ashamed of what I've become? Through the rest of the day she didn't mention the Club.

AAJ, she discovered, was only too eager to extend her leave. Ms. Henshaw filled out some papers, and now she had another six months to spend in "the big city." After her meeting with human resources, she had lunch with several of the women with whom she'd been friendly when she worked at AAJ, and they spent almost two hours laughing at stories of both New York City and Seneca Falls. One woman had a new baby and pictures were passed around the table. Looking at the infant Jenna became wistful, wondering whether she'd ever be snapping shots of her own child. She quickly brought herself back to the present.

Melinda Franks, her best friend at AAJ, asked the question the others were too tactful to ask. "So when are you coming back?"

Jenna was deliberately noncommittal. "I'm having a wonderful time in New York and I'm not sure what I'm going to do. I've gotten Henshaw to agree to extend my leave of absence for another six months, and then we'll see."

There was a collective groan around the large table. "You know how much we miss you, Jenna," one of the women said and Jenna found her eyes filling. It had been easy to leave the first time, but this departure seemed more painful. When she left the first time it was a lark. Now she realized that it might be permanent.

When they eventually separated, the women kissed cheeks and Jenna vowed to stay in touch. They all suggested that she visit with them again during Christmas week, but Jenna told them she was probably staying in New York for the holidays. It was already looking like it was going to be a busy week at Club Fantasy.

Jenna had called Glen on Thursday evening and they had made plans to have dinner Saturday at a steak place that had recently opened. He'd originally suggested that they meet at the same restaurant where he'd proposed, but they both quickly realized that was a bad idea.

Wearing a pair of brown, wool slacks and an off-white, cable-knit sweater that she had left in her old room, Jenna arrived at the restaurant to find Glen waiting for her at the door. She hadn't seen him in six months but she quickly realized that he hadn't changed a bit. Like Seneca Falls, he was warm and comfortable and—home. He hugged her and placed a quick kiss on her cheek. "I'm so glad to see you," he said. "You look fabulous."

"You've seen me in this outfit before."

"I don't mean the outfit. You're glowing and you look happy." He hung his head with a rueful grin. "I had hoped you'd look a bit thinner and maybe have circles under your eyes but New York City seems to agree with you."

"Thanks. It does."

Glen gave his name to the jeans-clad hostess who led them to a table off to one side.

"Wine?" Glen asked.

"I'd love some." As he signaled the waiter, Jenna gazed at him. He was so familiar, comfortable, and she loved him in her own way, whatever that meant. She knew his feelings so well. They were written all over his face, yet he was being a complete gentleman and had been nothing but casual in the months they'd been talking on the phone. Could they be friends? She knew that friendship wasn't all that Glen wanted, but that was what she wanted. Wasn't it?

She'd thought a lot about him in the months they'd been apart. There'd be something tiny, a moment when something happened that she'd love to share with him. He'd called her once despite a terrible head cold and she'd felt badly for him, suggesting remedies. She'd been feeling down one evening and he'd seemed to sense it when he called. He'd told her a joke he'd heard at work and it had made her laugh and eased the worst of her momentary depression.

Together after all the months apart, they spent a delightful dinner discussing everything and nothing. Finally, Glen leaned across the table, took her hands and said, "Jenna, what are your plans now? How long are staying in New York? Forever?"

Shit. Now's the time to say, *Yes, forever. I'm not coming back so find someone else.* But she couldn't. "I know that it's not fair of me to say that I don't know but I don't. AAJ has given me another six months. I don't know whether I'll use it all or come back or just quit one day."

She pulled her hands away and Glen didn't make any effort to stop her. "I thought this would be easy. I thought I'd just come back here and realize that my life was now in Manhattan. I'd pack a few more things, sell my car and decamp. Totally and without reservation. It didn't happen that way."

Glen sat patiently until Jenna continued. "I like it here too. My life in New York City is exciting, more exciting than you can imagine. I'm happy there."

"And . . ." Glen said, when she didn't immediately continue.

"But beside Chloe I have no friends there, no feeling of belonging. Sure, I know lots of people and I talk to lots of people every day but it's not . . ."

"Intimate?"

Jenna chuckled inwardly. In a way, though, he was right. She had clients and had lots of forms of intimacy, but it wasn't closeness, at least not the way it had been here in Seneca Falls. "That's as good a word as any."

"Marcy has told me that you have lots of boyfriends."

"She told you that?"

"I think she's been trying to be kind, to dissuade me from clinging to what we had."

Marcy was a wise woman. What better way to convince Glen to move on. "I've had dates. Lots of them."

"I've had a few too," Glen said.

Jenna felt an unreasonable stab of jealousy. *It's unworthy of you, Jenna*, she yelled at herself. You want him to move on, make a life.

Glen continued, "I realized about a month ago that I was obsessing about you. Marcy was right. I was clinging to some vain hope that you really did love me and it would just take a few months of sowing your oats in Manhattan for you to realize it and come back. To me." He huffed out a breath. "I fantasized the whole scene. Us in the same restaurant, you telling me how you'd made a mistake, me slipping the ring on your finger. I finally told myself to get over it and I made every effort. I think I'm succeeding. I've had a few dates and met a few very nice women."

Jenna swallowed hard. Why did she feel hurt? Isn't this what she wanted? "I'm happy for you, Glen." She forced the corners of her mouth upward in what she hoped would be the semblance of a smile. "I really am."

"I know you are," he said. "You're a wonderful, generous person and I'm happy to have you as a friend."

Glen straightened his spine and tried to make what he was saying sound genuine. True, he had had dates with a few women and each time he'd compared them to Jenna. Not as good a sense of humor, not as knowledgeable about politics, not as well read.

But he was going to have to move on. Jenna was making her position clear. Although she seemed truly confused, there was little or no chance that he would be part of her long-term future. So be it. Maybe he could keep her as a friend, although keeping a friendly relationship with an ex-lover was against all the odds.

Ex-lover. God, he still wanted her. She was still the sexiest woman he'd ever been with. He'd gone to bed with one of the women he'd dated only a few weeks ago. It had been good for her; he'd seen to that. He'd climaxed as well but it hadn't been wonderful, and he hadn't called the woman again.

They finished dinner with no more personal revelations. Finally, he paid the check, over Jenna's objections, and they walked outside to her car. "I care about you, Jen," he said as he opened the driver's-side door. "I care very much. May I kiss you good-bye?"

Jenna slipped her arms around his waist and kissed him lightly on the mouth. Without warning, all the old feelings resurfaced and her arms twined around his neck as his drew her closer. Passion raged inside him, a quick, consuming hunger for her. No! This wasn't supposed to happen. They were friends. Then her mouth was on his, hard, hot, filled with desire.

He pulled back so there was some space between them and looked into her eyes, now glazed with desire. "What's happening here?" he asked.

"I don't know," Jenna said, her voice breathy and hoarse. "I don't know." She kissed him again.

"Jenna, don't tempt me. I still want you, that should be obvious. Let's not confuse everything."

"I don't mean to confuse things, Glen. Really I don't."

He stood for a long moment, trying to regain his equilibrium. "I know you don't. Let's say good night."

"You're right," she said. "This is just messing with things we thought we'd settled. But I have to say it. I don't want to go home yet."

"I don't want you to, either."

*   *   *

Jenna couldn't believe the words that were coming out of her mouth. One week ago she had understood her life and where Glen fit into it, or didn't. Now, she was feeling nostalgic about Seneca Falls and the friends she'd left behind. She was wondering whether going back to Manhattan was what she really wanted to do. How can I feel so right in New York, she wondered, and so right here as well? She chalked it up to having a seriously split personality.

Glen. She couldn't, in good conscience, lead him on, go to bed with him when she wasn't sure where her head would be next week, or even tomorrow. God, I'm making this decision over and over. She heard Chloe's voice. Make the decision, then stop thinking about it. She squared her shoulders. "Glen, you're right. This is a bad idea," she said, but found herself locking her car door and starting to walk toward his. "I can't make any promises. There's so much about my life in New York that you don't know."

"Probably. You're undoubtedly having sex with other guys. That's okay. I think I really do understand."

Other guys? If he knew about Club Fantasy. "It's really not fair." They kept walking.

"I know, and I understand that this is tonight and means nothing in the long-run. Nothing has changed, or will change if we go back to my apartment. I also know that I want you and you want me. Right now. To hell with tomorrow, let's enjoy tonight."

A mistake. A big mistake. But she made it.

When they arrived at Glen's condo, Jenna felt surrounded by the warm, familiar feel and smell of it. They'd spent so much time here, talking, watching TV and rented movies. They'd shared a lot of cooking, experimenting with Chinese and Italian foods. She could almost smell star anise and oregano. One wall of the living room was covered with bookshelves stuffed with volumes they'd both read and discussed at length. Glen took her coat and hung it in the small closet in the entryway. Then he was behind her, holding her shoulders and turning her to face him.

"I want you, but that doesn't mean we have to do anything about it," Glen said.

Why had she gotten herself into this? Did she want to re-open things she thought were settled? She gazed at his comfortable, familiar face. "I know," she said. "Glen, I want you too but it doesn't mean anything's changed between us. I'm still going back to New York." He kissed her gently on the side of her neck where he knew she was vulnerable. "Nothing's changed." He kissed her again, taking small nips at the tendon. *God*, she thought, *he knows how to turn me on.*

"Glen, we really shouldn't do this. You'll just get hurt all over again."

"I know," he whispered, switching to the other side of her neck, "you've said that a zillion times. But for me, right now, tonight is all that matters. I'm so hungry for you that tonight's the only thing I want."

She tried. She really tried. Then she stopped trying. Of their own volition her arms slipped around his neck. Of their own volition her lips found his. Of its own volition her body pressed against his. Their lips met, tongues dueling, warm and soft.

And hungry. Her hunger was sudden and overwhelming. She grabbed the back of his shirt and pulled it off over his head. Skin. She wanted to feel his skin beneath her hands. So soft and smooth. His back, his shoulders, his lightly furred chest with the line of hair that disappeared into the waistline of his slacks.

He was obviously as hungry as she was. Quickly her sweater lay in a heap on the floor, her bra beside it. His hands were full of her, tugging at her nipples the way he knew she liked, while she found his belt and pulled it open. The button at his waist was stubborn so he helped her with it. Then his slacks and hers were tossed aside, along with shoes, socks, and underwear. Both naked, he picked her up and carried her into the bedroom.

Lying on the bed, she watched him lay down beside her. "Oh, God, Jenna," he whispered. "You're so beautiful." Then he could say no more. She dragged his mouth to hers and, smooth body against smooth body, they moved, feeling, just feeling.

The silky spread on his bed against her back, his body heavy on top of hers, they moved together. His hands cupped her face and he kissed her eyes, cheeks, ears, then devoured her mouth. She felt his hardness against her mound and the wetness between her thighs. She needed him but he didn't move to penetrate.

His hand found her sopping center and stroked, then two of his fingers plunged into her as her hips bucked upward to meet him. She wanted him to rub her clit so she grabbed his hand and showed his fingers where to touch. Higher and higher she climbed, moving her body to enhance the sensation. She ran her fingernails down his back, then found his hard cock. She squeezed, then slid from base to head. He quickly rolled away and pulled a small foil package from his bedside-table drawer.

She took it away, opened it, and ever so slowly unrolled the latex over his penis.

"Jenna!" he shouted, plunging into her. His hand was between them, stroking her clit as his cock thrust and withdrew. She cupped his buttocks, showing him her rhythm. She was aware of his restraint until she finally came, then he followed. Sweat soaked and exhausted, they collapsed on their sides, the entire length of their bodies pressed against each other.

Satisfied. Replete. All the words she'd read over the years in novels about the aftermath of lovemaking, this was all of that. She snuggled against Glen's warm body and draped an arm over his naked chest. What had she done? She'd think about it later. For right now she closed her eyes and floated in a delicious haze.

Glen lay against Jenna, his fingers lightly stroking up and down the arm that lay across his chest. He tried not to read anything into their lovemaking. It meant nothing, just a coupling of two hungry people. He tried to focus on that. And failed. They couldn't make love like this unless there was something still left of their relationship. He started to say something, then decided to leave well enough alone. They had made a memory, something for him to hold on to, something for Jenna to think about when she returned to New York City.

He closed his eyes and just enjoyed the moment.

Chapter
12

The following morning Jenna and Marcy sat in the sunny kitchen. Jenna hadn't slept much the previous night. Glen had dropped her off at her car, then followed her to the house to be sure she arrived safely. They had each struggled not to say what was uppermost in their minds.

"I really fucked it up, Marcy," Jenna said after she told her sister that she and Glen had been to bed together. "As much as I said it didn't mean anything I'm afraid Glen will expect too much of me, then have his hopes dashed all over again."

"You mean it didn't change anything?" Marcy mopped the last of her egg yolk from her plate with the last of her toast.

Did it change things? Jenna hadn't a clue. Why had she come back to Seneca Falls? Why had she had lunch with Melinda and the other women from AAJ? Why had she reminded herself of the good things she'd left behind? And the biggest why of all; why had she gone to bed with Glen? He's such a special man and they were really good together. He'd made sure she was satisfied before letting himself come. She'd showed him what she needed and he'd done it well. Had she ever showed him before? "I don't know what it changed, Sis. All I know is that I'm going back to Manhattan this afternoon more confused than ever."

"I can't say I'm unhappy about your confusion, Jen. I'd love to have you back here. I miss you like crazy. But more important, you need to make some difficult decisions and you need to understand as much as you can to make them, yourself more than anything."

"I wish you'd stop being so reasonable," Jenna said, wryly, pushing her empty cereal bowl aside.

Marcy's grin was quick and wide. "Dessert time." She picked up the jar of jelly beans at her elbow and held it out to Jenna, who reached in and picked out a coconut one. "You can't pick," Marcy said. "You've got to take whatever jelly bean jumps into your hand."

Jenna popped the white candy into her mouth. "I guess I can, and I did." Was there a lesson there? She couldn't pick the parts of her life she wanted to keep. It was Glen and Seneca Falls or Club Fantasy. Right now, it was Club Fantasy.

Jenna arrived back at the brownstone midevening. She'd thought about going back to her apartment but she found herself giving the address on East Fifty-fifth to the cab driver at the airport. She arrived, let herself in, and found Rock watching a basketball game in the living room. "How was your visit?" he asked.

How was her visit? Interesting question. She had decided not to think too much about Glen and Seneca Falls. "Confusing."

"Want to talk?"

Jenna looked at him and realized that, as he gazed at her with undivided attention, he would probably be a good listener. However, she didn't want to talk about her incredibly mixed feelings. "Not at the moment."

"I'm here if you want to unload. Any time."

She realized that he truly meant that. "I know, and thanks. Where's everybody?"

"Chloe's in the motel room and Anita, one of Erika's ladies, is in the Western room."

Jenna put down her suitcase, dropped into a chair, and fastened her gaze on the big-screen TV. "Are you a basketball fan?" Rock asked. She knew that he was a fan of every sport that had even been invented. He'd watch the World Poker Tour or a British snooker tournament if there wasn't anything more strenuous on.

Jenna had never been much of a basketball fan but she knew a little about the way the pros played. The New Jersey Nets were winning by four points over the Sacramento Kings. "Good game?"

"Yeah," Rock said. "Only three minutes to go. That should only take about half an hour."

Jenna laughed, knowing that he was probably right about the time. As the images played across the TV screen only a small part of Jenna's mind was on the game. She hadn't spent any time with Rock since their encounter in front of the mirror almost a week earlier and she wondered whether anything had changed between them. Fortunately, it didn't seem to have. He was still just a friend. With Rock occasionally pointing out a particular player and explaining the coach's strategy, they watched together in silence until the game ended with a Net victory almost twenty-five minutes later.

As she stood up to head home, whatever that word meant, Rock said, "I've been doing some thinking about the basement. Got a few minutes?"

"Sure," Jenna said, glad to have her mind occupied in a different direction.

"Great." He unfolded himself from the chair and took her hand as they walked downstairs. "Let me tell you what I think we might do."

At the foot of the stairs Rock flipped on the only light, a bare, hanging bulb. Jenna looked around. The room was only a half-finished shell, plasterboard walls, a ceiling with the lighting fixtures already in place but inoperable, and a tile floor that was always cold underfoot. It appeared as though sometime in the past Aunt Elise had thought of turning it into a play room, but had never gotten past the initial stages. Boxes and trunks were piled everywhere, now covered with a thick layer of dust. The room smelled musty and damp, the air thick with the odor of disuse. Jenna had always thought about going through the mess to try to find items for their fantasies, but so far hadn't worked up the energy.

"The room is large enough for us to wall off the water heater and furnace area," he said, motioning off to one side, "and still have enough space to work with. I think some dark paneling, with at least one wall entirely of mirrors." He grinned. "You know all about mirrors now, don't you?"

She tried desperately not to blush. "Enough," she said, laughing to cover her discomfort.

"I hoped you'd be able to laugh about that evening. It was wonderful sex and I enjoyed it thoroughly, but I don't want it to change our friendship."

"I don't, either. It worried me a lot."

Rock grinned sheepishly. "Me too. But I value your friendship enough to assure you that there won't be a repeat unless you want it. However, I would love a return engagement if you want to play some time. I'd really like to show you how this room works when we get it done."

Strange way to interact, she thought, as she felt the tension drain from her body. *I want to be friends, he says, but I want to fuck your brains out from time to time. What the hell. After all, I run a brothel called Club Fantasy. What could be stranger than that? What did they call it on* Sex in the City? *Fuck buddies? Why the hell not?* "I think I would too."

His grin was infectious and she found herself smiling with him. "Good." He draped a large arm over her shoulders. "Back to business. We can create storage space in the furnace area for whatever of this we want to keep. We'll need a table or a bed, depending on the situation, and lots of bondage equipment. I've never been able to create a specialty area like this from scratch and I've got dozens of ideas. Give me a budget and I'll get started."

She and Chloe would have to agree on the finances but they had so much money rolling in that Rock could pretty much spend whatever he thought necessary. And this room would bring in lots of additional business. "I guess we'll need to hire folks."

"Don't worry about that," Rock said. "I have friends who can do the work in exchange for an evening's entertainment when we're done and the use of the room from time to time, at your convenience. One's even a licensed electrical contractor, so we'll be up to code on everything."

"Electrical contractor?"

"We need extra outlets and better lighting. It needs to be dank and dim or brightly lit, depending on the client."

"Oh, right."

"I'd love to take you and Chloe shopping at a place I particularly like. Lots of fetish stuff."

"I thought I'd just check that kind of stuff out on the net."

"The net's fine, but I like to touch and play with things before I buy."

Touch and play with things. Her pussy was twitching and getting wet. This was going to be an interesting project.

The following day she and Rock talked with Chloe, and they arrived at a budget for the dungeon. Over the next weeks, several men came and went during the day and, when Jenna happened to be around, she could hear hammers, power tools and lots of macho male laughter. *God,* she thought, *Club Fantasy should consider a construction room for women's pleasures.* She giggled to herself. Muscular men and power tools.

Finally the room was finished and Rock suggested a grand-opening party. "We're usually closed on Monday and Tuesday so why don't we have a play party some Monday evening soon with a few of the guys who helped me build this thing. Are you ladies up for some fun?"

Jenna had to make one admission. "I'm not sure I'm ready to have sex in the same room as Chloe just yet. It would feel really bizarre to me."

"That's fine. You ladies will play separately, if that's what you two want. No problem."

With a bit of trepidation, Jenna and Chloe agreed to Rock's plans. "And no peeking at the room until then. I want it to be as much of a surprise as it would be for a new customer."

Before they could enjoy the new room, Jenna took on quite a different project. Chloe, using her club name Melissa, had taken a call from a man named Tony, well recommended and seemingly able to pay Club Fantasy's price for both himself and his wife.

In their interview, Chloe had learned that what Tony wanted most was to watch his wife with another man. Since his wife Nancy would be involved in this fantasy, Chloe met with her the following afternoon and discussed Tony's desires, and Nancy's. She and Jenna set everything up, then called Tony to outline the evening to him. Tony had wanted a peephole sort of thing, but Chloe explained that they had a video area set up and he could watch on closed-circuit TV. If he wanted the tape afterward, there would be an extra charge, of course, but he told her that he might be willing to pay it. After all, watching the tape should be almost as good as watching it live.

He arrived at the brownstone at the allotted time, and Chloe settled him in the "living room" and sat silently behind him, watching his reactions. She, Jenna, and Nancy had discussed the evening at length. They knew they were taking a chance with their plan but they had all decided that it would be worth it. They'd hired one of Erika's male entertainers, a gorgeous would-be actor named Jack, to help.

Tony stared at the big-screen TV, large enough that the images would be almost life-size. Chloe knew he was picturing naked bodies, hands, asses, genitals, all arrayed for his viewing pleasure, as they said in commercials. His cock was probably hard just thinking about it as he settled more deeply into his lounge chair, feet up, and waited for the fun to begin.

And begin it did. As Chloe watched, a woman walked into the room first, dressed in one of Nancy's floor-length, floaty robes that just hinted at her body beneath. It was a bit difficult to see the woman's face but Tony leaned forward and nodded. The woman was followed by Jack, a true stud with a great body, well-developed pecs and a tight ass, dressed in a very tight, black tee shirt, slim, black jeans, and black cowboy boots. He was about six feet tall with long, curling, dark brown hair tied at the back of his neck with a leather thong, and steel gray eyes.

Tony craned his neck to see how his wife was reacting to this hunk, but her back was to him, her head lowered, seemingly unaware that she was being filmed. "Do not speak," the man said. "You have told me all your secret passions and I will endeavor to give you pleasures beyond your wildest expectations."

"Thank you," she said, her voice already hoarse with passion. She started to look around at the camera but the man turned her away. "I don't want you to think about the camera or your husband." He paused. "Think only of me, of here, and of now."

Chloe and Tony watched her nod her agreement.

"Have you ever been blindfolded?" the man asked. When Tony saw her begin to speak, the man turned her and put his hand in front of her mouth. Understanding, she merely shook her head. "You respond well," he said, as he took a wide black scarf from his pants pocket and quickly tied it over her eyes. "Now you will think only of me and our lovemaking. Think of my hands, my mouth, my cock giving you pleasure."

The man obviously knew that Tony was watching, but he seemed oblivious. He slowly turned Nancy toward the camera, the wide scarf covering most of her face. He unfastened the neck of the garment and it slipped to the floor. He smiled as he gazed with appreciation at her lush curves.

The man's hands hovered over Nancy's body, not touching her skin. Rather he traced the shape of her breasts, her shoulders, her belly, and hips. "You are perfection," he purred. She raised her head and he kissed her, obviously drinking deeply of her mouth. His arms slid around her waist, drawing her closer. He cupped her buttocks, pressing his jeans-covered groin against her naked flesh.

Still fully clothed, he cupped one naked breast, then bent and took her nipple in his mouth. Tony was obviously entranced. Rock was controlling the filming from one side of the room. They had invested in a second camera and a circuit board that allowed him to change the one broadcasting and to pan and zoom without moving from the controls. Now and then the shot changed, zeroing in on the man's mouth sucking at Nancy's breast or her fingers threaded through his hair. They could hear Nancy's breathing become raspy and watch her tremble.

As the camera zoomed in tighter, until the mouth and nipple filled the screen, Chloe grinned as she watched Tony's hand drop to his crotch to rub his throbbing hard-on through his jeans.

With the camera following, the man's mouth moved to Nancy's other breast. While he suckled, the camera panned to his fingers, plucking and pinching. Tony obviously knew how much Nancy loved to have her breasts played with and when he heard the growling sounds she always made, his hand moved more quickly in his crotch.

Several moments later, the man guided Nancy to the bed and stretched her out, legs splayed wide apart. The viewers in the living room could see how the tall, angled mirror above the bed was positioned. The camera panned to it and Tony could see his wife as if from above, displayed on the bed, her hips moving, reaching for . . .

The man reappeared in the shot, naked now, his erection hard and thick. He crawled between Nancy's spread legs, his mouth moving toward her pussy. Totally oblivious to Chloe behind him, Tony unzipped his jeans, pulled out his cock and wrapped his hand around his erection and squeezed, unable to take his eyes from the TV screen. This was like the best porno movie he'd ever watched, Chloe thought.

The man's mouth moved closer to Nancy's pussy, slowly approaching, licking his lips. He fastened his lips against her crotch, his fingers again playing with her nipples. Smiling, Chloe watched as Tony's erection softened slightly as he watched Nancy writhe. She was seemingly enjoying this stranger's lovemaking as much as she enjoyed Tony. She was really hot, really turned on. For long minutes, the man sucked, licked, pinched, played. Tony's hand fell away from his crotch as he watched the man's fingers thrust into his wife's cunt until she moaned with increasing pleasure.

It was all Chloe could do not to laugh as she watched Tony's eyes narrow and his frown deepen. The man's hard cock, now covered with the required condom, approached Nancy's pussy, then slowly, as the camera panned in for a close crotch shot, slid into her. Chloe could almost read the thoughts racing through Tony's mind. He's sliding in so easily, Tony must be thinking. She must be so wet, so hot. He's gotten her so high and he seemed to do it so easily. Now they both could see the muscles of the man's ass tighten and flex as his cock drove into her. Over and over he thrust until, with a scream, Nancy came, with the stud not far behind.

Tony was visibly shaken and Chloe knew what he must be thinking. His wife had climaxed so easily with another man. True, it had been really hot to watch, but it now obviously made him very uncomfortable. Would he relive this scene every time he was fucking his wife? Would he see the man's ass driving into his wife's body? Fucking her? Would he hear her scream for a stranger when she screamed for him?

As Tony watched the man collapse on top of his wife, he heard a voice from behind him. "Was that what you wanted? Did it meet your expectations?"

Tony whirled and saw Nancy standing behind him, fully dressed. He turned and stared at the screen. What the hell was going on? As he watched, the woman on the screen removed her blindfold, stretched languorously and turned toward the camera. It wasn't Nancy.

"No, it's not me," Nancy said, settling on the arm of Tony's chair. "I hoped you'd be revolted at the sight of me with another man, and discover that your fantasy should remain that, just a fantasy. Melissa, Hillary—that's her you've been watching—and I set this all up. Hillary is built enough like me that we hoped you wouldn't notice. We used the blindfold to keep her face hidden and she's wearing a wig so her hair looks just like mine."

"I don't understand," Tony said, unable to grasp what was happening.

"This was never your fantasy, darling," she said. "It was mine." She leaned over and kissed her husband, then Tony felt her hand slide down his chest to his now flaccid cock. She knew just how to squeeze and rub so that he hardened quickly. "I knew you thought you wanted to see me with another man, but, baby," she purred, "I was also pretty sure it wouldn't end up being what you expected."

Chloe slipped from the room but couldn't resist a bit of eavesdropping. As she peeked, Nancy slipped to the floor between her husband's spread knees, gazing up at him through her lashes. "I hoped that you would eventually hate it." She licked the length of his now hard cock. "Did you?"

"Yes," he said, suddenly breathless, "but I love what you're doing now."

She sucked his cock into her mouth and tightened her lips around it. Ever so slowly she pulled back, then sucked again, driving him higher and higher with each movement. Back on her heels, she gazed at him. "Watching made you hot at first, didn't it?"

"Yes," he said, finding it difficult to concentrate. "But later—"

"I know." She took his cock again and brought him closer to orgasm, then sat back again. "And you wondered about making love to me after seeing all that." She licked her lips. "Now, when you think of what you watched, you'll also think of this." She wrapped her hand around the base of his erection and sucked the tip into her mouth. Squeezing and sucking, she aroused him past the point of no return. He came in her mouth, his hips bucking, his penis throbbing. He opened his eyes and watched a small bit of semen escape her lips.

Minutes later, he said, "You've never done that to me before."

"I know, but I decided that you did deserve to have at least one fabulous fantasy come true. And I surprised myself. I enjoyed doing that, much more than I thought I would."

"What about you? You haven't—"

She interrupted. "Let's go home. By the time we get there you'll be able to take care of me and my needs too."

"You know, that blindfold thing turned me on. Would you let me do it to you?"

"Sounds great. Let's get out of here." Without a backward glance, they grabbed their coats and left.

The following afternoon, Chloe, Jenna, and Erika sat around a small table in Alfredo's, a small restaurant where the three women often met. Chloe took a long drink of her coffee, having finally finished the story of Tony and Nancy. "I can't thank you enough for letting us borrow Jack for the evening," Jenna said. "He arrived and left so quickly we didn't really get to say thanks."

"I'm so sorry about that," Erika said. "He's very much in demand, as you can imagine from looking at him. He had an engagement before yours and another later that evening so he was really tight for time. I picked him because he sounded like the physical type your client was looking for."

"He certainly was and it came off just fabulously." Jenna winked. "I enjoyed him a lot. I've never made it with a professional before."

"You two might want to do it again some time, gratis. Jack commented on how responsive you were."

Jenna blushed beet red and Chloe laughed. "I've never seen you blush before, Jenna."

"Shut up," Jenna snapped, good naturedly.

"It all worked out," Erika said, playing with the stem of her wine glass. "Tony saw what he expected to see. It could have all backfired, you know."

"I know," Chloe admitted, "but having talked to both of them separately for quite a while, I thought I understood them pretty well. Luckily, I turned out to be right."

"I guess you were. That closed-circuit TV connection you set up will come in handy again too," Erika said. "Lots of men want to watch like that. You ladies have come up with some pretty creative stuff."

"We certainly have, and in this case I feel like we performed some kind of public service," Jenna said.

"You did," Erika said. "You certainly did."

Although some men easily discussed the details of the fantasy they wanted to act out, others found it difficult to talk about something so deeply personal. Jenna found dealing with these men somehow the most rewarding. Over a cup of coffee, she would take time to make the man feel comfortable, then lead him through the intricacies of his dreams.

When Royce Devlin made an appointment to meet her at a small bar in Midtown, she envisioned a dynamic businessman, three-piece suit, well-trimmed moustache, maybe rimless glasses. As she sat at a small table off to one side, she was approached by a very tall, gawky man of about thirty-five, with long, shaggy, graying hair, thick eyebrows, which his thick-framed, tortoiseshell glasses almost hid, and a long, thin neck that made him resemble a stork. She stood as he approached. "You're Royce," Jenna said, holding out her hand.

He took it, his palm damp and his grip weak. "And you're Hillary."

"Sit down, please," she said, retaking her seat. "Would you like something to drink?"

He turned as the waiter approached. "I'll have a beer." After the waiter finished reeling off a long list of domestic and imported beers and ales, Royce said, "Make it a Bud."

Smiling politely, the waiter disappeared into the late-afternoon crowd. "It's very nice to meet you, Royce," Jenna said. "How did you happen to call Club Fantasy?"

"I heard about it from several friends of mine," he said, then named several names she knew well. She would call one or two of course, but he sounded genuine. "They speak very highly of you and your organization."

"I'm so glad they do. What exactly can I do for you?"

Jenna watched his Adam's apple bob as he spoke. "I'm not really sure. I don't know whether you're going to do anything. I'm just not sure."

"That's fine." She lowered her voice and spoke conspiratorially. "I'm here to help you fulfill your deepest desires, but only if and when you want me to."

He looked her over. "You. Really, actually you? Not someone else?"

"It would certainly be me if that's what you want."

"You're exactly right. But I still don't know."

"Of course you don't. I understand how difficult this must be."

She saw the first glimpse of a smile. "You have no idea."

"Oh, but I do. I talk with men like you often and I can imagine how embarrassing it must be. Let me reassure you that nothing you say will shock me, and nothing will ever go any further than this table."

"If I decide to tell you about my desires, they *will* shock you." He squirmed in his chair. "They shock me."

She lowered her voice further. "Is that bad? Sometimes just telling someone about something so exciting can be enough to satisfy your desires for a while. You might find you don't really need Club Fantasy."

She watched Royce swallow as the waiter placed his beer in front of him, then slip away. "Telling someone," he said after taking a long drink. "I never envisioned telling anyone."

Jenna had deliberately worn a lightweight, rose sweater with a deep U-shaped neckline so that when she leaned forward to speak softly, directly to him, he would get a good view of her lacy, pink bra. "You can tell me."

Royce took another long swallow, then patted his mouth with his napkin. "I'm not a very handsome man," he said. "Not sexy or powerful."

Jenna caught the automatic *of course you are*, coming out of her mouth and stopped it. She sensed that he wouldn't want platitudes so she merely said, "Go on."

"I've never been good with women. Actually, I've got a lot of women friends on the Internet. I correspond with half a dozen—long, sexy chats. My screen name is roycefromny and I think the name fools them. Royce. It sounds so macho, masculine. They picture Royce as a bodybuilder from one of those exercise-machine commercials and I cultivate that image, as long as they can't see me." He shrugged. "It's not the real me, but it makes all of us feel good."

Jenna kept silent, waiting for Royce to continue. She had found over the months that men wanted to fill silences and Royce was no exception. "Anyway, in my dreams I'm a hunk."

"I wish I could do that for you," Jenna said with a slight sigh.

He picked up his coaster and began to tap its edge on the table. "I wish you could too, but you can't and I didn't expect it. In my dreams, I'm . . ."

When he couldn't continue, Jenna tried to figure out what he wanted. He wanted power. "You want to pick up a sexy lady in a bar and have her choose you over lots of other guys?" She'd acted out that scenario with another client about a week before.

"No, although that would be great." He smiled at the thought, then flipped the coaster over and tapped it again. "But it's not what I'm thinking about."

Jenna waited. "I want to be powerful. Strong." He took a long pull on his beer, flipped the coaster and continued tapping, remaining silent. Jenna waited. As if he'd suddenly made up his mind, he blurted out, "I want to rape a woman." She grimaced. "Shit. That sounds so horrible."

"No, it doesn't. Not at all." Without allowing him time to dwell on what he'd just said, Jenna continued. "It's a very common fantasy. Power is heady stuff, for both men and women. And I'm sure you wouldn't dream of actually raping a woman."

"God, no," he said, quickly. "Never. I love women and wouldn't ever do anything to hurt anyone."

"Of course not. I understand." She thought quickly, creating a scenario they could act out together. She watched his hands as they played with his coaster. "Maybe you're a burglar who breaks into a woman's bedroom and subdues her, then has his way with her." His fingers became still for several seconds before he continued tapping the coaster's edge on the tabletop. "Maybe he holds her down as she struggles. She's unable to break his hold. He holds her wrists with one hand and rips off her nightgown with the other." She watched his

Adam's apple bob and the tapping accelerate. "He ties her to the bed, then . . . Well, you know the rest."

Softly, he said, "You do know."

"If you arrive at my place next Thursday evening it can be real."

"I'll be there. Is eight o'clock okay?" He paid the usual thousand-dollar fee, then left.

Although she knew that Chloe had acted out a few similar situations, this would be a first for Jenna. At the appointed hour, Chloe showed Royce up to the empty motel room, now set up as a lady's bedroom, with fresh flowers on the night stand, bottles and jars taken from Jenna's and Chloe's cosmetics scattered around, and a collection of framed photographs on the dresser and walls. He was dressed in a black, long-sleeved tee shirt, black jeans and sneakers.

Chloe showed Royce to the closet, then whispered, "I think she'll be home soon. You'd better hide in here." Then she left.

Moments later, Jenna entered, wearing a navy blue, tailored business suit, simple navy pumps, and carrying a briefcase. "Long day," she said with a sigh, kicking her shoes off and perching on the edge of the bed. Slowly she slid her skirt up and peeled down her hose, then, in plain view of the slightly opened closet door, slowly undressed. When she was down to her navy, lace bra and bikini panties, she crossed the room to the large mirror over the dresser. She could see the reflection of the closet door and imagined Royce behind it, watching her every move. She wanted to give him a good show before the main event.

She poured a pool of body lotion into her palm and starting with her neck and shoulders, sensuously covering herself, making her skin slick and shiny. When she finished with her arms, she unclipped her bra and dropped it on a chair, then massaged her breasts with her slippery hands, paying particular attention to her nipples, twisting them until they stood out from her flesh.

Finally, she removed her panties and slipped into a soft peach-colored nightgown. She and Chloe had carefully snipped the seams at several places so that when grabbed, it would rip off quickly and easily. Jenna lit a thick, white candle and placed it on the bedside table, and then she stretched out in bed, pulled a sheet over herself, and pretended to fall asleep.

It took several minutes for Royce to emerge. Either he was playing the game of waiting for her to be asleep or he was summoning his courage. Keeping her breathing slow and even, Jenna finally heard him pad softly from the closet. Her eyes flew open and she started to scream. Playing his part, Royce slammed his hand over her mouth and hissed, "Not a sound and I won't hurt you."

"No," she mumbled around his hand, then started to thrash around, kicking her feet and grabbing for his arms. She tried to loosen his hold on her mouth but he was stronger than she had anticipated. She didn't have to hold back as she'd thought she would. He quickly straddled her hips and pulled at her wrists until her arms were stretched above her head. "Keep still," he hissed when she gathered a deep breath to yell. "It will go easier if you keep still." He grabbed the neckline of her gown and pulled it down to her waist. As planned, the garment came apart in several pieces. He took a small bit of nylon and stuffed it into her mouth, then used a longer one to hold it in place. Then he efficiently tied her hands to the headboard.

Jenna thought for a moment about her predicament. If he had been someone who wanted to hurt her, she couldn't have stopped him. She'd only allowed herself to get into this predicament after several phone calls to the men who'd sent him to her. She again blessed Erika for her very sound advice and for the presence of Rock downstairs.

Royce ripped the remainder of the nightgown from her

body and then gazed at her. She lay still, her legs decoratively arranged, her knees together. "God, you're so beautiful," he murmured. Then his hands were all over her, touching, probing. His mouth devoured her nipples, his hands threaded through her hair, pulling slightly. As her fluids began to flow, a small part of Jenna's mind considered it. She loved not having to do anything. She'd been with so many men with whom she had to think constantly: how fast, how hard, how loud, how everything? Now she didn't have to decide how to proceed. Royce was making all the decisions.

"Spread your legs wide," he said, his voice hoarse. When she didn't obey immediately, he snapped, "If you do what you're told I won't have to kill you." She nodded, widening her eyes and trembling slightly.

When she parted her thighs, his breathing quickened until she could hear each rasp of air. She was surprised that he didn't remove his trousers. Rather he unzipped and allowed his rigid member to spring free. "Now you're going to get what you've been asking for."

She shook her head violently and tried to scream through the gag in her mouth. Unable to make a sound, she wiggled her hips provocatively and watched as he covered his cock with a condom. When Chloe had answered his ring of the front door bell, she'd handed him the house rules, which included the admonition about condoms. Jenna knew he'd agreed. Otherwise Chloe and Rock would never have let him upstairs.

Still fully dressed, Royce knelt on the foot of the bed, then crawled between Jenna's legs, his cock in his hand. She felt him rub it on her heated, slippery flesh, then plunge inside. "You can't do anything to stop me," he said, pounding into her.

She fought him, squirming and kicking just enough to reinforce the fantasy, not enough to dislodge him. He grabbed her thighs and held her down while he rammed into her over and over. Jenna was nearing orgasm herself when he came with a deafening bellow, then collapsed beside her. Her pussy was pulsing and she knew that the minute he was gone she'd have to satisfy herself. God, she was hot.

Finally he rose and quickly removed the gag and untied her. "I'm sorry if I hurt you," he said.

Smiling, Jenna said, "You didn't." Not wanting to break the fantasy, she said no more.

He quickly cleaned himself up and headed for the door. "This was everything I'd imagined. Can we do it again?"

"Of course," she said.

"Good. I'll call Club Fantasy in a few weeks." He closed the door behind himself.

As Jenna lay on the bed, her fingers playing over her wet skin, she thought about power and the incredibly wonderful sensations she'd just experienced. She recreated the moments when she'd been powerless to stop Royce's actions and fantasized about a real burglar, with truly devious intentions, forcing himself upon her, powerful yet satisfying. She held on to the sensations while she drove herself to orgasm. She remembered the scene in the shiek's tent but there she hadn't been tied. This had been even better. She approached climax with the vision of Royce's body looming over her, straddling her hips, rendering her incapable of preventing his invasion of her body. She came, feeling his cock invading her cunt, and she couldn't stop him from doing anything he'd wanted.

She wondered how it would feel being on the other side of this power fantasy. What if she were in command? She might just enjoy that too. It was a whole new world.

Chapter
13

Jenna took a three-day trip to Seneca Falls over Christmas, arriving on the twenty-fourth and returning to Manhattan on the twenty-seventh. She made excuses to Marcy for the brevity—work, commitments for Christmas parties, plans with Chloe—but in reality she didn't want to get sucked into the holiday scene in Upstate New York. She'd always loved searching for a tree, decorating the house, and all the rest of the holiday preparations. When she'd planned her visit to be so brief she'd known how it would all confuse her. In addition, of course, was the fact that business was particularly hectic throughout the holiday season with people being given, or giving themselves, gifts of evenings at Club Fantasy.

She had Christmas dinner with Marcy, lunch with her girlfriends from AAJ, and had dinner on the twenty-sixth with Glen. They again made love and it was soft and warm and satisfying. She told no one about Club Fantasy.

When she returned to New York City, the final work on the basement had been completed. But before Rock could set up an evening with his friends to try the room out, she and Rock were asked to fulfill an unusual fantasy.

"I had a call from Erika yesterday," Rock said to Jenna one evening, about a week after her return. "She referred a couple to me and I just got off the phone with the wife. Her name is Denise and her husband's name is Walt. They have a fantasy and they are willing to pay to have us make it come true, but I'd need you to help me."

"Me?"

"Let me explain. They've been married for about five years and have recently become interested in the dominant/submissive lifestyle, but they have no idea how to make it work. They want experts to teach each of them, independently, how to behave and what to do. She's unsure about what she can demand and he's not sure how to respond. I thought you could work with Walt while I was with Denise. Is this something you think you might enjoy?"

"I'd love to do it, but I'm no expert. I've played with dominant/submissive fantasies a few times but I know very little except what those particular clients wanted to do. Until I learn, I certainly can't teach."

"Actually, you've got the easy part. All you've got to do is show him how to obey. You get to demand all the things you've always wanted. We can talk about it and I'll get you a few films. The basic question is, however, whether you feel you can be a dominant woman." He winked at her. "You do submissive wonderfully well."

She shuddered as she always did when Rock looked at her as if he'd like to eat her alive. "Yeah, well, I don't know about the dominant part. I've never tried."

For the following week she and Rock talked about domination, and she watched films and read stories. Doing it didn't seem too difficult, but to do it really well she'd have to find something inside herself to draw on. She only agreed when she was totally sure she could give Walt his money's worth, whether it truly turned her on or not.

* * *

The sessions with Denise and Walt were scheduled for an evening in mid-January. While Jenna made Walt wait, Rock entered the room where Denise waited.

"Good evening. My name is Rock," he said softly, "and I'm going to make you over into the woman you want to be." He took her hand and squeezed it lightly.

"Nice to meet you," Denise said. "I guess you already know I'm Denise, and who do you think I want to be?"

"You want to be in charge, have the power, rule your sex life, leaving no room for argument from your husband. You want to dominate him in the bedroom, and have him enjoy serving you. I can do that for you, by being both your teacher and your first subject. I will instruct you, and then give you the thrill of knowing how you'll feel with a man who's subservient, subject to your will."

He watched Denise rub her damp palms down the thighs of her slender, black skirt. Her breathing was shallow and rapid and he could see her pulse pound in her neck. "Can you really do all that?"

"I wouldn't be here if I couldn't." She smiled at that, and they settled down on a small sofa to one side of the room. "You're paying enough to ensure it. I have only one rule. If we do anything, or talk about doing anything, that you can't or won't do, you have only to say so. However, don't reject something because you think you shouldn't, or he couldn't, or it's not nice. Only speak if something repels you or you know it will be repellant to your husband. Agreed?"

"Okay. That sounds reasonable."

"Enough of reasonable," he said. "This concerns only what you want. Do you know what you want?"

"I think I do."

"What do you want?" Rock asked patiently. He needed to be sure she understood.

"I want to be in charge of our lovemaking. Mine and Walt's.

I want him to do what I tell him, when I tell him. He wants that too."

"What about outside the bedroom?"

"Outside?"

"Do you want him to do the dishes? Cook? Clean? Or is this just in bed?"

She paused and seemed to be considering. "I've read about master/slave type relationships and that's not exactly what I want. It's just in the bedroom."

"All right. We'll concentrate on that. Denise, let's begin with this. It's attitude. It's all attitude. Right now you see me as a sort of even-tempered, teacher type of guy, not necessarily much in the domination department. Right?" When Denise didn't answer, he continued, "Be honest. If you can't be honest here, then it's all over."

"Okay. Yes. That's the way you seem."

Rock, who had been lounging beside her as they spoke, stood up and straightened his back and squared his shoulders. Something in his expression hardened and he looked deeply into Denise's eyes. Everything about his demeanor changed in an instant. "Stand!"

Denise stood. "Straighten up and don't stand like a wimp!" She squared her shoulders and sucked in her stomach. Rock watched her for a very long moment, but she didn't relax. Then his body softened and his shoulders dropped. "See what I mean?" he said softly. "It's all in the attitude. You want to dominate your husband. So do it. Become a strong, powerful woman, first in your mind, then in your body language. We'll take care of the rest."

She grinned, then straightened and stood, not ramrod straight, but tall and almost stately. Rock stopped to have a good look at her. Denise was short, maybe about five-two, and slender, with an angular face and ear-length, brown, wavy hair. As he watched her body stiffen, he knew that she'd be as quick a learner as Jenna had been. "Remember," he continued, "it's all in the attitude."

"Attitude," she said. Then louder, "Attitude." She took a deep breath and nodded. "Like what?"

Rock crossed the room and opened the door to a large closet. "Here we'll make you appear as the woman you want to be." He looked her over and then rummaged in the closet for a moment. He pulled out several hangers and handed the clothing to her. All she could see was that everything was either red or black. "Try these. If anything doesn't fit, let me know and I'll adjust the size, but I think it will all be about right." He and Jenna had ascertained Denise's size, then gone shopping at a local erotic boutique. The cost of the clothing had been included in the fee they'd collected.

"Where can I change?" Denise asked, looking around.

Rock laughed. "Why, right here, of course. You've got to be proud of your body, both clothed and naked. It has to show in every line, every gesture." Rock took her hands in his. "You can do anything, make Walt do anything that gives you pleasure. He wants to serve you. Your body is the seat of his pleasures. Be proud of it, not for what it is, but for the way Walt perceives it."

"Right." With increasing comfort she took off her clothes and sorted out the garments Rock had given her. First, a red, leather bra with demi-cups that lifted and increased her cleavage, then black leather split-crotch panties with ties that fastened the sides over her hip bones, and, finally, black, thigh-high stockings with lacy tops and black boots with four-inch heels.

As she finished zipping up the boots, Rock took her shoulders and turned her toward a full-length mirror. "This woman can do anything."

She gasped as Rock admired his selections. She looked like something out of a porn magazine. "Yes," she sighed. "Oh, yes."

"We need to do a few things before you finish dressing. Come inside." He led her to the room next door, set up as a doctor's office, with an exam table in the center set up with gynecological-type stirrups. "Remove your panties, sit there and put your legs into the supports."

She climbed onto the table and wiggled until she found a comfortable position. "Now, let's take the next step in both your appearance and attitude." He moved a five-wheeled stool until he could sit between her thighs. With a small scissors, he clipped her pubic hair very short. "Now, I'm going to make you over into the woman you dream of being."

He positioned a mirror so she could watch what he did. As she gazed at the man, working so diligently between her legs, he washed her thoroughly, and then slowly shaved all of her pubic hair except a small patch in the front. "It's a heart," she said.

"Yes. And I'll give you some instructions to keep this from troubling your skin. As often as you like, even daily if you want, have your husband do this for you." He dried her, then smoothed on a soothing lotion. "This is not only good for the skin, but your husband will learn to love the taste."

"Taste," she said, her voice almost strangled. "I love oral sex, but Walt usually only licks for a moment or two."

"You'll change that immediately. Not only will he give you what you want, but he'll learn very quickly to enjoy it as much as you do."

"He will?"

Rock looked up and raised an eyebrow. "Attitude."

Denise grinned. "He will!"

"Yes, he'll love the taste the way I do." Rock poured more lotion on Denise's mound, then slowly began to lick her now swollen clit. He slowly moved his tongue until it reached all the places that felt so wonderful. Then he lifted his head. "Feel good?"

"Yes. Oh, yes."

"Then why did you let me stop?"

"Let you stop?"

"Yes. Remember your new persona. You're in charge. It's what both you and your husband want. So be in charge."

Denise hesitated, then said, softly, "Don't stop."

"Excuse me?" Rock said.

Denise took a deep breath. "I said, don't stop!"

"No, ma'am." Rock's mouth returned to her clit.

He teased but went no further than licking her. Eventually, she'd realize that she wanted more. It would be up to her to get it.

Finally, she said, "Put your fingers inside of me."

"Yes, ma'am. Anything you want. Should I keep tonguing your clit too?"

"Yes," she said, her voice stronger. "Do that too."

His fingers found her opening and, slowly, one finger slid into her sopping channel. "Not enough. You're too gentle. Do it hard!"

"Yes, ma'am." He slammed his fingers into her and, at the same time, sucked her clit into his mouth. Over and over he thrust his fingers into her channel. He knew that she didn't want to come, but he gave her no choice. She let go. Strong spasms claimed her pussy, clenching his hand, and her hips bucked, pressing his mouth more firmly against her mound. As he slowly withdrew, she shuddered, then calmed.

"You're content with only one orgasm?" he asked.

"Oh, that's usually enough for me."

"Enough? Ridiculous. It's never enough. You should be capable of many climaxes and of demanding your husband's services until you're exhausted. That's another thing we'll have to work on, but I think you're getting the idea. I'll let you rest for a few minutes, then you'll have another lesson. By the time you get home you'll be ready for anything." He grinned. "Or maybe you'll be too tired and make him wait until tomorrow."

"Oh, yes," Denise said, catching her breath, already excited by the thought of coming again. "I'm certainly getting the idea."

"Good. Next, we'll work on your makeup, then we'll continue with how to treat your husband, and finally complete your orgasmic training."

Jenna stood at the door of a room on the third floor and watched Walt as he sat on the edge of the bed. She was dressed in a red leather bra and shorts set, stockings with high, red boots and long, fingerless, red leather gloves that ended above her elbows. Her makeup was severe and her hair was pulled back tightly and heavily moussed.

From what she could see, Walt was of medium height and build, with graying hair and deep laugh lines around his mouth. He was slumped slightly, his elbows braced on his thighs, hands clasped between them. She squared her shoulders, remembered all of Rock's lessons, and knew she could do this. "No one told you, you could sit!" she barked. Reflexively, Walt stood. "Better, but not good. Eyes down. You may look at me only when I give permission. Is that understood?"

"I guess so."

"Wrong answer!" she snarled. "The only correct answers here are *yes, ma'am* and *no, ma'am*. Nothing more. Is that understood?"

"Yes."

"You're hopeless. I'm leaving!" Jenna knew he wouldn't let her go. He wanted this as much as his wife did. He just didn't know the rules yet.

"Please, no. I mean, *no, ma'am*. I can learn."

"Can you?"

"Oh, yes, ma'am," he said, his breathing rapid, his cock hardening just from her voice.

"You will do exactly what you're told. No more and no less. Is that understood?"

"Yes, ma'am."

"Kneel!"

Trembling from both fear and excitement, Walt hesitated only a moment, then he dropped to his knees.

"Not bad. There might be hope for you yet. Now strip."

This was a test of sorts and Walt looked dubious. She'd let him make the final decision. Would he undress in front of a stranger? Jenna watched his mind work, then he pulled his sweatshirt off over his head and tossed it onto a chair. He pulled his belt from the loops on his jeans and it followed his shirt. As he started to get up to remove his pants, the woman said, "Did I tell you, you could stand?"

"No, ma'am."

"Well then . . ."

Walt knelt back down, slipped off his loafers and socks, then struggled to pull off his jeans without getting up. Finally, he maneuvered them off, and, finally, with a few more wiggles, his shorts. Jenna smiled. He was actually embarrassed by the fact that he was fully erect, his cock sticking straight out from his groin. When he started to look at her, she snapped, "Eyes down." She knew that not only did he have to get used to keeping his eyes averted but he would be forced to look at his erection.

"Good. Now you will listen carefully while I outline the position you will assume at all times unless told otherwise. You will stand, feet apart, hands clasped behind your back, eyes on the floor. Your dick belongs to your wife or whoever else wants you, as does your mouth. Your hands will not touch your cock unless you are told to. Is that understood?"

Jenna watched his cock stiffen still more as her words aroused him. At the start she hadn't been sure how she'd feel being in charge, but she found she loved it. The power was, as Rock had said, a great aphrodisiac. "Yes, ma'am."

"What are you waiting for?"

Walt stood, mortified at the sight of his erection bobbing in front of him. He clasped his hands behind him, unable to cover his cock. He stared at the floor and waited. "That's quite good, actually," Jenna said. "Now just wait there. I'll be back. And don't move."

From behind him, she closed the door loudly but remained silently standing in the corner of the room, knowing how much he needed to come. Hesitantly, he unclasped his hands, reached down and grasped his cock. "I knew you couldn't be trusted," she said.

"I thought you left," Walt said, obviously knowing that he was violating the rules speaking to her. "Ma'am," he added, trying to save himself.

"This was a little test, and you flunked. Big time." She moved around behind him and pressed her breasts against his back. "Your wife paid to have you trained so I won't just boot you out, although I'm not sure there's any hope for you. Can you learn?"

Dejectedly, Walt said, "Yes, ma'am. I'm really sorry, ma'am."

"That will do for starters. Now here's another little test. You need to hold your cock, do you? Okay. Hold it. Feel how hard and hot it is in your hand. But just know this. If you come, there will be punishment. Serious, severe punishment. It might be the whip, or the paddle. No. You'd enjoy that. Maybe we'll just send you home, back to your humdrum, little life. Of course your wife will be ready to play my part, but she won't do it with you. She can stay here and act out her fantasies with men more reliable than you. Is that what you want?"

"Oh, no, ma'am."

"Then hold your cock. Are you right handed?"

"Yes, ma'am," Walt said, sounding puzzled.

"Then hold it with your left hand." Walt wrapped his fingers around his cock. Jenna assumed that he masturbated from time to time, but he undoubtedly used his right hand. Holding his cock now with his left hand would feel different, more like someone else, both on his hand and on his cock.

"Now, stroke it. Rub it just the way you do when you need to come, but don't you dare come." When he hesitated, she snapped, "Do it!"

As he rubbed, Jenna smiled, watching his discomfort as he tried to detach his mind from his hand and his dick, but she knew it was oh, so difficult. Rock had told her about this little game. He was a genius. "I'll come if I keep this up," he moaned.

"You have to learn control. Once you belong to your mistress, she'll tell you when you're allowed to come."

He kept stroking, gritting his teeth and biting his lip to keep his orgasm from bubbling out of his balls. "All right," she said. "I'll let you off the hook for now. Put your hands behind your back again and let's get you dressed properly."

She rummaged in a drawer, then held a black, leather thong with a small pouch for his penis and testicles, dangling from her long, bright red–painted fingernail. "Put this on."

As he fastened the Velcro straps at the sides and struggled to get the rear strap between his cheeks, she continued, "Your mistress might want ball spreaders or a cock ring, but this will do for now." He arranged his stiff erection inside the pouch and tucked his balls into their small pocket. The pouch was too small for him and he vainly tried to get comfortable. "Don't bother. I deliberately selected one several sizes too small so you'll always be conscious of your genitals. Hands behind you now."

He obeyed, staring past the bulging leather his cock created to his bare toes, which dug into the carpet as he tried to quiet his need to climax. "Your wife favors men with hairless chests. We can take care of that."

"She does?"

"Did I say you could speak?"

"No, ma'am."

Jenna spread a quick-acting lotion that Rock had suggested over his skin. "Just a few minutes and you'll be smooth as a baby's ass." After a few minutes, she guided him to a bathroom where she rinsed off all the lotion, chest hair and all.

"Now look at yourself," she said, her finger beneath his chin. He raised his eyes and saw himself in the full-length mirror on the wall of the bathroom. His chest was smooth and the black pouch stood out against his white skin. He looked pretty proud of himself, Jenna noticed. That was okay. He needed a bit of confidence too.

"Are you ready to serve?"

"Yes, ma'am," he said with enthusiasm.

"I like a man's hands on me so you're going to give me a massage." She pulled off her gloves, boots and stockings, and stretched out on her stomach on the bed, handing him a bottle of body oil. "Rub all the nonsexy places first and, if you do well, I'll let you get me off. Of course, if you do *that* well, I might, just might, let you get off too."

When he didn't begin immediately, she barked, "Get to it!"

He took the bottle of oil and covered his hands with it, rubbing them together to get the oil warm. Then he worked from the bottom of her body upward, beginning with her feet and legs, deep strokes using the heels of his hands and his thumbs, followed by feather-light caresses with the tips of his fingers. "You're very good at that," Jenna purred.

"I'm glad I can serve, ma'am."

Jenna nodded. He was learning quickly. He moved to her hands and arms, keeping the entire thing nonsexual. He kneaded her shoulders and pressed his way down her spine around the back of her bra.

"Unhook the bra and continue," she said, and he did as she asked, now able to use long strokes on her smooth flesh. "My ass too," she said, and he pressed and squeezed her cheeks.

"You do that really well. There's hope for you after all." She turned over, removing her bra and unsnapping the leather panties. "Breasts first, and, when I get really wet, you may rub my pussy."

He poured oil directly on Jenna's skin, then swirled his fingers from her ribs to her nipples, and blew a stream of cool air on them and watched them pucker. Over and over, he teased her tits. "May I suck them, ma'am?" he asked.

"I think so," she said. "I like it when a slave sucks my tits."

He lowered his head until he could take one now erect nipple in his mouth. He licked, sucked and bit until Jenna rewarded him with a moan. "Now my cunt," she said. "I'm ready for you to rub my pussy with those very talented hands. Make me come."

He added more oil and she was glad that he knew just where to touch. He squeezed her inner lips and pinched her flesh lightly. He tapped on her erect clit and probably used every trick he knew to push her over the edge, but she held back, not wanting him to make her come too easily. He needed to learn that climaxes take work.

"This *was* a test," she said, laughing, "and you passed. I almost came from your fingers alone and that's very rare. Actually, I can't come without a mouth on me and a big dildo fucking my snatch." She motioned toward the dresser at the side of the room. "In the drawer."

He returned with a long, thick dildo, which he touched to her opening. He rubbed the tip over her flesh, sliding over her hard clit again and again. Then, when she was writhing, he rammed the dildo into her and covered the front of her slit with his mouth. It took only moments until she screamed and climaxed. He was really good at giving pleasure, Jenna thought. His wife was a lucky woman.

As Jenna sat up, Walt put his hands behind his back and lowered his gaze to the floor.

"You're really all right. Would you like to come?" She saw that his cock was hard as stone and probably painful from his need for release.

"Only if it pleases you, ma'am," he hissed through gritted teeth.

She laughed. "You are a fast learner and I can see that you do need it. Well, you may do something about it. Use the oil and make your hands slippery. Then massage your cock so I can watch you jerk off. When you spurt, cover my tits with your cum, then rub it in. It's good for the skin, you know."

"Oh, yes, ma'am." He poured a small pool of oil into his palm then went to work on his cock. Jenna smiled as she watched him wrap the fingers of his left hand around the base, then squeeze as he pulled toward the head. He stroked his balls with his other hand, his eyes watching her stare at his fingers. Soon he couldn't prevent his orgasm and it boiled from his balls and erupted onto his mistress's breasts. Spurt after spurt of thick creamy cum splashed on her beautiful tits. His hands still oily, he spread his jism on her skin as she brought herself to another climax.

"Assume your position," she said, long minutes later. He stood tall, his clasped hands behind his back, and looked down. "Very good. Very good, indeed. I'll recommend you to your next mistress, Mistress Denise. I'm sure she's learned her lessons as well as you have. Tonight, after you leave here, you'll have your first lesson with Mistress Denise since she's completed her training. Obey her as you would me. Is that clear?"

"Mistress Denise," he mumbled. "Oh, yes, ma'am."

"Give her the same pleasures you gave me and I'm sure she will be well pleased."

"Oh, yes, ma'am. I will please her. It's my job."

Chapter
14

The work on the dungeon in the basement had been finished for several weeks and Chloe had already used it, with Rock and his friends and with a few clients. Finally Rock and Jenna had a chance to, as Rock put it, "christen it." Since Club Fantasy was closed on Mondays and Tuesdays, Rock had set everything up for the beginning of the third week in January. "The guys who helped me build it," Rock had explained to Jenna, "are going to play with us. It's their payment for the work they did, in addition to getting to use the room themselves from time to time, of course."

Jenna had a bit of hesitation about doing "dungeon things," whatever that meant exactly, with strangers, but then she laughed at herself. She did kinky things with strangers all the time, and Rock would be with her to insure that nothing got out of hand. She'd played both dominant and submissive, but she'd never played with more than one person at a time so this would be another new experience. Sometimes her mind boggled at how far a thirty-something from Upstate New York had traveled in the past eight months. She loved it, but frequently lamented that she couldn't tell the two most important people in her world about the Club. Marcy was too much of a prude and Glen couldn't be expected to deal with it.

For the evening, Rock had suggested that she dress in undies only, so she wore a deep blue, satin bra with matching bikini panties. Her legs and feet were bare. As she took one last look at herself in the bathroom mirror on the third floor, she grinned, sucked in her stomach, and thrust her breasts forward.

Rock met her at the door of the motel room and guided her downstairs. As they approached the door to the basement, Rock said, "One last and most important thing. The safe word is *Marigold*. Say it."

"Marigold."

"You've already agreed to playing with several guys, but it's vital that I know that you won't play martyr. I understand that you're a professional but your reputation isn't at stake here, and even if it were, there are lots of games we can play and still stay within your personal limits. Promise me that if anything gets uncomfortable for any reason you will say that word. If you won't agree to that we can't feel free to play any way we choose. All the guys know the safe word and will stop if you say it, without hesitation."

"I understand." Jenna's heart was pounding with a delicious combination of fear and anticipation. She trusted Rock implicitly and that was the only reason why she would play.

Rock opened the basement door and together they walked down the stairs to the room at the bottom. As they descended, she realized immediately that the slightly cool, musty atmosphere had been replaced with warmth and a slight antiseptic smell mingling with the odors of new wood and incense.

Jenna looked around curiously, surprised that there was nothing medieval about the room. Two of the walls were paneled in dark wood while the other two were covered with mirrored tiles, as was the ceiling, all reflecting the light from several ceiling fixtures and standing lamps. Jenna was surprised how bright the room was. Hooks of all sizes and at varying heights protruded from one wall and hung from the ceiling by chains of differing lengths. Whips, crops, and paddles of all sizes and shapes were displayed on the walls. She knew, of course, what they would be used for, but tonight? Was she ready for heavy stuff?

Areas of the floor were carpeted while others had shiny white tile. On one side of the room stood a table unlike anything Jenna had ever seen before, with rings and hooks along the sides and an enclosed space beneath containing who knew what. There were several cabinets along another wall, topped with highly polished counters, and a few closets, as yet empty, with their doors open. One contained hanging space, another about a dozen drawers. Everything made her wonder what they did or would contain. Cock rings and ball spreaders? Hoods and gags? Ropes? Nipple clamps, dildos and vibrators? Chains with large padlocks? She remembered someone once using the term *delicious fear.* Perhaps that was what she was feeling.

Two men dressed only in jeans sat on bar stools along one wall, holding wine glasses. One was a striking-looking, blond wrestler-type with a large gold hoop earring in one ear and a tattoo of a dragon circling one entire arm. The other man was surprisingly innocuous-looking, paunchy, with thinning, brown hair, and wearing rimless glasses with Coke-bottle lenses. A heavy set, dark-haired woman dressed only in a pale pink, breastless bustier and stiletto heels, sat at his feet with her head in his lap. As Jenna crossed the room she was greeted with light applause. "She's first rate," the blond said.

Rock shook hands with each of the men, introducing Jenna as Hillary Oakes. "This is Wayne," he said, as the man with the earring extended his hand. Wayne took Jenna's fingers and held them to his lips. As she smiled, he turned her hand over and circled the palm with his tongue, then lightly bit the tip of her thumb.

Rock shifted his attention to the other man. "This is Paul and his lady Diana." Paul nodded and tousled Diana's hair.

"Glad you could be here," Rock said. "And Diana, it's good to see you."

"I'm glad Paul brought me," she said, her voice soft and breathy. As Jenna's gaze flicked to her, she grinned. "This room is just fabulous. Paul had told me a lot about it but I never imagined it would turn out this perfectly." She squeezed Paul's thigh. "He did all the electrical work and the plumbing. He's so talented, don't you think, Rock?"

"I certainly do."

"I hope we can arrange to use the room from time to time," Paul said.

"Of course. It's going to be busy most evenings, but the house is closed Mondays and Tuesdays so if you make arrangements in advance we'll certainly make it available."

"I can already think of so many things to do here," Wayne said, leering.

As they crossed the room, Rock said, sotto voce, "I didn't know Paul was bringing Diana, Hillary. She might want to play with us. Is that okay with you? I know you didn't want Chloe here so don't be embarrassed to say no. This is my party and I can direct the activities away from anything you don't want to do."

Chloe was too much like a sister so playing with her would have felt incestuous. Jenna thought about playing with another woman and wasn't sure how she felt. Since she knew that she could call things off at any time, she decided to go along for now. If she hadn't trusted Rock, and by extension his friends, she wouldn't have agreed. She nodded.

Rock led her across the room toward a strange-looking X-shaped device that stood against one wall. It was almost as tall as she was, with fastenings of various types at the ends of each arm. Rock removed her bra and panties. Jenna watched the men's eyes as they stared appreciatively at her breasts. "Nice tits," the blond said. "Don't you agree, Paul?"

"Definitely. What do you think?" he asked the woman seated at his feet.

"She looks just delicious." The two man laughed at her choice of words. Delicious. *Hmmm*, Jenna thought.

Rock showed Jenna the X-frame. "Wayne built this for me," he said, motioning to the blond man, "to my specifications. Now we get to see how well it works. Notice that each of the four arms is moveable to any position and adjustable to any length. Let me demonstrate." Rock pressed her against a small padded area in the middle of her back, where the four arms joined, and fastened a nine-inch-wide strip of elastic around her waist and around the frame. The tight wrap was somehow erotic, something Jenna would remember for her clients. Rapidly Rock fastened her wrists and ankles to the ends of the frame, arms and legs splayed. She found she was a bit apprehensive. Was that part of the pleasure?

Rock placed a marble in her palm then leaned close to her ear. "There won't be anything terribly heavy tonight. I didn't think you'd be up to that yet." She didn't know exactly what she was ready for, either. "Remember what this is for?" he asked as he closed her fingers around the marble.

She didn't know why they were whispering, but she lowered her voice. "I'll drop it if I have any problems with anything anyone does."

"Good girl. No one has to know and you don't have to be embarrassed if anything disturbs you. This is supposed to be pleasure for everyone. If it isn't we'll stop and I'll take the responsibility. Okay?"

She nodded. Since she *was* in the business and in some way she had been trying to impress Rock's friends, she might not want to admit out loud that some activity made her uncomfortable. She began to click through activities that could be planned, but then she stopped and just allowed herself to roll with it. She squeezed the marble.

Rock pulled up a wide, padded rest for her head and attached her forehead to it with more elastic. She was in no discomfort, but she was totally immobile, naked and spread wide for anyone's pleasure.

"One of the things I want you to learn tonight," he said to her, loud enough for everyone to hear, "is how it feels to be more aroused than you've ever been, yet be unable to do anything about it—to be dependent on someone else to bring you to climax. I want you totally dependent on us for your satisfaction." Rock turned to the two men. "We're here to satisfy all your fantasies and Wayne, Paul, and I have discussed a few. Rock sounded like a professor giving a lecture to a room full of freshmen. *No*, Jenna thought, *rather like a carnival barker*. "I've used them to plan this evening. All things are possible here at Club Fantasy so if you desire an additional pleasure, let me know."

He took something from a small drawer, then returned his attention to the audience. As he walked toward Jenna, she saw that he held a small vial with a cork stopper. "I picked up this oil on a trip to Asia." He withdrew the stopper and, with his finger over the mouth of the bottle, inverted it. "It's an interesting substance." He rubbed his oily finger over Jenna's lips. "Tell me what you feel."

"It's getting slightly warm," she said, reflexively licking her lips.

"It does get warm," he said, "and more. It's a mixture of herbs, ground up bark from a tree that only grows—" He laughed. "Well it only grows somewhere. This vial cost me a small fortune but I think you'll see that it's worth it. Hillary? Are you feeling a bit aroused?"

"Yes," she said, but she wasn't sure she was more aroused than she had been merely because of the situation.

"Good. It's supposed to be an aphrodisiac but, of course, who ever knows since so much of arousal is mental. Maybe Hillary is getting hot knowing what the oil is supposed to do.

I've never done a double-blind, scientific study." He shrugged. "Well, who really cares as long as it works?"

He moistened his finger again and rubbed it over Jenna's left nipple. Whether it was mental or physical, she quickly felt the heat as it flowed from her breast to her vagina. It felt like liquid wax coursing through her veins, heating, exciting.

Rock walked over to the woman who sat at Paul's feet, and raised an eyebrow. "Sure, I'd love to try it," she said, and Rock spread a bit of the oil on her nipples, which tightened almost immediately. As she watched, Jenna felt the warmth spread, seeming to flow directly to her pussy. She felt her tissues swell still more and her juices trickle down into the crack between her ass cheeks.

"Has Diana ever made it with a woman?" Rock asked.

"Have you?" Paul asked.

"Oh, sure," she said. "If it's sexy, I've done it."

"Diana and I have only been going together for a few weeks but I can tell you that she's a very open-minded kind of woman," Paul said proudly, reaching down and palming one breast.

"This sounds like my kind of party," Wayne said. "As I told you, Rock, watching two women is one of my favorite fantasies." He adjusted his jeans to make his cock more comfortable.

"Mine too," Paul said.

"I had a few other things in mind for tonight but since Diana is here, why not fulfill a few fantasies."

Rock flicked a glance at Jenna and she knew he was wondering whether she'd drop the marble. She didn't. She'd go with it. Tonight all things were possible.

Jenna found herself getting hotter and hotter. Was it the oil or the atmosphere? "The oil is perfectly safe," Rock said, "but it's even more of an aphrodisiac when taken internally." He reached down and took Diana's hand, guiding her to a standing position, then over to where Jenna lay, totally unable to move. "Suck!" he said. Although his tone was gentle, there was something powerful in his words. Diana leaned over and took Jenna's nipple in her mouth.

This was a woman, Jenna thought, closing her eyes. She expected to feel something unusual but, to her surprise, it didn't feel unlike the men who'd done it to her. Maybe she should be repelled at the idea but she found she wasn't. It just was. As the dark-haired woman suckled, Rock spread oil on Jenna's other nipple and she found her arousal growing. God, she was hungry. She desperately wanted to rub her clit to relieve the need, but she didn't have the use of her hands. She could only feel and grind her hips.

"I'm going to spread just a little of this on your cunt, Hillary. Can you imagine how it will feel?"

She doubted that she could get any hungrier, but she quickly found that she was wrong. The heat inside her was a flame now, threatening to consume her as he spread a bit of the oil on her sopping flesh, then stood back and smiled. "Tell me, Hillary."

"I want, need, I don't know. I can't think of anything except my pussy. Please, fill it for me."

"Not just yet." He guided Diana to a spot between the legs of the frame, pushed her to her knees, and the woman quickly went to work on Jenna's cunt. Her tongue was wonderful, softer somehow, seeming to know exactly where Jenna needed it. She licked the length of her slit, then pushed the tip of her tongue into her. Diana actually fucked her with her tongue.

"Look up, Hillary," Rock said and she opened her eyes. The mirrored ceiling reflected the brown hair of the woman whose mouth was working so hard between her legs. She could also see the rapt attention the two other men paid to the scene being played out for their delight. As Jenna watched, Diana reached up and pulled at her nipples, her mouth not stopping its ministrations.

For what seemed like forever, Diana kept sucking and soon

her fingers joined, filling Jenna's passage and rubbing her clit. She wanted to hold back, prolong the intensely erotic moments, but she couldn't. Screaming, she came, colors soaring, spearing, flashing in all directions. Orange and electric blue swirled through her brain. Over and over she felt the spasms clench deep in her belly. With Diana's mouth on her, she felt like she could keep climaxing indefinitely.

Rock pulled the woman from her and tipped the frame so that Jenna's head was level with Diana's crotch. "She's in just as much need as you are, Hillary," Rock said. "Help her."

Jenna buried her mouth in Diana's crotch and licked. Since she'd never done anything like this before, she just thought about what she liked and did the same. From the woman's moaning she realized that she must be doing something right.

"Shit," one of the men said, "that's quite a sight." She couldn't see the mirrored ceiling, but she heard rustling, and then a mouth was on each breast as her tongue found Diana's erotic places.

"The oil is wonderful on the cock," Rock said. "It increases the size and hardness of the erection. I've tried it myself several times."

From the sounds, she imagined everyone stripping, then Rock painting the oil on the two men's eager cocks. "Since you can't fuck Hillary's pussy without a condom, how about this way." Jenna felt a cock in each hand and, as she sucked on Diana's clit, she used her fingers to spread the oil, and then called on all her skill to give the two men the best hand jobs she could.

The room reeked of sex. Grunts, growls, and moans filled her ears as she allowed the intense pleasure to overwhelm her. Eventually, everyone left her alone. As she watched in the ceiling, Diana got on her hands and knees, lowing herself onto Paul's rigid shaft while Wayne fucked her from behind.

"I told them that I wanted the pleasure of bringing you your ultimate orgasm. Jenna," Rock whispered. Calling her by her right name increased the intimacy as he removed his clothing, adjusted the frame so that her pussy was at the right height for his staff, then, with a condom in place, rammed his cock home, holding her thighs tightly as he thrust deeply.

When he was lodged fully within her, Rock lay full length on top of her as he thrust, stretching his arms over hers, his face filling her vision. As he began slow strokes, she came one last time. Her orgasm seemed bigger than anything she'd ever experienced, but whether it was the erotic aura or the oil, she neither knew nor cared. Rock came soon after.

When he was done, Rock used a warm, wet cloth to wash the oil, juices, and sweat from her drenched body.

"That oil is quite something," she said to Rock later, after everyone else was gone.

"I'm glad it worked out this way," he said. "I had something different in mind but since Diana came along . . ."

"It was wonderful. I wasn't sure why I was so hot but I guess I didn't care. It was a powerful experience. I only hope I can give some of that to my clients."

"I'm sure you can, and do. Sex is really a lot of fun, isn't it?" Rock said, grinning.

"It certainly is."

Later she thought about her relationship with Rock. She ought to be confused. She had very special feelings for Glen but couldn't have a relationship with him because of what she was, and she cared for Rock but it was all friendship and lust. How she knew the differences she wasn't sure, but she knew.

Chapter
15

Marcy saw it all, felt it all that night. Faces, men with huge erections, hands on bare breasts and penises. A woman with her mouth doing unspeakable things—things that felt exciting, arousing, but were so wrong. She was struggling, trying to get up but she couldn't. Her wrists and ankles were bound. She tried to scream but no sound escaped. She was being violated and there was nothing she could do about it. Through it all, the same face she'd seen before filled her mind. Bald, dark, with a diamond in his ear.

She sat bolt upright, panting, sweat pouring from her body. She was both terrified and aroused. It was a dream, she told herself, it was a dream. But it felt very real, so real that she couldn't slow her heartbeat or breathing. So real. She looked at the clock. It was almost 3:00 A.M. She needed to call Jenna. Maybe she was in trouble. Maybe this was that twin thing they had always kidded about but couldn't deny, either. She had to call her sister. She reached for the phone, but then let her hand drop. This was silly. Jenna was home, asleep. It was just a nightmare.

She rubbed her thigh where the woman's hands had touched her, then looked down, almost surprised to see the same white, flabby flesh. She threaded her fingers through her hair, then lay back down, knowing she wouldn't get back to sleep.

At seven in the morning, she dressed and made herself a pot of coffee. When she couldn't wait any longer, she pressed the quick-dial button to call Jenna. "We're sorry, the subscriber you've called does not answer. Please try your call again later."

Damn. She's turned the phone off or she's in a dead spot. Maybe she'd let the batteries drain as she often did. It's nothing to worry about. Marcy paced the floor of the kitchen, staring out at the snow falling on the yard, then tried Jenna again. She couldn't shake the dream and the belief that Jenna was in some kind of trouble. "We're sorry—" She pressed 'end.' By eight-thirty, she was dressed for work, but then she reconsidered and called in sick. She was getting more frantic by the moment, all the time telling herself she was being silly. Silly or not, she couldn't shake the fears or the dream.

By nine, she had tried Jenna's number a dozen times with the same results. "Okay," she told herself. "I'm obsessing. This is ridiculous. Jenna's fine." With those thoughts in mind, she changed into warmer clothes, climbed into her car, and headed for Manhattan.

Six hours and several dozen, useless, phone attempts later, she parked in a garage on East Fifty-second Street and walked through an inch of slush to the brownstone. The man who opened the door was huge, tall and muscular, with a completely shaved head, striking blue eyes and an eerily familiar diamond stud in his left ear. He was dressed all in black, but then she somehow knew he would be. Although she had never met him, she knew him. She'd seen him often in her dreams. "May I help you?" he asked.

"I'm looking for Jenna. Jenna Bryant." When he seemed about to close the door in her face, she added, "Please. I'm Marcy. Marcy Bryant."

The smile on his face changed him from a menacing figure to a . . . Well, now he was a smiling menace. "Yes, of course.

Now I see it," he said. "You're her twin sister." He held out his hand. "I'm Rock. I'm so glad to finally meet you. I've heard a lot about you." Ushering her inside, he took her coat and hung it in the closet.

The house looked the same as it had when she'd visited over Labor Day weekend, but who was this giant? "Is she here?"

"I'm sorry, she won't be in for at least an hour. Is there something I can do?"

"Where is she?"

Looking suddenly wary, Rock said, "Maybe I ought to let her explain that."

"Explain what? I don't understand." He seemed so at home in Jenna and Chloe's house. "Are you visiting?" she asked.

He seemed puzzled. "I live here."

Now Marcy was completely confused. "I thought my sister lived here."

The doorbell rang and Rock moved to answer it. He admitted a tall, good-looking man with carefully blow-dried, totally white hair. The man looked her over. Marcy was wearing her standard outfit, an oversized, black sweatshirt with a black turtleneck shirt beneath, and matching sweat pants. "I guess I'm a little early," the man said. "You're not dressed."

"Me?"

"No, Mr. Phillips," Rock said gently, "she's not your partner this evening. Melissa is waiting for you upstairs in the living room."

"Oh." Mr. Phillips looked Marcy over again. "I'm sorry. I like women with meat on their bones," he said. "If you're free next time I come, miss, I'd love to have you."

Marcy was so puzzled that she kept silent as Rock showed Mr. Phillips up the stairs. When Rock returned, he said, "I'm sorry for the interruption. If you'd like to wait in the living room, I'm sure Jenna will be here within an hour. She's got someone at six."

"Got someone?"

"I think I've said more than enough," Rock said, his cheeks coloring slightly. "Maybe you should wait for her."

While she waited, a lovely looking woman arrived, kissed Rock on both cheeks, and disappeared up the stairs, followed only a few minutes later by a rumpled man in a leather coat and jeans. "She's in the motel room," he told the man.

It didn't take a rocket scientist to figure out what must be going on. Her dream. The men and women coming and going. This was a whorehouse, and Jenna must be part of it. Another couple arrived, and Rock guided them to something called a Western room. Marcy seethed. Her sister was a whore. There couldn't be any other answer. But it couldn't be. She knew her sister and she wouldn't do a thing like that. There must be something she was overlooking. This can't be what it seems. Maybe it's something Chloe's doing and Jenna had to move out because of it. Yeah, that must be it. But why didn't Jenna tell her about it? And what about the man called Rock who'd disappeared up the stairs?

She stood, paced, then sat back down. She fiddled with her purse, then went to the tiny bathroom in the hall. She didn't dare go anywhere else in the building. Who knew what was going on? Finally, about three quarters of an hour after she arrived, Marcy heard a key in the front door. Wondering where she should be when Jenna walked in, she stood, then sat, then stood again and walked toward the door. If she hadn't been so upset she would have been amused at the shocked expression on Jenna's face as she walked in.

"Marcy," Jenna said, dropping her pocketbook on the floor and splaying her hand over her chest. "You scared the hell out of me. What are you doing here?"

Marcy rushed forward and hugged her sister, then held her at arms length and stared at her from head to foot. She wasn't hurt, although she'd been assaulted the previous evening. Or had she? "I scared *you?* I was terrified. You're all right."

"Of course I'm all right. Why wouldn't I be?"

"I thought you'd been hurt, then I tried to call over and over and I couldn't reach you."

"Shit. I'm sorry. I must have left my phone here, turned off."

Marcy stalked into the living room, then back to the entrance way. "I drove all day, terrified that something had happened to you." She couldn't decide what made her angrier, the fact that Jenna was okay or that she'd been so frightened by her dream.

"What's gotten into you, Sis?" Jenna said, looking mystified. "We've been out of touch before and it's never freaked you out like this. If you'd just given it time, you'd have reached me. You know I misplace my phone now and then. And if you had left a message, I'd have called you back."

Through gritted teeth she hissed, "What had me freaked out, as you put it, is that I had one of those twin things we have occasionally, in the middle of the night last night. There was a woman with you, then you were being assaulted by a man who looked exactly like that bodybuilder type who says he lives here." By the time she reached the end of the sentence she was almost shrieking.

Jenna leaned back against the front door and Marcy watched her body deflate. "You met Rock?" she said softly.

After a deep breath, Marcy answered, her voice deceptively soft, "I met Rock. I also met a man named Phillips who said that if I was free the next time he came, he'd like to—how did he put it—have me. What the hell is going on?"

Jenna recovered her equilibrium enough to usher Marcy into the kitchen. In silence, Marcy sat down while Jenna put coffee on to brew. "If you're trying to figure out how to answer that question," Marcy said, as Jenna settled opposite her, "let me say that the truth would be refreshing." There was an acid tone to her voice that matched the taste of bile rising in her throat.

Jenna hung her head, then, as if she'd made up her mind about something, straightened up. "Marcy, I've wanted to tell you all about this for a long time but I was afraid of your reaction. I can see that keeping secrets was worse. We call this place Club Fantasy and I haven't lived her for a few months."

Club Fantasy? She stared at her sister, a woman she suddenly didn't know.

Jenna looked her straight in the eyes. "Men come to us to fulfill fantasies and we do a damned good job of it. Men who have nowhere else to go to live out things they've dreamed of all their lives come here and enjoy. We get well paid for it and both Chloe and I love what we're doing."

"You're a prostitute?" She wanted to say whore but that word sounded so disgusting. Prostitute sounded a bit less like some hooker hanging out on a street corner with a needle in her arm.

"I'm a woman who has sex with men for money," Jenna said softly.

Marcy stood and paced the length of the kitchen, unable to think clearly. This was her sister, her twin, a woman she'd been closer to than anyone, including their parents. This was a stranger. Her heart pounded and she couldn't catch her breath. She couldn't decide what name to put on what she was feeling. Disappointment? Embarrassment? No, too mild. Shock? Repugnance? Yes, and revulsion. "I don't even know you."

"I'm the same person who was bored in Seneca Falls and needed something new in my life."

"But, Jenna. My God. What's come over you?"

"I'm sorry you had to find out this way, Sis, but frankly, I'm not doing anything I'm ashamed of. You know that I love you and I want you to understand." She glanced at the clock on the front of the microwave. "I have a client in about fifteen minutes and I need to get ready." She rummaged around in the bottom of her purse. "Here's a spare key to my current apartment." She scrawled the address on a piece of paper. "Please. For me. Go over there and think about everything. Try to react with your brain, not with your heart. If we're going to part company let's do it after you have some time. Don't go back to Seneca Falls before we talk again. Please." Jenna stood and hugged her sister. "I'll be there around midnight."

Marcy put the key on the table. "I don't think so."

"Marcy, it can't end like this. Please." Before her sister had time to turn away, Jenna bent down and kissed her cheek. "I love you, Sis, and we have to talk but I can't continue this right now. I have an obligation to people who've paid a great deal of money and have expectations that I have to fulfill." With a heavy sigh, Jenna walked out through the kitchen door.

After Jenna left, Marcy sat at the kitchen table for a long time, playing and replaying their conversation. Jenna had treated it all like some kind of public service and it wasn't. Okay, so what was it? She tried to concentrate on the evils but she kept coming back to the rationality of all of Jenna's arguments. Her head spun.

At about nine, Rock walked in. "I see you're still here," he said gently.

Marcy stood and picked up her purse. "I was just leaving."

"Don't judge her too harshly, Marcy. She's a wonderful woman and it would be a shame for you two to go your separate ways without talking it all out."

"She told you?"

"Only the rudiments. She's devastated."

"I'm sure," she said, unable to hide her bitterness. Marcy glared at the huge man who she'd never seen before outside of her dreams. "And what the hell are you, a male prostitute?"

"Yes," he said softly, "and I'm very good at what I do."

Marcy could only gasp. A male hooker? It went against everything she'd ever considered. Women didn't need sex the way a man did, so why should they go to someone like him?

What was more deeply embarrassing was that she'd been attracted to him in her dreams. It was disgusting. She didn't understand any of it.

"Talk to her. Try to cut her a little slack." Rock poured himself a cup of coffee and left without another word.

Marcy picked up the key Jenna had left on the table. Rock was right about one thing. They did need to talk.

While Marcy was taking a taxi to Jenna's apartment, Jenna was in the doctor's office "examining" a new customer. It took all her concentration to play the part of a sexy doctor giving a man a physical. She managed to shove all her worries to the back of her mind and give the client everything he'd paid for. Although much of it was on autopilot, she must have done a good job since the man departed with a big smile and left her a hundred-dollar tip.

Later she entertained another customer in the second motel room, one they'd set up recently since the first one was occupied all the time, with a waiting list of men with fantasies that played there. By the time she grabbed a cab across town it was almost twelve-thirty. She'd checked the kitchen table, almost afraid to find her key still there, but it was gone. There was hope.

Jenna opened the door to her apartment and found her sister sitting in the living room deep in thought. "I'm glad you stayed," she said softly, draping her coat over a chair. She looked around for Marcy's but she quickly realized that her sister would have hung it in the closet.

"I never did find out what the hell happened last night." Marcy's voice was tight, her hands now fisted in her lap.

Marcy had used the word *hell*. *She must be in some state*, Jenna thought. Well, at least she hadn't rushed back to Seneca Falls. Maybe there was a chance to patch some of this up. It might never be the same as it had been, but maybe it wasn't totally ruined. She sat at the opposite end of the long sofa and tucked her legs beneath her, as usual a mirror image of her sister's pose.

What had happened last evening? How could she answer Marcy's question? I was part of an orgy? I fucked several men in several different ways? I had my first experience with a woman and got off on it? "I had a very enjoyable evening."

"Can it. I saw some of it, and felt some of it. You were raped."

"Actually, no, I wasn't."

"I couldn't move. You couldn't move. I can't sort it all out but there was all sorts of strange stuff going on. I know that much."

"Nothing happened last evening that I didn't want, didn't consent to and participate in willingly. There was nothing that I didn't totally enjoy."

"Enjoy? I saw you, no, felt you, tied down, grabbed here," she said, touching her upper thighs, "and more. I saw several men including that Rock guy."

"That's true."

"And a woman."

"Also true."

"Jenna, what's become of you?"

She sighed. Marcy would never understand, but she had to try. "I've learned to enjoy lots of off-center stuff with clients and with friends."

"I don't get it."

Of course you don't, Jenna thought. She gathered her thoughts. "I don't know what to say, Sis. On the outside, I'm different in lots of ways from the woman who left home to come to Manhattan, but inside I'm still the same person. I think some of this was in there all along, but I didn't know it. The only thing I knew was that I couldn't marry Glen and settle down to a white-picket-fence life. It was only when I moved here and met people, did different things in bed, that I discovered what I had been looking for."

"So you became a hooker."

"If you want to put it that way."

"What other way is there? You were looking for kinky sex when you said no to Glen. It wasn't just about being tied down."

"It was so many things that I couldn't sort them all out but, yes, sex was a big part of it."

"You didn't tell me that part."

"I know. I didn't know whether you'd understand."

Jenna watched the color rise in her sister's cheeks. "Right. Sweet, uptight, sexually repressed Marcy wouldn't have a clue about wanting something more in bed."

Jenna hadn't meant it like that but it was closer to the truth than she wanted to admit. "I'm sorry. It wasn't like that."

"We're being honest, or at least I think we are. Tell it straight. You didn't think I'd understand because I've never had a sex life."

She was right, of course. Jenna wondered how far to take this, then said, "Okay. Here's honesty. You're plain vanilla or at least that's the way you've always seemed to me. I wanted rocky road, heavenly hash, something more."

"But you slept with Glen when you came home. Twice, if I've been counting right."

"I did, and it's been a lot better since I got away. I accept that a lot of what went wrong with Glen was my fault. I didn't know how to ask for what I wanted and there was no way he could have guessed. Doing what I've been doing has taught me a great deal."

"I'll bet," Marcy said, her voice snide.

Jenna grinned. "Don't knock it, Sis. I've had some great sex."

"I'll bet." After a minute, Marcy added, "Tell me about Club Fantasy."

Encouraged by Marcy's softened tone of voice, Jenna spent a long time telling her sister about the way it had all started, the movies, the motel room, and then the venturing out into other types of fantasy fulfillment. "We've had a lot of help from a wonderful woman named Erika who's been doing this sort of thing for a long time."

"Another hooker?" she said sharply. There was a pause, then she continued, "Sorry, maybe I should stop using that word. It sounds so terrible. Okay. What about this Erika person?"

"Thanks for being patient, Sis," Jenna said. "You can't imagine how much I've wanted to share this with you."

"God, Jenna, this is so difficult for me. I'm trying to be reasonable and listen."

Jenna explained Erika's history and told her sister a bit about Courtesans, Inc. "She's such a wonderful woman. I'd love to have you meet her."

Marcy shook her head. "I don't think I'm ready for that right now. Jen, I'm trying to deal with all this, mostly because I love you and I know you've got the same basic morality I have, but you can imagine how difficult it is for me. It goes against everything I've ever believed."

Jenna reached across the sofa and hugged her sister. "How can I expect you to understand when it took me weeks to come to terms with all of this? It makes sense to me now, however."

"It doesn't to me, but I can live with that. From what you've said this is a thriving business and you're having fun with it. I guess that means that you're not coming back home."

"I don't know whether Club Fantasy is a life or just a temporary pleasure. For right now, it's such fun and there's so much money involved that I'm going to stay here."

Marcy leaned forward and her voice dropped. "How much money?"

"I've added more than ten thousand dollars to my bank account in the past few months."

Marcy's eyes widened. "You're kidding. Isn't some of that from your work?"

"Sis, I haven't taken a translation assignment for about six weeks. It's all from Club Fantasy, and the business is growing all the time." She spent several minutes filling Marcy in on the details.

Marcy seemed to be digesting all the information. Finally, she asked, "Don't you worry that you're cheating yourself somehow?"

"Cheating myself?"

"How are you going to be able to get married, have kids, like that, after what you're doing here?"

"I've thought about that and I don't know the answer. I want a family, husband, kids, but for right now I'm not going to worry about that. Erika's married and several of the ladies she works with are as well."

"What about Glen?"

"That troubles me a lot and it's difficult for me to know what's right."

The two women stayed up for another hour, then Marcy bedded down on the pull-out sofa. They had breakfast together, then took a cab to the garage where Marcy had parked the day before. The twins hugged and, although Jenna knew that Marcy still didn't totally understand, they were still friends when she left.

Chapter
16

Marcy didn't mean to tell Glen about Club Fantasy. It just happened.

"Where were you last Wednesday and Thursday?" Glen asked her as they sat having a quiet dinner the following Sunday evening. Since neither of them had an active social life and since they had Jenna in common, they'd been having dinner together once or twice a month. "Joe Stewart told me you'd suddenly taken two days off. That's not like you."

"I took a quick trip down to see Jenna," Marcy said, unable to think of a lie quickly enough. She didn't want to get into this with Glen, afraid she'd say something she shouldn't.

"Oh?" he said. "That was really sudden. I hope nothing's wrong. She didn't mention anything when I spoke to her last Friday."

"I thought there was a problem, but I was mistaken." Marcy had been thinking about her visit and all the things she'd learned. She hadn't adjusted to the idea that her sister was a prostitute, but she'd decided to cut Jenna some slack and let things ride.

They'd spoken several times since her return to Seneca Falls and, at times, Marcy had wanted to preach, to tell Jenna all the reasons why what she was doing was wrong, but she found she had an increasingly difficult time finding those reasons. She also found herself a little intrigued. None of this, however, was Glen's problem.

"Did you have a nice visit?" Glen asked.

"Great, actually." She decided to be as honest as she could. "I tried to call her several times and got her voice mail. As it turned out, she'd just misplaced her cell phone so I got all worked up for nothing."

"How is she?"

"She's fine, enjoying New York City in the winter. I have to say that I like it here better. The snow in Manhattan is seldom white. Central Park is pretty, though. I took a cab through the park to her apartment. It was really lovely. I guess it's the only part of the city where the dirt doesn't show."

"Her apartment? I'm confused. I thought she lived with Chloe in a brownstone."

Damn, Marcy thought, *I knew I'd louse this up.* "Oh, didn't I tell you?" she said brightly. "She's got an apartment on the West Side. It's really cute. So, how was your week? I gather there's a merger in the works."

"Something's not right here," Glen said, not letting her change the subject, "and frankly, Marcy, you're a lousy liar. What's going on? Is she in some kind of trouble? Is that why you raced down there?"

"She's not in any trouble, Glen. Let it go, will you? Please!"

"She's not just a casual acquaintance and I don't just ask about her because she's your sister. What's going on?"

Marcy heaved a deep sigh. Glen was right, she was a lousy liar. Slowly, with the help of several pointed questions from Glen, she told him the whole story. "She's a hooker with a high-priced clientele," Glen spat. "That doesn't make her any different from a streetwalker. What the hell is wrong with her?"

As Marcy told Glen about Club Fantasy, she realized that,

although she didn't understand it, if it was what Jenna wanted, she would try not to judge. Her sister was a grown woman and Marcy wouldn't reject her, even if she didn't like what she was doing. But for Glen, maybe this was just the reason Glen needed to move on with his life. "Let it go, Glen. Admit that she's not the woman for you and get on with the rest of your life."

Glen remained silent and the meal ended awkwardly. When she told her sister about her mess-up the following day, Jenna was understanding and resigned to the loss of her relationship with Glen. "It's probably for the best," she said, echoing Marcy's words. "It's probably for the best." As she hung up, Marcy thought she heard her sister cry.

For nearly a week Glen couldn't deal with what he'd learned about Jenna so he tried not to think about it. He managed to suppress it during the day, but at night, as he lay in bed, he pictured Jenna, the woman he'd asked to marry him, in lewd poses with men of all sizes, shapes, and colors. Mixed with those images were ones of himself and Jenna making love, as recently as Christmas. He'd been so receptive and the sex had been good. He remembered that he'd noticed that she was more willing to show him what she wanted.

How could she have changed so much in such a short time? Or had she changed? Was this Jenna inside the one he'd proposed to all the time? For another week he alternated between puzzlement and just plain fury. How could she do this to him? How could she do it to herself? He hated her, and hated himself for still loving her. It made no sense and he couldn't sort it out, as much as he tried.

It gnawed at him and he kept revisiting his conversation with Marcy like a tongue touching a sore tooth. Club Fantasy. Men. Lots of men. Some guy named Rock, of all things, living in the brownstone in which Jenna and her friend Chloe were supposed to be. He hadn't gone to visit because he was giving her space. She sure took her space, all right. And look what she did with it.

It was illegal and dangerous. What was to prevent some pervert from doing all kinds of things to her? Marcy had alluded to all kinds of kinky stuff. He knew what that meant. S&M, bondage, orgies. Orgies. Jenna and who knew how many men. His Jenna.

Not his. Not anymore. He wanted to choke some sense into her, to attempt to make her understand what she was doing. She couldn't continue this way without getting hurt, injured, battered. He knew what went on. He read the papers and watched TV.

By the third week he was starting to formulate a plan. He had to show her how dangerous this was. Things would never be the same. There was no future for them, but he had to admit, if only to himself, that he still cared deeply about her and wanted her safe. Not with him, of course, but safe.

Slowly, he figured out what he had to do. He took a few days off from work and, telling no one where he was going, drove down to Manhattan the following, bitterly cold Monday morning. He arrived in the late afternoon, parked, and found the brownstone in a lovely side street with trees planted every few feet. He'd been in the city on business several times but he'd never really explored its more residential neighborhoods. It was an exciting city and, even with all its problems, it managed to have charming areas like this one. He could certainly understand why Jenna enjoyed her stay here. Not what she was doing, of course, but the city itself.

He climbed the two steps to the front door and knocked. The huge, totally bald, sightly menacing man who answered the door must be the man Marcy spoke of, the one called Rock. "Hello," Glen said. "I'm looking for Jenna and something called Club Fantasy." He thought that knowing about the Club might help him get to talk to Jenna if she wasn't there at the moment.

"I'm sorry, I've no idea what you're talking about."

Glen didn't expect such a quick rejection. "Jenna. Jenna Bryant. She doesn't live here anymore but I really need to talk to her."

The man shook his head slowly. "I'm really sorry but I'm afraid you have the wrong house."

Glen knew he had the right house. He'd checked the address several times. And this was the guy Marcy had spoken of. What now? Maybe he needed a bit more honesty. "You're Rock, aren't you?"

"That's my name but there's no one here called Jenna. I'm really sorry."

As he started to close the door, Glen said, "Please. I'm really an old friend of hers from back home. Can't you help me?"

The wary look on the man's face relaxed slightly. "Back home where?"

"Seneca Falls. Upstate."

He raised an eyebrow. "Tell me more."

"My name's Glen Howell and Jenna's sister's name is Marcy."

Slowly, the giant opened the door. "There's no one here right now but me. Why don't you come inside and tell me why you're here?"

Glen entered the comfortable house and, while Rock put his coat away, he looked over the living room. It seemed no different from any other living room, sofas, plants, a very comfortable lounge chair in front of a great-looking, big-screen TV. He sat on a side chair as Rock stretched out on the lounger, ankles crossed, looking like king of the realm. "Want to tell me about it?"

What could he say. "Why were you so suspicious?"

Rock's laugh was warm. "Let me count the ways." He raised his first finger. "I knew you weren't a customer. No one arrives here unannounced and everyone is cleared six ways from Sunday before they even get the address." He raised a second finger. "Jenna doesn't use her real name. She's Hillary Oakes to all the customers." He extended a third. "We're closed on Mondays and Tuesdays and anyone who knows about Jenna and this place would know that. Shall I go on?"

"No." He was amazed. She had taken lots of safety precautions. "Who are you and what do you have to do with all of this?"

"Me? I live here and I'm here whenever we have customers. Sort of a bouncer." He flexed a muscle. "Who would mess with anyone when I'm around?"

"Have you ever had to bounce anyone?"

"No, I haven't, but I'm not the issue here. What are you doing here?"

"I'm her ex-boyfriend."

"I know that. She talks about you a lot."

Amazed, Glen said, "She does?"

"That's the only reason you got in the door. She's been really upset since her sister showed up unexpectedly a few weeks ago."

Who the hell was this guy and what was he to Jenna? Maybe everything had been a lie despite their wonderful dinners, phone conversations, and sex. "You two talk about . . . things?"

"Yes. We talk. And no, I'm not the new boyfriend. I'm a guy who happens to be a friend to both Jenna and Chloe. Until Jenna and her sister reached an understanding about what goes on here, she had only Chloe and me to talk to, so I'm pretty well informed."

Curious now, Glen asked, "What did she tell you about me?"

"You want me to share secrets? I don't think so, but I will tell you that she cares about you a great deal. How do you feel about her?"

"I hate what she's doing here." Was that the entire answer?

Rock smiled and nodded. "I don't blame you. It must seem bizarre to an outsider like yourself."

Glen found himself warming to this strange man. "It passed bizarre a long while ago."

Rock laughed. "I'll bet."

"Are there any more guys like you hanging around?"

"No, but it's a pretty busy place."

With a deep sigh, Glen said, "I thought she was in danger here. I didn't realize what a professional operation this was. She's got another name and everything." He sighed again. "I thought it was just her and I believed I could talk her out of it and lure her back home."

"I don't think she'd leave here right now."

"I guess not."

"I'm sorry this is so difficult, but it is what it is," Rock said.

"I know. The trouble is that she's been with so many men. That bothers me as much as everything else."

"True enough. Let me ask you this. If you met her today and all those men were in her past, would you love her, anyway?"

"I didn't say I love her."

"You didn't have to, but answer my question."

"I guess if it were in her past, then what business would it be of mine?"

"Good man," Rock said, nodding. "That's the way I think it should be."

"But they're her present."

Rock smiled softly. "I know and that's the real problem isn't it." It wasn't a question. "What was your sex life like?"

Glen gasped. "That's not any of your business."

"Maybe it isn't but it might be something for you to think about very seriously."

Their sex life had been fine. He'd always seen to it that Jenna was satisfied. Wasn't that enough? It had been a bit more creative since . . . oh, shit. That's why it was better. She's learning from all those other guys. There's no hope.

Glen slumped in his chair. "Help me understand," he whispered. He and Rock talked for a long time, then went out to a local Irish pub for a sandwich and several beers. Finally, after ten, they were back in the brownstone. "I hear what you're saying and part of me really gets it, but part of me can only think that this is Jenna. The woman I wanted to marry, to have my children."

"That can still happen, you know."

"I don't think so. I just couldn't. Not now."

"Can I make a suggestion?"

"Sure. Anything."

"Why don't you make an appointment with Hillary? Experience what she's like here for yourself."

"Excuse me?"

"Be a customer. See what all the shouting is about. See what she's all about. I don't know whether this is the real her or the one you know in Seneca Falls is, but I think you need to find that out, if only to put a period at the end of this phase of your life."

"I don't think so. I just wanted to see her, talk to her, not play sex games with her."

"Don't knock sex games. Remember, they are just that: games. Have you got a place to stay tonight?"

"No," Glen said, a rueful smile on his face. "I guess I hadn't thought that part out. I thought I'd see her and some kind of magic would happen. She'd realize that she'd been wrong and we'd spend the night at her place, have wild, wonderful sex, then drive back to Seneca Falls together." He scrubbed his face with the palms of his hands. "I'm not thinking straight at all."

"Probably not. Why don't you stay here? There's no one here but me until Wednesday and there's an empty room upstairs. I can lend you whatever you need. Do some serious thinking and maybe we can figure out some way for you to deal with everything. Or at least take a few steps in that direction. If that's what you want."

"I don't know what I want."

"Then that's the first thing you need to settle in your own mind."

Glen spent a sleepless night in a simple bedroom Rock had called the motel room. He thought about Jenna, Club Fantasy, and all the men she had sex with. He balanced that with what Rock claimed to be her feelings toward him, and his feelings toward her. When he met Rock in the kitchen the following morning, he was no closer to understanding what he wanted than he had been the previous evening.

"I still think you should be a customer and experience what she's doing firsthand," Rock said. "You'd learn a lot about your feelings, and hers."

"How could I do that? She'd know me in an instant."

"Not if you were someone who was very nervous about all this and insisted on being masked. We could set it up so that the room was quite dark."

"What about my voice? She'd know that right off."

"You could disguise it as best you could and speak very little, if at all. You could use my toiletries so you'd even smell different."

"Okay, so maybe I could pull it off. So what? What would that prove?"

"It might prove something to you and it certainly would make up your mind one way or the other. Can you make love to her without thinking about other men? Without thinking about what she does to earn a living? Is she still the woman you love?"

"It might help, I guess."

"What have you got to lose? You can't just go back Upstate and leave everything no more settled than it was."

"Okay, let's give it a go."

Rock called Jenna and asked her a favor. "I got a call from a guy who needs some of what you do best. He's new at this, needy and nervous as hell, but he's such a nice guy it's difficult to turn him down. Would it be okay to make a date with him for tonight? He's only got this one evening in town and he's willing to pay extra. Have you got other plans?"

"No," Jenna said. "I guess it would be okay."

"He's really shy so he wants low lighting and he'll wear a mask. Actually, I think he's afraid of being recognized. He might even be famous. I don't have a clue. I just know that Erika vouched for him, so he's legit."

"Okay. What fantasy does he want?"

"He wants a knowledgeable woman to teach him about good, creative sex. A Mrs. Robinson type. You know, show him all the bells and whistles."

"I've done that one often enough. Sure, set it up."

At dinnertime, Glen went around the corner to a sandwich shop and sat for more than an hour over a meal he couldn't eat, giving Jenna time to set up for the evening. At seven-thirty, the time Rock had arranged, Glen entered the brownstone. He was wearing one of Rock's black shirts with his jeans, so there was no possibility of Jenna recognizing his clothing. Rock handed him a Halloween type of mask that covered only his eyes and nose, and fastened tightly to limit the risk of falling off. "You both know the set-up so say very little and just roll with it. You might learn more than you expect."

Glen shook Rock's large hand. "Thanks, Rock. Whatever happens, thanks for all the advice."

"No sweat."

Glen made his way upstairs to the room in which he'd spent the previous night. As he opened the door, he saw only dim, flickering light coming from the adjoining bathroom. "I hope this is okay," Jenna said from her seat on one side of the room. "I gather you want anonymity and that's fine with me. My name's Hillary."

"I'm Bill," Glen said, dropping the pitch of his voice and sounding a bit hoarse. Being politically savvy, his choice of pseudonym was obvious.

She grinned. "Ah. Bill and Hillary. I don't know whether that's the good news or the bad. But you're not here for a political discussion. Come on in and shut the door."

As Glen crossed the room, Jenna turned on a CD player. Soft music filled the room. "Let's dance," she said.

Glen and Jenna had never danced together back home so this was new for him. He wrapped his arms around her and held her close, breathing in the familiar scent of her hair. He was glad now that he'd taken Rock's suggestion and used his soap, shampoo, and after-shave when he'd showered that morning. "Mmm," she purred. "You feel nice." She pressed her cheek against his shoulder. "I love slow dancing. It's so intimate without being threatening. Don't you think so?"

"I guess," he mumbled.

"You know, if you hum along with the music I can feel the rumble in your chest. It's really sexy."

"Mmm," Glen said, agreeing with her. Then he found himself humming the familiar song.

"Nice." After several minutes, she said, "Would you like a drink?"

"No, thanks." Alcohol would only dull his senses.

After another song and lots of body contact, Jenna slowly slipped her hand up to his neck and pulled his face toward hers. The kiss was unexpectedly soft, a light touching of lips and teasing of tongues. She nipped lightly at his lower lip, then changed the angle of the kiss to make more intimate contact. "You taste nice."

He'd chewed a mint before he'd arrived just in case she could recognize his taste, although he didn't know whether that was possible. Somehow, now, even though all this must be phony, he was glad she was pleased.

"Tell me a little about you. I know you don't want to talk

much, but maybe you can help me a little. Have you had sex before?"

He chuckled. "Yes," he said, keeping his voice to a hoarse whisper.

"That's good. Was it nice?"

"Very."

"That's even better. I'm here to teach you whatever you want. What do you want? Could the sex have been even better?"

"Maybe. I don't really know," he said, unsure how to answer her question. "What do you enjoy?"

"This is all for you," Jenna said. "What I enjoy is irrelevant."

"But if you're not enjoying it, then how can I?" Glen realized that he was talking too much, but he kept his voice unnaturally low and continued, "I need to know about women."

"Okay. I don't know about other women, but I guess I like pretty much everything."

"Cop-out answer."

Jenna chuckled. "Right." She paused. "Okay, I guess I like soft, slow lovemaking best. The kind with lots of touching and stroking." She pulled his shirt from the waistband of his pants and ran her hand over his back, her feet still moving idly to the music.

"I like that too," Glen said, stroking her back through her soft, thin sweater. For long moments they moved and touched, her hands sliding over his body. She scratched her long fingernails down his back just enough to leave a tingle. "If I like something I usually think the woman does too. Is that true?"

"Usually. I think men like it faster and harder than women do, but maybe that's a stereotype."

"Well, I like this," he said, reaching beneath her sweater and making a path down her back with his nails. She arched her back and pressed her pelvis against his.

"I do too." She looked up at him. "You're wearing too many clothes."

"So are you," he whispered. While he pulled her sweater over her head, she unbuttoned his shirt. Soon her bra was draped over a chair and they danced, bare chest to bare chest. She undulated so the heat of her nipples scorched a path over his bare skin. He pressed his groin against hers, letting her feel his arousal. "I'm all for delaying gratification but I'm getting very hungry for you." As Glen said it, he realized it was true. Despite his doubts about Club Fantasy, he still loved her and wanted her. How could that be? She was a prostitute. Okay, Rock had told him about Erika and her husband but that was them and he couldn't be like that.

While he'd been musing, Jenna had been removing the rest of his clothing and hers. Soon they were naked on the cool satin bedspread. How many men had she been with in this room? When she wrapped her fingers around his cock, however, he ceased caring. He reached for her breasts and filled his hands with her flesh. He leaned down and sucked one into his mouth, pulling on them the way he remembered she liked, and listened to her moan. This wasn't a con. She was truly enjoying what he was doing. How could she? To her, he was a stranger.

Conflicted, yet aroused, he stroked and fondled, finally reaching between her legs and combing his fingers through her carefully trimmed pussy hair. She was writhing beneath his hand, thrusting and stroking his fingers with her wet flesh. God, she was so wet. She couldn't fake that. She obviously enjoyed lovemaking. The fact that she got paid for it was less important to her than that, he reasoned.

"I want you," she said, biting his earlobe. "I hope that's what you want."

"God, yes," he growled. She took a condom from a bowl on the bedside table and unrolled it over his erect cock. He wanted to be repelled as he drove into her. So many men had done this, but she was still Jenna, and he found that he didn't care about the others.

He found her clit with his fingers and, while he thrust, he rubbed her the way he knew would push her over the edge. It did, and as she screamed her pleasure, he came as well.

They lay side by side, her head cradled on his shoulder, his fingers idly running through her hair. "That was fabulous, Jenna," he said.

Immediately he felt her stiffen and he quickly realized what he'd just done.

"You called me Jenna," she said, then sat bolt upright and pulled off his mask. "Glen. My God." She leaped off the bed and grabbed her sweater from the chair and clutched it to her breasts. "My God. What the hell are you doing here?"

Shit, shit, shit. Glen. Jenna couldn't sort out the jumble of her thoughts. She got a lightweight robe from the closet and wrapped it around her, then dropped into a chair. "What the hell are you doing here?" He looked so sweet, the lying son of a bitch.

"I originally came to talk to you and get you to give this all up and come home."

"What do you think gives you the right?"

"Nothing gives me any rights. I realize that all too well. I just know that I love you." His voice was soft and so warm. "I know now that this was a crazy idea. I'm sorry. I know that isn't enough, but I'm so very sorry. God," he said, dropping his head into his hands, "coming here was a totally dumb idea but I couldn't think of anything else to do."

"How did you find out?" she asked, but she knew. "Marcy."

"Don't be mad at her, Jenna, she didn't mean to tell me. It just slipped out. She mentioned your apartment and one lie led to another until she couldn't deal with them any more and she told me. Please. She's your sister. Don't blame her."

Jenna sighed, her initial fury cooling. "I could have expected it. She's such a lousy liar." She swiped at the tears that were streaming down her cheeks. "I'm sorry you had to find out this way, but I guess I knew you would sometime."

He laughed lightly. "I was just about to ask you why you didn't tell me, but that's the dumbest question I've ever thought of."

Jenna smiled through the tears. "Right." She had to be honest. "I thought about just breaking it off with you many times, and I kept trying to, but I couldn't. I was totally selfish, but I wanted space so I ran off to the big city. I thought I didn't love you; then you called and sent the flowers and it was all so sweet. I've been so torn, Glen." She shook her head and grabbed a tissue from a bureau drawer.

"I think I understand much more than I did twenty-four hours ago," Glen said, sliding up so his back was against the headboard. "Rock and I have talked a lot."

"You met Rock?"

"Of course. You don't think he would have let just anyone be with you. I got here yesterday."

"Yesterday?" She sounded like an idiot but it was all too much to absorb.

Glen told her about the previous twenty-four hours. "He was the one who suggested I become a customer to see what it was like for you."

"Fuck him!" she exploded.

"It was the right thing to do, Jenna," Glen said. "I might have just gone home yesterday and never spoken to you again and that wouldn't have solved anything. He said something about walking a mile in your shoes." Glen paused. "Actually, he said I should walk a mile in your garter belt."

Jenna chuckled through her tears. "That sounds like him."

"Yeah. He's an unusual man. At first I thought he was your lover. The new boyfriend and all, and I was ready to hate his guts. He won me over."

"He's really a truly special man."

"I know." He huffed out a breath. "Jenna, I don't know where we go from here."

Jenna was stunned that they were having this conversation. He seemed so calm, so reasonable. Why wasn't he ranting about getting her out of this business? "Where can we go? Glen, let me be as honest as I can. I care for you. A lot. That's why I've allowed my feelings to overrule my better judgement and continued to see you. But this—" She waved her arm around the room. "—This is very important to me too. I love what I do and I don't have the usual ugly feelings about it. I understand men's needs and I cater to them. I do lots of kinky stuff."

"Do you enjoy it all?"

"Most of it. Sometimes I just do it because I give a man his money's worth and I love to see a man enjoying good sex."

"I can understand that. Even when I thought it was all phony, I loved seeing the look of joy on your face."

Touched, Jenna said, "I don't want to give it up. At least not right now."

"I didn't ask you to."

Not ask her to give it up? "I don't understand what you're saying."

"This evening has taught me a lot. I love you and I want you to be happy. I'm suggesting that this will wear off eventually and I'm hoping you'll come back to Seneca Falls. Until that happens, if it happens, I would like to continue seeing you on vacations, both here at Club Fantasy and back home, and let's see how it goes."

"You're not demanding that I give this up if we're going to be together?"

"Not right now. I don't know how I'll feel a month from now, but for the moment I'd like to just leave it the way it is, with the hope that eventually we can be together, and exclusive."

"God, Glen, I love you, and I can't believe how understanding you're being." She found she was crying harder. "It's so good between us. Damn, I'm getting all schmaltzy, but it's so good, so special."

Glen smoothed the pad of his thumb over her cheeks and then kissed her lightly. "I love you when you're schmaltzy."

Jenna smiled a watery smile. "I never thought of schmaltz as love words."

"When you say them, they are. Pay careful attention to what I'm saying. What we have is special and it's worth fighting for. I can't let you go, and I'll deal with Club Fantasy as best I can."

"We'll make it. I know we will."

Marcy and Glen had both been more understanding than she could have imagined. She took off her robe and climbed back into bed beside Glen. As she drifted off, in Glen's arms, she knew that it would work.

Two years later, as she gazed at her three-month-old daughter, Isabel, resting contentedly in her husband Glen's arms, Jenna knew that she had it all.